Jan Schoelzel

JOHN WRAY is the author of the critically acclaimed novels *The Lost Time Accidents*, *Lowboy*, *The Right Hand of Sleep*, and *Canaan's Tongue*. He was named one of *Granta*'s Best of Young American Novelists in 2007. The recipient of a Whiting Writers' Award, he lives in Brooklyn, New York.

ALSO BY JOHN WRAY

The Right Hand of Sleep

Canaan's Tongue

Lowboy

The Lost Time Accidents

ADDITIONAL PRAISE FOR *GODSEND*

One of *The Wall Street Journal*'s Top Ten Books of the Year
Named a Best Book of the Year by *San Francisco Chronicle*, *The Guardian*, and Oprah.com

"John Wray's lean, bristling novel is filled with startling transformations: the teenage girl at its center disguises herself as a man and leaves the suburbs of California for the Taliban army in Afghanistan. Yet the most unsettling change is the way it shifts the reader's perspectives on 9/11 and the war on terror."   —*The Wall Street Journal*

"None of the Anglophone post-9/11 novels have been as ingeniously involved with the question of conversion to Islam and with the determination to take one's acquired belief into the realm of violence as John Wray's new novel, *Godsend* . . . He does an outstanding job in depicting a protagonist who has studied Islamic theology with a mix of avidity and simplicity, has taken the lessons of Qur'anic verses to heart without having matured enough to approach faith seriously . . . The novel's highest achievement is to show how each one of her insights is nothing but an illusion."

—Amir Khadem, *Los Angeles Review of Books*

"[*Godsend*] has no right to work at all, but Wray's storytelling is so taut, his prose so laser-etched, his psychology so audacious, and his wisdom so much the opposite of conventional, that it ends up working brilliantly."   —Jonathan Franzen, *The Guardian*

"John Wray conjures up an extraordinary character: Aden Sawyer, Californian girl, pre-9/11 Muslim convert, cross-dressing imposter, Pakistani madrasa student, and, finally, Taliban militant in post-9/11 Afghanistan . . . With a novelist's perception, Wray sees through jihadism's political garb."   —Tanjil Rashid, *Financial Times*

"Wray's audacious fiction is clearly steeped in painstaking research, offering a devastating portrayal of the Taliban while finding a place of compassion for his profoundly misguided protagonists . . . The feat Wray pulls off is to seek understanding without ever becoming sentimental." —Dawn Raffel, Oprah.com

"Wray regulates the excitement levels, from tense to explosive, with a sure hand for narrative momentum . . . Wray's prose is hard, clipped, and precise—a hammer to move this grim story forward. Yet it can expand into something like Hemingwayesque eloquence in describing the terrain that opens its arms to Aden . . . [*Godsend* is] a work of great power, seamlessly elucidating the seductions of faith and violence." —Dan Cryer, *SFGate*

"[A] disturbing image of disaffected youth and the lures of extremism." —*Publishers Weekly*

"For a while now, John Wray has been writing as if let in on the secret history of the world, paying attention to moments we all know, but at the point we've stopped looking . . . This is literature as high-wire act without the net; epic in scale, even bigger in heart." —Marlon James, author of *Black Leopard, Red Wolf*

"I've just spent every spare moment in a fever heat reading *Godsend*, and I'm truly dazzled by its daring literal and psychological border crossings, its tonal complexity, and its pitiless compassion. Nothing is foreign to John Wray's imagination. I hope I can write half as fearlessly one day." —Karen Russell, author of *Vampires in the Lemon Grove* and *Swamplandia!*

"John Wray is making a place for himself among our greatest living writers. *Godsend* is a wonder to me: a fearless book about a terrifying subject. The elegance and daring of this novel left me dizzy." —Akhil Sharma, author of *Family Life*

"This novel crosses lines that fiction should, stretching the imagination from suburban California to a jihadi training camp in the foothills of the Hindu Kush. Wray's taut prose propels a gripping narrative that stands head and shoulders above most fiction about America's war on terror."   —Hari Kunzru, author of *White Tears*

"This is a great book about a time and a place that I lived through. I was nostalgic, reading *Godsend*, for the days when I was a young girl in Afghanistan, going to the madrasa with my friends. This came as a surprise to me. But there was beauty in that life. And there is beauty in this story."   —Shamila Kohestani, recipient of the
Arthur Ashe Courage Award

GODSEND

JOHN WRAY

PICADOR   FARRAR, STRAUS AND GIROUX   NEW YORK

GODSEND. Copyright © 2018 by John Wray. All rights reserved. Printed in the United States of America. For information, address Picador, 120 Broadway, New York, N.Y. 10271.

picadorusa.com • instagram.com/picador
twitter.com/picadorusa • facebook.com/picadorusa

Picador® is a U.S. registered trademark and is used by Macmillan Publishing Group, LLC, under license from Pan Books Limited.

For book club information, please visit facebook.com/picadorbookclub or email marketing@picadorusa.com.

Designed by Abby Kagan

The Library of Congress has cataloged the Farrar, Straus and Giroux edition as follows:

Names: Wray, John, 1971– author.
Title: Godsend / John Wray.
Description: First edition. | New York : Farrar, Straus and Giroux, 2018.
Identifiers: LCCN 2017058629 | ISBN 9780374164706 (hardcover) | ISBN 9780374716097 (ebook)
Classification: LCC PS3573.R365 G64 2018 | DDC 813/.54—dc23
LC record available at https://lccn.loc.gov/2017058629

Picador Paperback ISBN 978-1-250-23480-3

Our books may be purchased in bulk for promotional, educational, or business use. Please contact your local bookseller or the Macmillan Corporate and Premium Sales Department at 1-800-221-7945, extension 5442, or by email at MacmillanSpecialMarkets@macmillan.com.

First published by Farrar, Straus and Giroux

First Picador Edition: October 2019

10 9 8 7 6 5 4 3 2 1

To the men and women of CAIR
and to the cause they serve

GODSEND

DEAR TEACHER here I am now where you said I'd never be.

I'm writing this from the place that you told me about and it's as beautiful and terrible as everything you said. You said blue sky and cold and bad roads and worse water. You said snow in the houses and shit in the streets. A *godfearing people* you said. All those fancy descriptions. All that talking down to me like I was six years old.

It's cold here ok but I never feel cold. I'm with people that know me. I'm with people that will die for me and on my best days when I'm not afraid I know I'll do the same.

Can you think of one thing you can say that about?

You were right about this country and the way that it would take me. Dear Teacher I should have known better. I should have been careful. You were right about all that but you were wrong about one thing.

You said I'd never make it to this place. And here I am.

1

The day her visa arrived she came home to find the pictures on the mantelpiece turned to face the wall. She felt no urge to touch them. They'd looked fine from the front, catching the light in their brushed-nickel bevels, but from the back their inexpensiveness was plain. Puckered gray cardboard, no stronger than paper. These were no sacred relics. They held meaning for three people only, of all the untold billions, believer and unbeliever alike. And not even for those three people anymore.

She found her mother in the bedroom with the ridgebacks and the pit. The room smelled of old smoke and Lysol and beer. The dogs raised their heads when she opened the door but her mother kept still, both hands slack in her lap, staring out the window at the cul-de-sac. The T-shirt she wore said SANTA ROSA ROUND-UP and she sat upright and prim on the high queen-sized mattress with her bare feet planted squarely on the floor. The girl studied that proud ruined profile from the foot of the bed, trying as she often did to find her likeness there. For the first time in her life, in all their eighteen years together, she had no need to guess what her mother was waiting to hear.

—It came, she said.

—What did?

—You know what did. My visa.

Her mother made a gesture of dismissal.

—I thought maybe it wasn't going to get here in time. I really thought it wouldn't. If it hadn't got here—

—You told me you'd be home by five. Five o'clock at the latest. That's what you told me and I fixed my day around it.

The girl looked down at the pit. —I know I'm back late. I went for a drive.

—Don't think I don't know where you've been, Aden Grace. Don't mix me up with somebody who can't tell shit from taffy.

—I'm sorry. She reached down to scratch the pit between the ears. —I'm not trying to keep anything from you, Mom. I guess I'm just excited or whatever. Maybe even—

—I've asked you not to lie to me. You owe me that kindness. Don't you owe me that kindness? I've asked you not to complicate my life.

—I'll be gone this time tomorrow, said the girl. —I guess that should uncomplicate some things.

Her mother turned toward her. —You think I'm just counting the minutes till you're up in that plane? Look over here, Aden. Is that what you think?

—No. I don't think that.

—All right, then.

—I think you're waiting for the next bad thing to happen.

Her mother gave a clipped laugh. —Your old dad said the same thing to me once. You know what your trouble is, Claire? he told me. You're always expecting some failure. The failure of a person or the failure of a given situation. She laughed again. —The failure of a given situation. Those were his words exactly.

—You're drunk.

—Right again, girl. Pat yourself on the ass.

—I didn't even have to tell you. I'm old enough now. I could have packed up my stuff and just walked out the door.

—That's exactly what you're doing, far as I can see. Walking right out the door. Or am I missing something?

The light above the cul-de-sac lay thick against the hillside and glimmered down through air gone dim with pollen. The same air she'd moved through and breathed all her life. A hummingbird circled the feeder by the pool and found it empty. It had been empty for days. She asked herself how long that small bright bird would keep on coming.

—Try to remember to fill up the feeder, she said.

Her mother dragged three fingers through her hair. —You going to see him before you jet off? Is that part of your plan?

—I don't know.

—You don't know much, do you?

—I might go and see him.

—I never asked where you got the money for the ticket. I guess I must already know the answer.

—You're wrong. I asked him for money at Christmas. He told me it was out of his purview.

—His what?

—That's what I said. He told me to go home and look it up.

—Well doesn't that just sound like our professor. She coughed into her fist. —I tell you what, though. I bet it gooses him in all the right places, this life plan of yours. I bet he feels fulfilled and justified.

—He's got no reason to feel one way or the other about it. None of this is on account of him.

—Who do you think you're talking to here, Aden? Who do you think you're fooling?

—I'm telling it to you as clear as I can. I can't help it if you don't want to listen.

—For those with ears to hear, let them hear, said her mother.

—That's about right.

—That comes from a different book, though. Not the one in your pocket. She curled her toes into the carpet. —I should have made you learn that book by heart.

—You tried to, said the girl.

—Noticed that, did you? I guess that counts for something.

—It's not your fault I turned out like this. She bit down on her thumbnail. —You did what you could.

Her mother turned back to the window. —I'm tired. Go on out and leave me alone.

—I will if you promise to sleep.

—I'll sleep when I'm ready. She arched her back and lit a cigarette.
—I can't say I'm going to miss your goddamn fussing.

A jet passed overhead as the girl turned to leave. The house was on the flight path up from SFO and she'd always loved to hear the planes go by. It was a carelessly built house, cheap as the frames on the mantel, but when it shook she felt less separate from the world.

—I'm going for a walk, she said. —I'll be back in an hour. I'll make us some dinner.

—Whatever you say.

—He never paid a cent for it. I saved up from work. The church got me a discount on the ticket.

—Don't you call it a church. There's a word for that place you go to, Aden. Even I know the word.

—You can forget it as soon as I'm gone, said the girl.

Her mother's face caught the light as she pulled the door closed. Impassive and prideful, prepared for the worst. She recognized her likeness there at last.

She walked down Hidden Valley Drive to the cemetery, past Carmen's Burger Bar, past Ramirez Pawn N Carry, then up Pacific toward the junior college. On Mendocino she stopped in front of a shop window and shaded her eyes and looked in through the glass. A pyramid of mobile phones, leather protective cases for the phones, matching plastic belt clips for the cases. She imagined a world in which she might possibly enter that shop—in which she would work and save to buy the items offered there for sale—and it was not a world in which she cared to live.

Some kids from school walked by and snickered, and she allowed herself, for the last time, the luxury of picturing them dead. She watched them in the glass until they passed out of sight, then took stock of her own reflection, frail but straight-backed in a white shalwar kameez. Not a girl, not a boy. Just a ghost in a body. She felt a passing pang of sadness, perhaps even pity, but whether for herself or for the kids who'd laughed at her she couldn't say.

The campus was quiet and dark and unnaturally flat, a painted back-drop in a silent film. Her father's was the only office lit. She picked up the ancient security telephone at the service gate and waited for Ed Aycker's sleepy mild voice and the sharp double tone of the buzzer. It had excited her once, this clandestine transaction: it had put her in mind of coded entry to a military compound, or the vault of a bank, or the visiting room of a prison.

—You came in the back way? said her father before she could knock.

—Same way as always.

—I'm surprised Ed let you in with that crew cut of yours. Not everybody gets past him, you know. Must be a sign that you are pure of heart.

—You made that joke last week, she said, lifting a stack of legal folders off a stool.

—As I recall, you didn't laugh then either.

—I guess I haven't changed my mind about it.

—Fair enough. He brought his hands together in an attitude of prayer, an unconscious salaam, a gesture he'd newly adopted. —You haven't changed your mind about anything else, I suppose.

—I fly out tomorrow.

He lowered his hands to the desk. —And your mother? How's she handling this, would you say?

—She turned all the pictures around. Even ones you're not in.

—Don't play dumb with me, Aden. It doesn't suit you. He looked down at his hands. —How's she handling this trip of yours, I mean.

She watched him for a time across the great round-cornered teak-wood desk that took up half the room. He had brought her with him to work on certain rare afternoons of her childhood, a reward for good behavior, and she'd often napped beneath its creaking eaves. In her imagination and occasionally even in her dreams she'd sat behind it, poring over parchment scrolls and penning learned studies. It seemed unwieldy to her now, a monument to some forgotten culture, an ocean liner stranded in the desert. Her father's soft complacent face was hard to get in focus.

—It's not a trip, she said.

—Of course it's a trip.

—Not the way you mean.

—No? Maybe you should explain.

—I shouldn't have to explain. Not to you. She shook her head. —I'm not going over there just to see the sights, Teacher.

—I've never liked it when you call me that.

—I know.

He nodded for a time. —You're traveling to the Emirates to study, he said finally. —To improve your language skills, to broaden your perspective, to see for yourself what the fuss is about. I appreciate that. You're a serious girl, Aden. An asker of questions. You always have been. He pressed his palms lightly together. —Or is there some other reason?

She stared down at the floor between her feet, at divots in the carpet where a less stately desk had once stood. She wondered whose office the room had been then. She could picture no one but her father in that space.

—Have you given any further thought to your plans for the future? he asked her. —To your education?

—This is my education.

—I've spoken again with Dean Lawford. He's agreed, very generously, to permit a deferral—

—I know all about that.

—I'd like to speak frankly with you, Aden, if I may. He arranged his features into a smile. —This past year has been hard on all of us. I was distracted when you asked for my help with this adventure of yours, and I do regret that. But things have stabilized now, as you're no doubt aware, and I hope that you'll regard me as a resource. I have friends in Dubai: people you may find it good to know. I've prepared a list.

Her father pushed an index card across the desktop.

—There will be some adjustment required, needless to say. A great deal of adjustment. And in the matter of your return ticket—

—Don't worry about that.

—Sweetheart. Look at me for a second. You'd do well to consider—

—How are things with Mrs. Al-Hadid?

He hesitated. —Ayah is well, Aden. Thank you for asking.

—Ed Aycker ever give her any trouble?

—I wonder how your Arabic is coming, said her father.

—It's coming just fine.

—I wonder if you can read the verses on the wall behind me. In the little brass frame.

—In the name of God, she said. —Merciful to all. Compassionate to each.

—Those are good words to remember. Especially where you're going. Her father coughed and shifted in his chair. —Merciful to all, he repeated. —*Compassionate* to each.

She could hear students in the hallway outside, at least half a dozen, making high-pitched theatrical chatter. A hand was pressed against the glass as if in greeting. She gave her father the nod he expected.

—Good words to remember, he said. —There's a reason they're the first words of the Book.

—I know more words than that.

—I don't doubt you do.

—The woman and man found guilty of adultery. Flog each of them a hundred—

—Shut your mouth, said her father. He spoke in a lighthearted voice, as if amused. —I was a student of sharia before you existed as a thought in your poor benighted mother's mind or in the All Creator's either. What you understand about scripture could fit in a tub of eyeliner. Go to the Emirates with that attitude and God have mercy on your soul.

She leaned back on her stool and studied him.

—What are you grinning at?

—Eyeliner doesn't come in tubs, she said. —It comes in sticks.

—I see. He bobbed his head. —This is a joke to you.

She watched him and said nothing.

—What about that boyfriend of yours? Does he have the slightest idea what he's getting himself into?

—Decker isn't my boyfriend.

He flapped a hand impatiently, a quick dismissive gesture, the same one her mother had made not an hour before. —What do his parents say?

—They're proud of him, actually. Supportive, I mean. They've got family there.

—I was told the Yousafzais were Pakistani.

—They're Pashtuns, she said. —From near the Afghan border.

—I see. He watched her. —They emigrated to Dubai at some point, I'm assuming. Looking for work.

When she said nothing he sat back stiffly in his chair. Again his palms came nervously together.

—Your hair was so lovely. So curly and dark. You were terribly vain about it when you were small. He looked down at his hands. —Do you have any recollection of that?

—None at all.

—Are you doing this to hurt us, Aden? To punish us? Your mother and myself?

She gazed up at the scroll above the desk, letting her sight go dim and out of focus, watching the letters writhe and curl together. Those fluid voluptuous letters. No language on earth was more beautiful to look at, more beautiful to speak. She knew it and her father knew it. The difference was he saw the beauty only. She herself saw the grief and forbearance and hope behind the brushwork, the suffering brought to bear on every calligraph. But beauty was its first attribute and the most dangerous by far. The beauty of austerity. The beauty of no quarter. She felt its pull and saw no earthly end to it.

—You think everything comes down to you, she said at last. —That everything's on account of you, or thanks to you, or coming back off something bad you've done.

—Aden, I—

—But you're wrong. I don't think about you much at all.

The students were louder now and more numerous but if anything the room seemed more sequestered than before. It seemed airless and dank. Her father's eyes were closed and he appeared to be asleep.

His chest rose and fell. When he spoke again she had to strain to hear him.

—I apologize, sweetheart. I'm trying very hard to understand.

—That's all right. I forgive you. The first part of my jihad—

—For God's sake, Aden, don't call it that.

—*Jihad* means struggle, that's all. Any kind of a struggle. You taught me that yourself. Don't you remember?

—It's a new century now. A new world. He interlaced his fingers. —Things are taking a turn.

—I don't know what that means.

—It means you need to be aware of the rest of the world, not just Claire and myself. Are you listening to me? You need to take its fear and its prejudice into account. You need to consider other people's ignorance, Aden. He let out a breath. —You need to consider your own.

—I'll leave that to the experts. I'll leave that to you.

—You're still not hearing me, apparently. I'm endeavoring to explain—

—If they want to pass judgment they can go right ahead. They do it all the time anyway. At school and everywhere else. Even in my own house. But you wouldn't know about that.

—Aden—

—Try and stop me if that's what you want.

—I don't want to stop you, her father said tightly. —That's not my position at all.

—Don't talk down to me, then. It doesn't suit you.

Before he could answer she took up her pack. An army surplus model, sun-bleached and tattered, with squares of darker cloth where the insignia had been. She'd found it in the attic of her father's house the day before Thanksgiving, the day she'd decided to take up her jihad. She sat up and cleared her throat and raised the pack so he could see it, thinking even now to ask his blessing. But her father's eyes were dull and flat and blind.

—The religion I've spent my life studying teaches deference to one's elders, he said slowly. —It teaches the child to venerate the teachings of the father.

—Not if the father is an apostate.

—Aden, do you fully understand what that word means?

She got to her feet. He shook his head at that, regretfully and stiffly, as though forbidding her to take another step.

—I'm sure you're aware that I could put a stop to this adventure with a phone call. And the more I hear you talk, sweetheart, the more inclined I am to do so.

—You did this yourself when you were my age. You've been talking about it my whole life. It's the only thing you've ever talked about.

—I'd just turned twenty-two when I went to Kandahar. Twenty-two, Aden, not barely eighteen. And there's a more significant issue than your age.

—I don't know what you mean.

—You're being childish again. The possibilities for a woman in that part of the world are limited, as you know very well. You have disappointments in store, I'm afraid.

—Well Teacher you're wrong about that.

—We're fighting again. Let's both just take a moment—

—I'm going to get to places that you've never been. All kinds of places. I'm going to see things that you couldn't even dream of.

She met Decker on the airport bus at noon. He was dressed in a tracksuit and a Giants cap and his sneakers sat beside him on the seat across the aisle. His duffel was black and his high-tops were the same acidic orange as his tracksuit. An unlit Camel dangled from his downturned boyish mouth. When he saw Aden coming he picked up a book.

—You don't smoke, she said.

—I'm an international man of mystery, Sawyer. There's things you didn't know about me yet.

She nodded. —Like that you can read.

—I'm just reviewing this here list of conjugations. He puffed out his chest. —I happen to be traveling to Pakistan today.

She glanced across the aisle at his high-tops. —I thought you might be traveling to a kickball game in Oakland.

—This look is like American Express, he said, adjusting his cap.
—It's accepted worldwide.

—There's a lot of places don't take American Express. She passed him the high-tops and sat where they'd been. —La Tapatía, for example.

—La Tapatía? Decker said, raising his eyebrows. —That taco place back of the Costco?

—Lots of places don't take it.

—They'll take it in Karachi, he said as the bus began rolling. —What did you think people wear over there, Sawyer? Turbans and pointy slippers?

—I couldn't care less.

He frowned at her. —Why's that?

—Because Karachi's not the place I want to be.

It was hot on the bus and Decker nodded off quickly, his forehead propped against the greasy glass. She looked past him at outlets and drive-throughs and strip malls and cloverleaf ramps. The light on the hills was the light she knew best, the embalming golden light of California, and it lay thickly over everything she saw. Already looking out at that land-scape was like watching footage of some half-forgotten life.

Decker started awake just as they reached the airport. —What time is it?

—We're all right.

—Did we miss our one o'clocks?

—It's okay. We can pray when we get out.

The terminal was the last part of America she'd see and she made a point of paying close attention. The guideways, the acoustic tile, the sterility, the equivalence of every point and feature. She'd loved it as a child, seeing her father off to Islamabad or Ankara or Mazar-i-Sharif, and the child that survived in her loved it there still. The most American of places. A luminous blank.

A flight crew hurried past—the genteel blue-eyed pilots, the co-quettish attendants—and an usher with a bindi waved them forward with a bow. The scene might have been choreographed for her express instruction: the quick servile gesture, the noblesse oblige. She felt the old childish thrill and did nothing to curb it. It posed no danger anymore. Her eyes were open.

—What are you smiling at, Sawyer?

—I used to come here sometimes.

Decker stopped and adjusted his sneakers. —Tell you what. I've never even been inside a plane.

—You'll like it.

—What does Swiss food even taste like?

—Swiss food?

—We're taking Swiss Air, right? It's a sixteen-hour flight. They've got to feed us something.

She took his hand. —Let's go, man of mystery. We're late for prayers.

They found a small bluish room labeled INTERFAITH CHAPEL past the food court and set their bags in a neat row beside its entrance. A family of Mennonites rose to leave as soon as they came in. A limping old man and his wife and two toddlers. Decker held the door for them. Their dark formal clothing rasped and whispered as they moved. The wife seemed barely older than he was and she smiled at him sweetly as she sauntered out. Decker watched her until she was out of sight.

—I'm not supposed to say this in here, but that old Hasid is one lucky bastard. Did you see the look I just got?

—You're right.

—Damn straight I'm right. Did you even—

—You're not supposed to say that in here.

—Okay, Sawyer. My bad. Seriously though—

—And those weren't Hasids.

Decker sucked in a breath. —I'm getting a tater tot kind of smell. Tortilla chips maybe. I'm guessing from the Taco Bell next door.

—Shut up and help me move these chairs around.

They cleared a space at the front of the room and laid their prayer mats on the stain-resistant carpet and cleansed themselves with water from a bottle. Decker's prayer mat matched his tracksuit and his sneak-ers. Aden watched him for a moment, then shifted slightly to the left.

—How do you know that's east, Sawyer? There's no windows in here.

—It's east.

He nodded dubiously. —We're praying at the food court, basically.

—I'll tell you what I'm going to do, Decker. I'm going to go ahead and say the prayer we missed. What you decide to do is totally your call. Maybe your Mennonite's waiting at the Taco Bell. Maybe you guys can split a quesarito scrambler.

—Is that what you think she was? A Mennonite?

She gave him no answer. Eventually he kicked off his high-tops and knelt next to her.

—That's better, said Aden, prostrating herself.

—So long as you're happy. I think this is south.

When they came out of the chapel their luggage was gone. They stood blinking wordlessly down at the carpet, listening to the crackle and hiss of the PA. She felt no panic, only a coldness mustering under her ribs. Her passport and visa had been in her duffel.

—Those motherfuckers, said Decker. —We were praying, for shit's sake.

—It's all right. It's all right. We just need to find security. They can't be far.

Decker let out a groan. —I bet it's illegal, leaving bags around like that. Do you think they'll—

—No I don't. We were stupid, that's all. I was stupid.

Lost Baggage was in another terminal altogether and by the time they'd found it both their shirts were dark with sweat. Its foyer was the same jaundiced blue as the chapel. The guard at the window knew what they'd come for before they said a word. Their passports lay face-down on the countertop in front of him.

—You kids might as well take it easy. No one's flying anywhere today.

They waited for him to go on, wavering slightly in place, struggling to master their breathing. The guard looked down at them from on high, remote and unmoved, like a judge at some inconsequential trial. He took off his glasses and began to clean them with a wrinkled handkerchief. He seemed to consider the matter resolved.

—I'm not sure I understand you, sir, said Aden.

—Leaving two unmarked black duffel bags in the busiest part of the international terminal, right outside of the chapel. And a backpack. The guard shook his head. —Right next to the food court, for Jesus' sake. Neither of you been in an airport before?

—I've been to this airport eighteen times, sir, not counting today. With my family. We live in Santa Rosa.

The guard squinted down at her passport for a time. —Aden Grace Sawyer, he said thoughtfully.

—That's right.

—You've cut your hair since this passport was issued, Miss Sawyer.

—So what? said Decker.

—I wouldn't of recognized you, the guard went on. —You look like a boy.

—We're students, said Decker before she could answer. —We're on our way to Pakistan for school.

The guard flipped through her passport with an elaborate show of disinterest. He seemed unsurprised to find its pages blank. —What kind of a school?

—A madrasa, said Aden.

—A what?

—It's a religious school, said Decker. —Like a Catholic school, but for the study of the Holy Qur'an. It's actually—

—Just do what you're going to do to us, said Aden.

—Excuse me, Miss Sawyer? I'm not sure I heard you quite right.

—There's nothing illegal in those bags. You've searched them already so you ought to know.

—I wouldn't say nothing, Miss Sawyer. I wouldn't say that. He lifted Decker's duffel onto the counter. —*Defense of the Muslim Lands*, he said, bringing out a paperback without a cover. He brought out another. —*Join the Caravan.*

—Those are religious texts, she said. —They're for our course of study.

—These books are on the State Department watchlist. They're recruitment texts for militant jihad.

—We bought them from the campus bookstore of the University of California at Berkeley. There's nothing illegal about having those books.

—Her father's the dean of Middle Eastern studies, Decker cut in. —You know what a dean is?

—Tell your Arab friend to shut his mouth, said the guard.

This is what it means to live with open eyes, she thought. This place was here when I came with my father and we passed it by without even noticing. This same man sitting here at this same window. People stood where I'm standing but I never saw them. Where are those people now.

Decker was shouting something about freedom of religion.

—If you're not going to give us our bags back, tell us, Aden said. —Tell us that and we'll go.

The guard's drawn and bloodless face regarded her through the window, so leached of human feeling that it barely seemed a face. The waiting area smelled of exhaust and toner cartridges and sweat. The noise of traffic carried in from the outside. He hears this all day, Aden said to herself. All day long he hears these sounds and breathes this air. No one ends up here by choice. Not even him.

—I never said you couldn't have your bags, the guard said finally, shutting Aden's passport with a shrug. —I don't think you've heard a single word I told you.

By some undeserved miracle they reached the gate at final boarding call and were rushed aboard the plane like VIPs. People glared at them but she was used to worse. As they made their way up the aisle, disheveled and short of breath, a rush of jubilation overtook her. They were headed to Dubai and after that to Karachi and more of the faithful surrounded her than she'd ever seen outside a mosque. The plane would soon be airborne, a sovereign state, accountable to no laws but its own. Her country had relinquished her without a hint of protest. She was gone.

—I expected that to be rough, Decker whispered once they'd gotten to their seats. —The scanners and the pat-downs and the questions and all. But that was— He shook his head. —I don't know what that was. Son of a bitch, Sawyer. They made me unbuckle my pants.

—They do that to everybody.

—It's because we're Muslim, isn't it? They think I'm going to set my beard on fire.

—I'm kind of hoping you will, to be honest.

—Fuck you.

—Might not be worth the trouble, though. I'm counting maybe fifteen hairs.

—Better than you can do, Sawyer.

—No argument there.

—You look about six with that haircut. Like they had to shave your head at school to check for fleas.

She smiled at him. —What was up with all that b.s. back there? My father isn't dean of anything. You know that.

He shrugged. —You told me that he used to be. Back before his, shall we say, romantic complications.

—You were lying, she said. —You were bearing false witness.

—Your virtue does you credit, pilgrim. But it would be a hell of a lot more convincing if you stopped grinning like a monkey.

She closed her eyes and settled back into her seat. —I can't believe we're on this plane, she said.

She came awake in the dark to the sound of her name. She was far from herself and returned only slowly. The voice she had heard was not her mother's or her father's, not exactly, but the same silvery thread of worry ran through it that her parents' voices had. She waited with her eyes closed but it did not speak again.

—You are traveling to the Emirates? said a man across the aisle.

Blearily she turned to take his measure. He was portly and bearded and he blinked at her kindly. His voice was not the voice that had spoken her name but he seemed a remnant of her dream regardless. He wore a blue chalk-striped blazer over a shalwar kameez and a Qur'an lay open on his seatback table. She sat up and made an effort to seem boyish.

—Just to change planes, she said. —We're going to Karachi. My friend has family in Pakistan.

—Ah, the man said. —Karachi.

He pulled the Book toward him and asked no more questions. He sat spotlit and solemn, the only passenger in sight who wasn't sleeping. His thin lips moved subtly. He seemed to be reciting from memory.

—We're traveling to Peshawar, she said. —To a madrasa there.

—A madrasa! the man said. —That is very fine. He spoke a musical and British-sounding English. —Your intention is to memorize the suras? To learn them to heart?

—Yes, sir. It is.

He nodded gravely. —You are embarking on an honorable spree.

—I am, she said, biting her lip to keep from smiling. Beside her Decker mumbled in his sleep.

—But it is soon for you, I think, to leave your family. You can't have many more than fourteen years.

—My family can spare me, she said.

The man inclined his head. —You do them credit.

—Thank you, sir. I'm not sure they'd see it that way.

He let this pass without comment. —Peshawar is an uncertain place. But in the madrasa you will have your security. They will see to your case.

—To my case?

The man smiled and said nothing.

They sat for what seemed a great while without speaking, listening to the sighs and protestations of the plane. Underneath or behind the man's amiable manner was a quality that set him apart from the passengers around him. Or so it seemed to her as she watched him in the artificial twilight of the cabin.

—We hope to continue on from Peshawar, she said. —After we've finished our studies.

The man nodded politely.

—My friend says Pakistan is not an Islamic state. Not in the true sense of the word.

He gave what might have been a laugh. —Ah! he said. —Of course. It's very far from that.

—We're hoping to visit Afghanistan.

—Yes?

—Yes, sir. To cross into Nangarhar by the Torkham Gate.

The man's expression brightened. —But that is my own country! The Nangarhar province. We have a saying on the road when you arrive, a kind of advertisement: Nangarhar, House of Knowledge, Cradle of Peace. He nodded to himself. —It is warm in Nangarhar, and very green. Green all the year. We have another saying there: Forever Spring.

Of course this man is an Afghan, Aden thought. Of course he is. She waited respectfully until he spoke again.

—My work is in fabrics. I reside in Karachi. I have not seen Nangarhar in quite some years.

—I would like to see it, Aden said. —I'm excited to see it.

—You must see it.

—It's safer now, I think. My friend tells me it's safer. The warlords have all been pushed back to the north.

The man made a gesture she couldn't interpret.

—Isn't that true?

—The animals of the north have been given a kick, he said, repeating the same cutting movement.

—Yes.

—By other animals. By other beasts.

—By students, she said. —By the devout. By a learned coalition.

—Young man, he said slowly. —Where have you heard of this?

She held her breath and counted down from ten. It was hard to speak calmly. —My friend told me about it. He gave me a book.

—A book? said the man. —Not the Qur'an, I think.

—They're talibs, sir. Students. They're fighting to bring faith back to the country. They're fighting against the godless, like the mujahideen did against the Russians. Am I wrong about that?

—I will ask you a question.

—Please.

—Why do you care to pass over the border?

—I told you already, sir. I— She hesitated. —I just want to see it. A place ruled by believers. A country full of people living by the word of God.

—Your friend fancies himself an adventurer, does he? A bearer of arms? He glanced past her. —He has this ambition? To join in the fight?

Reflexively she turned to look at Decker. His mouth was working quietly as he slept.

—He told me he doesn't, she answered. —He promised me that.

—I see.

It struck her now that the man's manner had changed. Though he remained civil he no longer looked at her. —No such ambition, he said, letting his eyes rest on Decker. —I am satisfied to hear it.

—Why is that?

—Because he is still very young.

He opened his Qur'an and did not speak again. For the rest of the flight he remained as he was, sitting straight-backed and serene with the Book in his lap. Each time Aden awoke she looked shyly at him in his warm pool of light and found him exactly as he'd been before. When they arrived in Dubai he asked her help in bringing down his rolling suitcase and thanked her and wished her good fortune with her study of the Recitation. She never saw him again.

—Who were you talking to? said Decker as they came out of the gate.

—A Pashtun from Nangarhar. Can you believe it?

He let out a yawn. —That explains that.

—Meaning what?

—He had that sort of tribal shuffle. Like this. Decker took a few waddling steps. —It comes from walking barefoot over rocks.

—You've never seen an Afghan in your life. You're just being ignorant.

—There's an Afghan kebab place in Santa Rosa, Sawyer. You've been there yourself. What the hell kind of mood are you in?

She'd wanted so badly for things to be different. The place and the people. She'd hoped for grace and dignity and unity of purpose. Instead she felt the same disgust she'd felt at SFO, the same dismay, the same remove from everything she saw. Certain details had changed but the place was no different. The same shadowlessness, the same array of gaudy shops, the same sterility. She'd been a fool to think her country had released her.

They were sitting at their connecting gate before she spoke again.
—I hate it here. We might as well still be in California.
—It's an airport, Sawyer. Decker yawned into his sleeve. —What did you expect?
—I don't know. She pressed a thumb to her teeth and bit down on the cuticle. —I don't know, she repeated. —Not this place.

A group of Saudis passed them on their way to a neighboring gate, the men in tunics and keffiyeh and open-toed expensive-looking shoes. The wives walked a few steps behind their husbands, chattering and ignoring their overfed children, encumbered with bright bags of luxury goods. She felt sick to her stomach. The children clutched their own bags to their chests or dragged them indifferently across the polished floor. The smallest boy carried a bottle of cologne in a starfish-shaped box.

Decker sighed and cracked his knuckles as he watched the Saudis pass. —Are we just going to sit here for the next six million hours?
—I don't like it any better than you do.

He gave her statement due consideration. —All right then, he said. —Let's get up to no good.

They spent the next hour in a shop called Golden Ali Baba Duty Free. The prices were displayed on sliding vinyl tabs beneath each item and while Decker engaged the saleswoman in conversation Aden went stealthily to work in Scotch & Bourbon. The twelve-year Macallan that had been on sale at €59.99 was now offered at €99.95 and the eighteen-year at €00.99. The Glenlivet was €6,779.02 and the Jameson cost nothing at all. On the highest shelf, in a velvet-lined case previously occupied by Laphroaig Original Cask Strength, she set a starfish-shaped bottle of cologne. Then she noticed the saleswoman standing behind her.

—You are helping with my work? That is generous. But first to learn the difference between whiskey and perfume.

—Where we come from they're the same, she heard Decker answer. —They're both made from the devil's urine. The dreaded Al-Kool.

—And where is this place? said the woman, beckoning to security.

—Nangarhar, said Aden.

—Don't judge us, miss, said Decker. —We're mujahideen. We were born in a cave.

To their amazement they were ushered out of the shop without further questioning and left to disappear into the crowd. Decker whispered that they should take this as a blessing, maybe even an omen, which did not sound like Decker at all. She spun slowly in place in the bustling concourse and everything she saw and heard surprised her. The distance she'd felt earlier had passed without her noticing and now she fought the urge to laugh or to dance or to shout at the top of her lungs. She saw women in niqab and men in keffiyeh and blinding white vestments and began at last to understand how far she was from home. It made her feel as weightless as a bird.

Sometime later they found themselves in a magazine shop and her sight fell on a row of books in Arabic and Persian. She saw no English names or words at all. To have traveled so far. To have crossed half the world. She ran a thumb across the richly colored spines.

—We made it, she heard Decker say. —We finally made it, Sawyer.

She chose a book at random and studied its cover. The word embossed there in silver foil was one she did not know. It lay dead on her tongue when she tried to pronounce it. She grew aware of Decker close behind her.

—Not yet, she said.

He hooked a finger through her belt and turned her toward him.

—The hell with that. We made it, girl. We're gone.

—That old man, she said quietly. —The one on the plane.

—What? He drew her closer. —Don't talk to me about some fat old man right now.

—He asked if you were an adventurer. That's what he called it. If you planned to go and fight.

—Of course not.

—That's what I told him.

—Admit it though, Sawyer. It would be—

—It would be stupid.

—For you, I guess. He gave a shrug. —Because you're not a man.

She said nothing for a moment. —You're just pretending now. It's make-believe. You're trying out a part.

—Of course I am, he said. —And so are you.

She stood there unflinching and let him appraise her. He'd earned this much, surely. This modest concession. His face too close to hers to get in focus. His warm smoker's breath on her lips and her neck. She felt his thumbnail through the linen of her shirt.

—Sawyer, he whispered. —Let's go find a place.

A shiver ran through her as she braced the heel of her right hand against his ribs. He smiled and leaned closer. She pushed away and saw his eyes go dark.

—Careful, Decker.

—What for?

—Use your head for a second. All right? Think about where we are.

He frowned and slid his hand under her shirt. The heat of it felt good after the chill.

—This is the Emirates, she whispered. —Not some park bench in Berkeley.

—I don't—

—Not a place where you want to get caught with a boy.

—Don't be an idiot, Sawyer. You're not as convincing as that.

—Take a look for yourself.

He turned his head and as he did she watched the understanding hit. —How long have they been doing that?

—Doing what?

—You know what goddamn it. Staring like they want to hang me from a flagpole by my balls.

—I'm guessing probably since you got a boner.

He didn't laugh. —Just get me out of here.

She led him by the sleeve past the cashier and a knot of hard-eyed patrons to an empty gate across the corridor. He followed her tamely. His expression was that of someone lost in thought.

—You're angry at me, she said as they sat down.

—I'm not angry. He squinted at the floor. —I don't know what I am.

—Listen to me, Decker. You came all this way and I'm grateful. I'm so grateful to you. I never could have made it by myself.

He shook his head. —You'd have made it fine without me. Better, probably.

—You're the only friend I have. Do you know that?

—I do, actually. But you're the kind of person who doesn't need more than one. He grinned at her. —One might even be too much.

—Would you stop for a second?

—I'm not—

—Stop trying to be funny. She pushed his shoulders back as she bent toward him. —This is going to come out wrong.

—What is?

—It's not too late for you to go back home.

His mouth came open but he made no sound.

—Because it isn't going to happen, she said gently.

—What are you talking about?

—What you wanted back there, in that shop. It isn't going to happen, all right? Are you listening? Not ever again.

She'd thought her roundabout way of talking might confuse him but he understood at once. —But you like it, he mumbled. —You told me you liked it. You never once said no to me before.

—That was before, she told him. —That was in a different country.

—What does the *country* have to—

—Look at me, Decker. Do I look like the person you did that stuff with? Do I even still look like Aden Sawyer?

—You look like Aden Sawyer with a haircut. He bowed his head. —It doesn't matter anyway. I know who you are.

—You know who I used to be, maybe. When I had long hair and smoked pot and washed the piss out of my mom's sheets every day. But I'm not even sure you knew me then.

She watched his features slacken. He put up no argument, said nothing at all, and she gave a silent thanks for the reprieve. She couldn't have explained it any better. She was still trying to explain it to herself.

—All I'm saying is that you can change your mind. You don't have to get on this next flight, even. You can do what you want.

Decker didn't answer.

—I'll tell you what, though.

—What?

—I can't think of anything back home I'm going to miss.

To her astonishment he looked at her and laughed. —And here I thought this trip was my idea. All those chatrooms. All those books I made you read. *Join the Caravan* and whatnot.

—I'm not joining any caravans. I'm not joining any armies. Don't go trying to change the game on me. Okay?

She sat back and waited for his grudging nod.

—Okay. Thanks. And one more thing.

—Holy shit. What?

—I won't be using swear words anymore. I won't be cursing.

He let out a breath. —You're really fucking doing this.

—Of course I am. Just like we said.

—Hold on. He cocked his head. —Did something happen with your voice?

—What do you mean?

—Your voice sounds lower. Are you doing that on purpose?

—Took you long enough to notice. She grinned at him. —I've been practicing forever. Like a month.

He sat back in his seat. —And this whole time I've been worrying that you'd have second thoughts. I've got to be the dumbest shit there ever was.

—I didn't think you'd come at all, she said, taking his hand in hers.
—I was so surprised to see you on that bus.

Half an hour before boarding she dug her toiletries bag out of her father's pack and followed the backlit signage to the restrooms. The men's and women's entrances were separated by a frosted glass partition and she stopped in front of it, flushed and lightheaded, waiting for her fear to die away. Men passed to the right of her, women to the left. The women glanced at her reflexively before averting their eyes but the men paid her no mind at all. She waited and watched, drawing courage from their obvious indifference. A boy of no more than ten shuffled by, fiddling sleepily with the zipper of his jeans. She gritted her teeth and followed him inside.

The restroom seemed more harshly lit even than the corridor and she was about to turn and bolt when she saw that the men at the urinals took care to look at no one but themselves. She hadn't expected such a show of modesty. She had a dim but sharp-edged memory of being taken into a lavatory by her father years before, of staring up at the urinals in wonder and confusion, and she pictured him guiding her forward now, his strong square palm between her shoulder blades. The farthest stall was empty and she locked its door behind her.

The floor of the stall was littered with bunched wads of paper, the damp debris of bodies in extremis, worlds different from the brilliance of the terminal outside. She gave thanks for the mess: it made the space less frightening, less perfect. She might have been in any public restroom in the world. She lowered the lid of the toilet and sat—tentatively at first, then with all of her weight—and quickly pulled off her kameez.

She sat motionless then with the shirt in her lap, listening to the sounds from the urinals and the stalls and the sinks, so different from the noises women made. She heard no restraint or even self-awareness in the grunts of effort and relief around her. She was sitting on a toilet in a place reserved for men. No one had tried to stop her. She stared down at her fish-white arms and faintly freckled shoulders. The thrill of secret knowledge made it difficult to breathe. She pulled her pants and panties down and pushed her knees apart. The lure of invisibility. The power of deceit. These pleasures were ungodly and she endeavored to suppress them but they racked her with excitement all the same. She was no one in that instant, an animal with neither name nor history, which also meant that she was not a child. Her childhood meant less to her now than the wads of paper littering the floor.

A man came to the door as she sat there entranced and tried to force it open with his shoulder. He was wearing espadrilles and chinos and he abused the door in Arabic before he stepped away. He seemed to think that no one was inside.

She still wore a tank top that Decker had lent her and when the man had gone she looked down at her chest. Though the air in the terminal was perfectly conditioned she was sweating and her nipples stood out plainly through the cloth. The man was two stalls down from her now and she heard him muttering and fumbling with his belt. She pulled the tank top over her head and hung it from a hook and held her breasts in her hands, as she sometimes did to lull herself to sleep. Her hands could still cover them, but only just. She felt secure again and let her mind wander for a time, listening to all the pissing men. Then she opened her toiletries case and brought out an Ace bandage that had once been her mother's and wound it carefully around her ribs and chest.

Karachi proved a greater disappointment than the airport in Dubai. It reminded her of Oakland and Sacramento and the handful of other cities she knew, but it was hotter and more desperate and smelled of things she couldn't put a name to. The housing complexes and vacant lots and even the construction sites seemed primeval to her, the ground cracked and septic, the packed bazaars and thoroughfares a scrim over some underlying ruin. It disgusted and dismayed her and the shame this triggered brought her close to panic. The fault was hers, she knew, and not the city's. She was seeing it as her mother would have seen it.

She hailed an unmarked taxicab and rode with Decker to the terminal for buses headed north and bought two tickets. She'd expected him to protest, to insist that they spend that first night in the city, but he followed her like someone half asleep. He made no mention of his cousins in Karachi.

A bus left for Peshawar that same afternoon and they waited in the diesel-smelling courtyard of HINDUKUSH HI-WAYS, dipping flatbread into bowls of tepid dhal. The buses that passed as they sat on their duffels were garishly colored and slathered in images painted by hand: diamonds and horses and crude constellations, pomegranates and tigers, bluebirds and mountains and all-seeing eyes. She marveled at the profusion of graven renderings in a nation of Muslims but reminded herself how far from the true faith the country had fallen. She pictured the buses' interiors as richly upholstered and smoky with incense, smelling of anise and cinnamon, like the restaurants she'd gone to on Sunday evenings with her father and mother, long ago and on the far side of the world.

Eighteen buses passed through the yard, each more ornate than the last, before the Bannu Line to Peshawar arrived. The passengers ignored them but the man who filled their teacups watched them closely. He watched her when she stood to use the toilet and he watched as she returned. When they settled their bill he gave an elaborate bow, leering frankly at Aden, and rested his right hand on Decker's shoulder. He said something in Urdu as he took the cups away.

—What did he say to you?

—Didn't catch it, Decker muttered, stepping past her.

—What was it?

—Stop looking at him damn it. Let's just go.

The bus to Peshawar was empty when they climbed aboard, as though some disaster had struck the north without their knowledge. They sat down and waited with their bags on their knees, neither of them speaking a word, and her stomach began to cramp from the fumes and the dhal. Men boarded singly or in pairs, many of them holding hands, and seemed to fall asleep as soon as they sat down. They had a forsaken look to them, chagrined and defeated, though it was possible that they were only tired. Many of them were wearing freshly store-bought shirts with creases at the collars and the sleeves. It was the day before Juma'a and she imagined them bound for villages along the northwest border, in the tribal regions, to pass the Day of Assembly with their families before returning by that same reeking bus to whatever form of work it was that had left them so expressionless and still.

As they drove northward out of the city, past tarp-covered bazaars and ornate mosques and slime-clogged aqueducts, she began by degrees to recover. The sun rode low over the shining alluvial fan of the Indus and a line of cranes flew gracefully across its red disk as if the sprawl the bus moved through were no more than a trick of the eye. Decker's head came to rest on her shoulder. His touch was innocent in sleep and drew her back into her body and she felt safe inside her clothes again and comfortable and calm. A sentence she'd read in some chatroom came back to her as her own head grew heavy: *You can either touch each other's skin or you can touch the face of God.* She slid nearer to Decker and felt his coarse disheveled hair against her neck. He was beautiful and she wanted him against her. For the briefest of instants she wanted not to disappear. Then she thought of the waiter in the exhaust-stained courtyard and the look on his face as he'd whispered in Urdu. She thought of the way his tongue had come to rest against his teeth.

She came awake in the night to Decker's breath against her neck. —Did you say something?

—Tell me, said Decker.

—What? I just woke up. I don't—

—Tell me why you're here.

—I don't know what you're talking about.

—On this bus. Heading north. Here with me.

She willed herself to think clearly. —I'm sticking to the plan we made, that's all. The one we made in Santa Rosa.

—The hell you are.

She kept quiet and watched him. He seemed to be smiling.

—When you got your hair buzzed and started wearing those clothes I thought it was for both of us. For you to follow me. For us to keep together. He shook his head. —I was wrong about that. Or else you were lying.

—I wasn't lying. Not to you. I've never lied to you.

He nodded to himself, considering her answer. —You like girls.

—Come on, Decker. That's not even a question.

—What's the answer?

She looked past him out the window. His round head hung reflected there with her own head behind. In silhouette she saw no difference between them.

—I don't know.

They were in high country now with the least curve of moon. She thought of her conversion and the vows that she had made. As always the fact of it calmed her. A fire smoldered in the courtyard of a newly finished mosque and she saw herself arriving for the first prayer of the morning, the dawn light behind her, all heads turning as she stepped across the threshold. She imagined their indignation, then their wonder, then the voice of the mullah calling their attention back to prayer. She saw herself taking her place among them, gracious in her modesty, sovereign in her devotion. She turned the image back and forth in her mind, letting each of its brilliant facets catch the light. Then she imagined herself in her little room in Santa Rosa, staring up at the ceiling, listening to her mother's labored breathing through the wall.

—I'm going to ask you a favor, she said. —No more questions.

—You don't have many favors left to ask.

—You can go home any time you want. I told you that.

He shook his head. —Bullshit. You don't speak Urdu or Pashto, maybe two or three words, and that fancy Arabic of yours won't cut it anywhere outside a mosque. If I go home you're done.

—You said yourself that I'd have made it—

—I don't see you fooling this country for six whole weeks, Sawyer. I'll tell you that much for free. You'd better have a story ready for them when they catch you in your panties and your bra.

She hesitated. —You said they have a custom here. Remember? Of girls being dressed up as boys. You said they even have a name for it.

—That's got nothing to do with what I'm talking about. Nothing.

—Tell me the name again, Decker.

—You know it yourself, he said. —*Bacha posh.* But that's something parents decide for their children. Fathers decide it. It won't do a thing for you if you get caught. He gripped her arm. —Why the fuck are you smiling?

—Just about what you said.

—What I said?

—The six weeks.

—Listen to me, he hissed. —I plan to make it back to Santa Rosa with all my parts in mint condition. I plan to come home with my head on my neck and my dick in my shorts.

She smiled in the dark. —I can't blame you for that.

—Then why are you so goddamn happy?

—I'm not sure I'll be going back at all.

The next time she awoke it was morning and the sun was high and pale above the Indus. She looked out at the water, faster and deeper and blacker. A true northern river. The road ran hard by the bank and followed every cut and furrow of the hillside. The tribal zone was perhaps fifty miles to the west and she told herself that she could feel its closeness. Then she told herself that she felt no such thing.

Dust filled the air even at that early hour and wraithlike men and oxen staggered through it. The bus overtook flatbed trucks hauling propane and rock salt and chickens in blue wicker cages. Three boys on a moped passed them on an incline and threw fistfuls of sand at her window. They stuck out their tongues at her and she salaamed.

—We'll be there in an hour, said Decker.

—Who says so?

—My best buddy Khalid, he said, pointing across the aisle. He lowered his voice. —He's been trying to sell me hashish.

—An hour, she said, sitting forward. —That's soon.

She reached up sleepily to arrange her bangs and was surprised for a moment to find her head shorn. She turned back to the window to hide her confusion. The bedlam outside was so all-encompassing that it put her in mind of a mass exodus, or some great northward pilgrimage, or the aftermath of an enormous wedding.

—This is what you wanted, Sawyer. Decker reached past her and rapped on the glass. —Seven thousand miles from where you're from.

She felt herself nodding. —This is what I wanted.

A group of women stood balanced on the highway's shoulder, indifferent to the chaos, holding firmly to each other through the rumpled blue silk of their burqas. She imagined their eyes staring out through the lacework. She imagined them sightless, then faceless. A tremor ran through her.

—I've been picturing you in one of those things, said Decker. —With nothing on underneath. What do you think?

—Shut up.

—We could pick one up for you in Peshawar. It sure would make things simpler.

—What the hell would it make simpler, Decker? What part of our plan? Our coming here? My studying with you at the madrasa? She waited for him to answer. —Or is there something you're not telling me?

He shrugged. —I was thinking you could hide me up in there sometimes when things got scary. Would you deny a brother in his time of need?

She pushed his hand away and turned back to the window. An even gaudier bus was passing in a rippling haze of diesel.

—When did you stop laughing at my jokes?

—Just stop talking.

—You didn't use to be this pissed off, Sawyer.

—You're wrong. I always was. Just not at you.

Peshawar was no less abject than Karachi had been but this time she was not to be deceived. She saw through or past the stained concrete and armed checkpoints and sewage troughs and red-lipped unveiled women leering down at her from billboards. She saw it for the holy fortress it had been. The bus passed a mud lot so crowded with tents that there looked to be no open ground between them. Sun-bleached tarps and kilim scraps and siding weighted down with broken bricks.

Limping mange-marked dogs and creeks of yellow filth and ravaged faces. The man across the aisle let out a sudden angry laugh.

—Those were Afghans, she murmured to Decker.

—Who was?

—Back there in the tents. Those refugees.

—That's not what my boy here called them.

—What did he call them?

—You don't want to know.

At a bazaar near the station they bought water and biscuits and Decker grudgingly put on his shalwar kameez. The few women she saw were in burqas and the men wore brown homespun headcloths or pleated hats of heavy beaten felt. Here and there she saw young men in the pillbox-like skullcaps of students of scripture and she wondered whether any might be from the madrasa where she and Decker meant to study. So far away, she said under her breath, too quietly for anyone to hear. So far away. So far away. So far. Again a wave of triumph seemed to lift her off her feet. Decker whispered to her to stop laughing but no one in the jostling crowd around them seemed to notice. She wanted them to notice. All of them. She wanted everyone to see how far she'd come.

The university was nearby and as they made their way there she tried to interpret the slogans spelled out in chalk or in housepaint wherever she looked. Some were obscene, at least in Decker's rendering, and some were advertisements for auto parts or rice or gasoline, but most were exhortations to jihad. Many invoked the name of the Prophet himself or of those blessed enough to have fought and died beside him. The letters were familiar but the words they formed meant nothing to her. Some were followed by quotes from the Recitation or by columns of precisely stenciled numbers.

—What are those numerals for? Do they mark the citation?

—Phone numbers, Decker said, making a dialing motion with his finger. —Join the caravan, pilgrims. One call does it all.

They had arranged to meet Decker's cousin Yaqub at the east gate to the university but though they waited there in plain view, standing on their duffels and scanning the crowd, by afternoon no one had come.

In his downy beard and brown kameez Decker looked no different from the locals but the locals seemed to keep their distance from him. His hesitancy marked him as a stranger, she decided. His uncertainty made him someone to steer clear of.

—Maybe we should change some more money. How much have you got left?

—I gave you all my money, Decker. You know that.

—All of it?

He picked up his duffel without waiting for an answer and cut headlong into the crowd. Between a tobacconist's and a bakery they found a window across whose shutters the symbols of various currencies had been neatly scrawled in pink and yellow chalk. A man with teeth stained red from betel nut took the money Decker handed him and passed back a fistful of tattered rupees. She'd never seen so fat a wad of bills. Decker counted the money, then counted it again, then said one word sharply in Urdu. The man broke into a wide grin, disclosing his blood-colored gums. He reached into his shirtfront and brought out a small stack of sweat-blackened coins.

—Take them, Decker said, gesturing with the rupees. A group of boys had gathered while she stood at the window and now they closed ranks, pushing between the two of them, blessing her softly and begging for coins. Suffer the children, O believers, for theirs is the greater need. Their blessings grew shriller as the ring of bodies tightened.

—What are you doing, Sawyer?

—We don't need all this money.

—Like hell we don't. What are you—

—They're little kids, Decker. We can't just ignore them. What kind of Muslim are you?

There were more of them now and they pulled at her outstretched arms and clung to her shirtsleeves. Decker's panicked voice was swallowed by their flattery and pleading. Not all of them were children and they came from all directions and she felt herself pulled backward toward the window and the wall. The money she'd offered had long since been taken and still the crowd around her clutched and pressed and clamored. They hung from her shoulders and worked their fingertips into her belly and her armpits and the gaps between her ribs. They were pulling at her collar and her shalwar's linen drawstring. She shouted at them in Arabic and they answered her in English. She seemed to hear the words *bacha posh* whispered behind her but she couldn't be sure. They were laughing at her openly and parroting her speech. The voices grew dim and the light seemed to fade and she saw herself as they must surely see her. Blood rushed to her head and her body went light and she heard a small voice asking God's forgiveness. She saw herself stripped naked. A shutter clattered open and she felt herself wrenched back into the dark.

The rupee merchant kept her in his shop until the mob dispersed and Decker came to claim her. The merchant seemed embarrassed by her gratitude, or by his broken English, or simply by her presence in those spare and unlit rooms. She sat with her arms around her knees in the corner, painfully aware of her girlish body in its sheath of rumpled linen. When Decker came she asked him to thank the man in Urdu and to offer him some form of payment and he shook his head and told her to shut up.

She followed Decker mutely back to the university gate and made no objection when he left her there and wandered off alone. He came back with a packet of chips and two lukewarm cans of Farsee Kola and they took turns standing up so Decker's cousin wouldn't miss them. As the hours passed she felt her courage dwindling. She began to feel hollow. She took care to speak softly, to give no offense. She knew nothing and understood nothing. Even on that paved and cobbled street there was dust in the air and she found herself longing to shelter behind it. A woman in a burqa passed them, gliding measuredly across the pitted ground, and she watched her move with something close to envy.

—I'm tempted to try one of those on myself, Decker said, watching her watch the woman. —If you won't then I will.

She drank the last of her cola. —I don't see anybody stopping you.

—Maybe my cousin got the date wrong. Maybe he thought we were on the Islamic calendar.

—Very funny. She frowned at him. —That's not possible, is it?

—Everybody else's damn number is tagged around here. I bet the madrasa doesn't even have a phone. We should probably sign up with one of these militias.

—I'm not ready to get blown up yet.

—I was born ready, brother.

—I'd like to take a shower first.

—Martyrdom Is Your Desire and Ours, he said, squinting at a slogan on the wall across the street. —That's a pretty good description of our day.

—You don't even have an address? Just the last name of the mullah?

—I've got what town he's in. He took out a folded scrap of yellow paper. —Half an hour's drive west. That's what Yaqub told me. Feeling up for a hike?

They waited one more hour at the gate. She fell asleep for a time with her back to the wall and her legs gripping her duffel like a saddle. She had a dream that drops of blood were running down her calves into her shoes. There was no pain, only embarrassment. When she awoke Decker was holding the scrap of paper up to the light, like a shopkeeper checking a counterfeit bill.

—Rise and shine, Sawyer.

She blinked up at him. —How much money did you change back there?

—Enough for a hotel room. The kind where you shit in a bucket.

She nodded and got to her feet. —Let's get going.

—You have somewhere in mind?

—If it's enough for a room it's enough for a car.

The driver they hired had heard of the village but looked doubtful when they asked about the school. He seemed to speak neither English nor Urdu and shook his head regretfully when Decker showed him the name on the paper. They drove for an hour on a paved road and as long again on none at all and he deposited them at sundown at a cistern between crumbling sandstone bluffs. Not a house was in sight. He refused their rupees with a shake of his head, letting them fall through his hands to the ground. They offered him an American five-dollar bill and he bobbed his bald head and allowed them to take their duffels out of the trunk and drove slowly away after calling down God's blessing on their studies.

It was dark enough to make out a weak wash of light up the slope and they followed it stumbling and cursing to what looked like a child's or an idiot's rendering of a town: high mud-walled compounds, bowing outward and cracked at the corners, with pale blue gates of corrugated steel. A dog in the deserted square barked halfheartedly at them without getting to its feet. From somewhere nearby came the smell of boiling dhal. They went from building to building in search of a bell, too exhausted and timid to knock or call out. Eventually a gate swung inward and a man appeared and beckoned Decker closer.

She watched the two of them converse in cautious murmurs, guarded and formal, keeping their arms at their sides. After what seemed a great while the man pulled the gate shut behind him and led Decker hastily around the corner. Instantly she felt as helpless as a toddler. She followed their voices to a stucco-walled compound abutting the first, lit at its entrance by the headlights of a truck. Only then did she notice how completely night had fallen. She had no option but to make her way across that floodlit ground.

She closed her eyes for a moment and felt someone touch her. She was trembling and her steps were unsteady and her body felt outside of her control. A small hand found her arm and pulled her forward. A boy no more than six years old was leading her into the compound by the wrist.

The man who shook her awake the next morning spoke both English and Arabic in a voice almost too decorous to hear. He carried a cup of green tea in one hand and a plate of flatbread in the other and he watched her raptly as she ate and drank. He did not ask why she had crossed half the world to study at his dirt-floored madrasa, or whether she had found the room comfortable, or why she had slept in her clothes.

—The bread is to your liking? said the mullah in English.

—Thank you, mu'allim. It's wonderful.

The room was bare and windowless and the sound of voices joined in recitation carried faintly through the wall. She had a memory of Decker sleeping beside her but Decker was nowhere in sight. The mullah wore bifocals and a yellow homespun shawl and a wine-colored birthmark ran from his left ear to the collar of his shirt. His lips moved as he watched her, as though in sympathy with the disembodied voices. A second pair of glasses hung from his neck by a loop of plastic fishing line. It occurred to her now that Decker had told her almost nothing about the man before her or about the school itself. She had trusted him blindly. She'd been told the mullah's name and nothing more.

—I've allowed you to sleep through the first prayer, said the mullah.
—For travelers an exception can be made.

She sipped her tea and gave a tight-lipped nod. Her voice seemed to have failed her.

—My name is Mufti Khizar Hayat Khan. You and your friend are welcome to this house. While you remain I am father and mother to you. He pointed at her. —Now you tell me your name.

She set her cup down circumspectly on the floor between her feet.
—Aden Sawyer, she said.

—Yes. This is what I have been told. Is it your full and only name?

She shook her head. —My middle name is Grace.

—Ah! said the mullah. —And what does it mean?

Again her voice failed her. Her feet were bare and she was suddenly afraid that they might attract the mullah's notice. They were slender and delicate, her most girlish feature, not yet ready to be seen. She felt herself flinch.

—You needn't be afraid of me, child. We have no cause for fear inside this house. He brought his heavy hands together. —Outside is another matter.

She swallowed the last of the flatbread and found the word in

Arabic that she'd been seeking. It rang strangely in her ears, deeper and angrier than she'd intended. She wondered whether all boys' voices sounded harsh to them.

—*Na'ama*, the mullah repeated. —*Na'ama* is Grace.

—Yes, mu'allim.

—This is a common name in California?

—It was, mu'allim. In more religious times.

He nodded again. —And your father?

—What about him?

He tipped one hand upward. —His name. His vocation.

—Martin Isaiah Sawyer. She took in a breath. —He's a professor.

—Of what?

—Of Islam. Of Islamic studies.

The mullah sat forward. —Ah! He leads a madrasa?

—No, mu'allim. The students he instructs are not believers.

—Not believers?

—They are not, mu'allim.

—Then why do they study the Book?

—My father would say— She hesitated.

—Yes?

—My father would say, because they find it interesting.

—Interesting, said the mullah.

—Yes, mu'allim. Like visiting a foreign country.

He pursed his lips as though he'd eaten something sour. —And your father himself? Has he been rewarded with faith?

The voices in the next room had risen. The sura was one she knew well. *Should you slip after clear signs have been revealed to you, be assured that God is Almighty, All-Wise.*

—I don't know the answer to that question, mu'allim.

His expression clouded further. —How do you not know?

Are they truly waiting for God to come to them in the shadowy folds of clouds, with His angels, when judgment is pronounced and all revert to God?

—Because he never told me.

—Does he not pray in your home?

For those who disbelieve, the present life has been made to appear attractive.

—My father and mother live in two different houses, mu'allim. I don't see him much.

—Tell me about your mother.

—I'd rather not, mu'allim.

—Ah, he said. —And why not?

—Because she's a drunk.

The mullah cleared his throat and ran his fingers through his beard. He seemed to be observing something just beneath her cot. He seemed to be considering its merits.

—I see now why you came to us.

—Yes, mu'allim.

—Let me ask you something more. Have you elder brothers?

She shook her head.

—You are the oldest in your house?

—I am, mu'allim.

—Then why do you not bear your father's name?

—I don't— She stopped herself. —I can't say, mu'allim. I've never asked.

The mullah nodded thoughtfully. She kept straight-backed and solemn and watched him considering her answers. It was a sign of disrespect to stare but the mullah seemed indifferent to her rudeness. She tried to look away but could not do it.

—I see, he said a second time, taking the cup back from her and getting to his feet. —Perhaps it is well, given what you have told me, for Martin Isaiah Sawyer's name to go no further.

—Yes, mu'allim.

—In this house you will be called by a new name. One of your own choosing. You will find this is best. He took her by the hand.

—I beg your pardon, mu'allim. I—

—Yes, child?

—I don't like to be touched.

He seemed not to hear her. —You are a young man of gumption, to travel so far. Is this what you say? Of gumption?

—Some people might say that. It's an old word, mu'allim. Like grace.

—I see. He bobbed his head. —Do you have need yet of a razor?

She opened her mouth and closed it.

—Feel no embarrassment, child. We have boys in our care of less than seven years. He straightened and turned toward the door. —I'll see that a copy of the Book is brought to you, that you may choose your name.

—I don't need the Book, mu'allim.

—No need of the Book? Why is this?

—I chose my name the day I left my mother's house.

He gave her a Qur'an regardless and led her down an unlit corridor with his hand at the small of her back. He was temperate and mild and did not rush her. It was she who was rushing. The Recitation grew brighter as the daylight receded. God guides whomsoever He wills to a path that is straight. Though the voices were high-pitched and lilting they were the voices of men and men only and this thought forced the air out of her lungs and made her head go hot and empty. She could no longer make out the walls or the floor. She was listening her way forward.

At the corridor's turning the mullah stopped her and opened an unpainted door. The hall they passed into was narrow but deep and though it was filled with skullcapped figures not a man among them raised his head to look. Fluorescents bathed the kneeling men in quavering yellow light. The Recitation was of the two hundred and fourteenth verse of the second sura of the word as revealed to the Prophet by the Angel Gabriel. Or do you imagine that you will enter the Garden without undergoing that which befell those who came before you? Violence and injury did touch them and they quaked, until the Messenger and the believers with him said: When will God's victory come?

—Children, said the mullah in Arabic when the sura had ended, letting his hand come to rest on the declaimer's shoulder. —Join with me in greeting Brother Suleyman. He comes to us from California.

Now their heads lifted. She had dreamed of this instant and feared what might follow but she saw no malice in that field of upturned faces. A welcome was murmured in Arabic and a language she guessed to be Pashto. The youngest sat elbow to elbow in the foremost row and she noted to her amusement that their expressions were the most dignified of all. She tried and failed to find Decker among them. She had never felt so closely watched or so unseen.

—Find a place for Brother Suleyman. We receive him this day as our honored guest.

A shoulder's-width interval opened before her and she took her place among the youngest children. They were ten years of age at the oldest, some much younger, and she tried to make herself as small as possible. Tattered brown prayer books lay before them on bookrests and their shoulders pressed against her through the linen of her shirt. Sweat was gathering in her armpits and at the small of her back and she imagined the men behind her watching first with curiosity and then with outrage as the body her clothing hid from them came gradually into view. But of course the men were doing no such thing. They stared down at their prayer books and she did the same. When she raised her head again the mullah was gone.

The declaimer coughed into his fist and turned the page.

—The Messenger believes in what was revealed to him.

—The Messenger believes in what was revealed to him by his Lord, came the answer. —As do the believers.

All believe in God, his angels, his Books, and his messengers. We make no distinction between any of his messengers. They say: we hear and obey.

We await your forgiveness, O Lord. To you is the journey's end.

God charges not any soul except with what it can bear. To its credit belongs what it has earned: upon it falls the burden of what it has deserved.

—Our Lord, said the declaimer.

—Our Lord, Aden answered. —Do not lay upon us a heavy burden, as You laid upon those who came before us. Our Lord, do not lay upon us that which we have no strength to bear.

———————

They recited without pause until the noon call to prayer and when their prayers were done they gathered in the courtyard. She relieved herself in the latrine on the far side of the building, taking care no one saw her, then went looking for Decker. She found him crouched in the shade of a mulberry tree with two beardless men she hadn't seen before. As she approached them the men got grudgingly to their feet, mumbled a few words in greeting, then drifted away. Decker sat back on his heels and watched them go.

—Your friends don't seem to like me much, she said.

—They can't figure you out.

The blood rushed to her head. —Figure me out how?

He yawned and shrugged his shoulders.

—Did I do something wrong at recitation?

—I wasn't at recitation.

—Why not?

—I slept in.

—Do you want to let me know what's going on? Are you trying to impress your new friends? Is that it?

—Don't wig out on me, Sawyer. I'm sure you can guess.

Her back was to the yard now but she felt herself observed. —Tell me what you're trying to tell me, Decker. Just say it in words.

—These kids grew up poor as shit. They've never seen— He stifled a yawn. —I don't even know where to start. A Corvette. A laptop. An American up close. You might as well have a pointy tail and horns.

She nearly laughed with relief. —Is that all it is? That I come from the States?

—It's enough.

—Don't scare me like that again. Okay?

—Just quit worrying so much. That won't help anyone.

She put a hand on his shoulder and felt him pull back. —Are you going to tell me why you're treating me like this?

—Like what?

—Like you wish I was dead.

He squinted into the sun. —I'm trying to figure out why I should lie for you, I guess.

—Coming here was your idea, remember? Lying was always going to be a part of it. Nothing's changed.

—You've changed, Sawyer. You cut off your hair and you talk in a fake voice and you won't even say fuck. Won't say it and won't do it. So don't go trying to act like I'm the one that's different. Don't you dare.

She gripped her knees and listened to the ordinary sounds around her. The clatter of teacups. The call of a magpie. The whining of a generator on the far side of the wall. —I'll make this right, she said at last. —I'll make this up to you.

—Sure thing, Sawyer. Whatever you say.

—What are you going to do, Decker?

He shook his head tiredly.

—It won't just be me that gets in trouble if someone finds out. We came here together.

—I could leave anytime.

—That doesn't make what I just said less true.

The look he gave her brought her precious little comfort. It was less a look of cunning or resentment than one of calm indifference. It made no sense to her.

—Don't turn on me, Decker. Don't do it.

He looked away from her. —You've got things switched around again. You turned on me.

They chanted through the afternoon until the third call to prayer and when their prayers were done they chanted on till dusk. The declaimer's reedy singsong never wavered. The Arabic of the others was colored by Pashto or by Urdu or by languages of which she had no knowledge. She sat in the midst of them and recited in a halting, breathless voice, so softly that not even she could hear. The talibs rocked in rapture to the verses. In the very best moments her own sight seemed to dim and she could feel the verses buzzing as they passed between her teeth and that was all she wanted or could ever want.

After the fourth call to prayer Decker appeared in the doorway and found a place for himself at the back of the hall. They had reached the two hundred and sixtieth verse of the sura and each voice seemed distinct and known to her. His California twang cut through sharpest of all: the voice of privilege and vanity and everything else she'd hoped to put behind her. Her own voice was just as grotesque, just as incongruous, subdued though it was. She did her best to ignore it. She pictured herself reciting as if from on high, a small still form in all that sway and tumult. She imagined herself and the others, bowing and rising and bowing again, rippling like a field of windswept grass.

When Saul set out with his soldiers he said: God is about to test you at a river. Whoever drinks from it is not my follower. Whoever drinks not is my follower, save one who scoops a scoop into his hand.

They drank from it, all but a few.

When he passed across the river, he and those who believed with him, they said: We have no might today against Goliath and his troops.

Those who believed they would meet God said: How often a small force has overcome a numerous force, by God's leave. God is with those who stand fast.

After the fifth prayer they took their evening meal of flatbread and dhal in the courtyard and when she'd finished she was sent for by Hayat. She found him in a sunlit room at the school's southwest corner, humming unmusically to himself, sitting on a leopard-spotted cushion in the middle of the floor. Apart from a tea set and a padlocked metal cabinet the little room was bare of ornament. A matching cushion faced him and he gestured toward it grandly.

When she was seated the mullah arranged the pot and cups between them. A small boy with a harelip came to serve the tea but Hayat waved him off. —I'm not too decrepit to pour my own tea, praise God, he told her in English. She nodded and gave him a tentative smile.

—I take buffalo's milk with my tea, Hayat said as he poured. —The English prefer cow's milk, I understand.

—Yes, mu'allim, she said. —But I'm not English.

—Of course! He let his head tilt forward in what might have been a bow. —And yet you do take cow's milk with your tea.

—I don't take anything.

The amusement that was never entirely gone from his countenance was conspicuous now as he sat and observed her. She found herself smiling to mask her discomfort. She was tired and unsure of herself and her throat was raw from chanting. She raised her teacup to her lips and drank.

—To your fine health, the mullah said, raising his cup.

She stopped in mid-sip and returned his good wishes. —Pardon my rudeness, mu'allim, she said in Arabic. —I have many things to learn.

—You know a great amount already, Suleyman. An astonishing amount. Are many American boys like you?

She took another sip. —I don't think so, mu'allim.

—Your Arabic is better than that of most of these country block-heads God has given me to teach. Much better. It pleases my poor half-deaf ears to hear it.

—Thank you, mu'allim.

—It is formal, of course. Not the everyday way of speaking. And there are traces of the English, especially in the *qaf* and the *ha*. He smiled. —Which only reminds us of how far you've come.

She bobbed her head and said nothing.

—Never have we had a visitor from such a distance. *California.* He pronounced the word carefully. —You do us a great honor. You and Brother Ali.

—Yes, mu'allim. Who is that?

—Your companion, of course.

—My companion? I don't—

—Ali is the name he selected.

She looked at him blankly. He took the cup from her and re-filled it.

—I'm sorry, mu'allim. I guess I'd have expected him to tell me.

—You are bosom friends with Ali. Is this so? He beamed at her. —Friends of long standing?

—I'm not sure how to answer, mu'allim.

—You may answer directly. By saying the truth.

She hesitated. —Decker Yousafzai is the best friend I have in the world. Without him I wouldn't be sitting here now.

—That is well, said Hayat. —It is well to have such a friend. But in this house his name is Ali Al-Faridi.

She felt the blood rush to her cheeks. —Yes, mu'allim. Of course.

—I've had Brother Ali with me here, in this room. While you were reciting. I asked him the question I've just asked of you.

She sat back on the cushion. —And what did he say?

—Why are you here, Suleyman?

Her scalp began to prickle. —To learn the Holy Qur'an, mu'allim. To memorize it. To learn it by heart.

—To learn it by heart, he repeated. He took in a breath. —Yes, that is what we practice in this house. You have not been misled.

—Excuse me, mu'allim?

—No one has misled you.

She was unsure what if anything he wanted her to answer. He seemed to want nothing. She drank from her teacup.

—Of course, this school of mine is not exceptional. We are believers but we can in no way—what is the word in English? He frowned. —We can in no way *contend* with the great madrasas. Ashraf-ul-Madaris in Karachi, for example, or Jamia Ashrafia in Lahore. Their fame is glorious and well deserved. You have heard of these schools?

—I have, mu'allim.

—Yet you chose to come here. To my village madrasa of fewer than forty heads. Truly, we feel ourselves blessed.

She found herself nodding.

—Does it not say in scripture: Whoso emigrates in the cause of God shall find on earth many places of emigration and abundance? And elsewhere: You will surely find that the nearest in amity toward the believers are those who say: 'We are Christians,' and that is because they do not grow proud? He raised both arms toward her. —How true are those words, Suleyman, in this case!

—Thank you, mu'allim.

—Is it perhaps also true that you came to my school because it is close to the border?

—Excuse me, mu'allim? I don't—

—Perhaps you are not aware that we are situated a day's march from the border here, well within the tribal regions. Many young men pass through this district, and in fact through this village, on their way to the camps of the mujahideen. Was this fact known to you?

She shook her head stiffly.

—But you have seen their advertisements in Peshawar, I am sure. Their slogans of recruitment.

—I've seen them.

—I would advise you kindly, Suleyman, against this course of action.

As in every other room of that thin-walled house the sound of muffled voices carried to her. Behind or below them she heard other sounds: a motor backfiring, the laughter of children. It occurred to her for the first time, as she sat straight-backed before the mullah and struggled to reply, that there might be children in the village with no interest in the school.

—May I ask a question, mu'allim?

—You may.

—Why are you telling me this? About the mujahideen?

—I have been engaged in the instruction of young men for nigh on thirty years, Suleyman, and my eyes have been made keen, all thanks to God, to certain signs. He cupped his palm and tipped it upward, as she'd seen him do before. —You have a restlessness, child, although you take pains to keep yourself still. Your feeling for scripture is— He paused. —Your feeling for scripture is a desperate one, he said finally. —And such feeling can tip easily toward violence. I have seen this often. I have grown attentive to it.

—I came to you to learn, she said. —That's all. To get nearer to God.

—I can have no objection to jihad, he continued, as though she hadn't spoken. —The Prophet himself tells us: Fighting has been prescribed for you, although it is a matter hateful to you.

He sat forward and lifted his teacup and drank.

—But the jihad of the Kalashnikov may be the least useful, Suleyman, both to us and to God. Many young men have departed this house for the camps. No small number of them left in the dead of night, leaving everything behind—even the Book they had come here to study. As though it had outlived its usefulness. Few of them have graced this house again.

He took her cup and refilled it. She had been threatened before in the guise of advice—her father had done so many times, especially since her conversion—but she had no sense of what the mullah's threat entailed. The threat had not been expressed in words or even by his voice but it hung in the air between them like a wisp of colored smoke.

—You may sleep here, Suleyman Al-Na'ama. You will do me that honor.

—Here, mu'allim? But this is your—

—We are not so fine as the schools in Lahore but you will find that you are treated with respect. You have perhaps seen the rooms—the dormitories, yes? Is this the term?—where the men have their beds. You have passed by these rooms?

—I have, mu'allim.

—Then you've seen that they differ from what you are used to. This room is more suitable. The cushions can be joined to make a bed.

—May I speak, mu'allim?

—You may.

—I'd like to sleep in the dorms if that's all right. With the others. I don't want anything the rest don't have. I don't want anyone to think of me as strange.

Hayat was watching her closely. —And yet you are strange, Suleyman. Even to me.

—But not forever, mu'allim. Not if God wills it. I can get to be as normal to you as this pot of tea.

The mullah ran his fingers through his beard. He smiled at her and nodded. —You will sleep in this room, Suleyman, he said.

She slept fully dressed and when the call to prayer sounded she awoke to find a bowl of water and a washcloth on the floor beside her feet. She listened for a moment, holding her breath, then got up quietly and barred the door. She opened her pack and found its inner pocket and brought out a handkerchief neatly folded to the size and thickness of a deck of cards. The cloth lay cool and dry against her palm. She unfolded it and drew out a silver wheel of pills in its envelope of foil and tore it open. The brittle sound it made was somehow pleasing. She laid the first of the pills on her tongue and packed the handkerchief away and knelt down to perform her dawn ablutions. She performed them with care because her presence in that house was a pollution and an outrage. She was a liar and dissembler and she'd never been so happy in her life. The pill had no taste at all. She ran down the corridor to join the others in the freezing unlit courtyard, placing her mat in the last row so no one would see her. But the mullah nodded to her all the same.

At midday she found Decker where he'd been the day before. He sat slouched in the mulberry's dappled shade and watched her blankly as she crossed the yard. Again she tried and failed to grasp the change in him. The same two men sat beside him and this time they remained. She greeted them both and they smiled in return. She had no memory of seeing them in recitation or at prayer.

—These here are my cousins, said Decker. —Altaf and Yaqub. Altaf used to be a talib at this school.

She shifted from one foot to the other, unsure what to do next.
—I'm honored to know you, she murmured in Arabic. They nodded and touched their right palms to their chests.

—My brother has no Arabic, the one called Altaf said.

—That's all right. She smiled at him. —I have no Urdu.

—Urdu is a dirty language. You are better for not having it. It is the language of the ignorant. Of vagrants.

Decker gave a laugh she hadn't heard before. He's laughing in Urdu, she thought. Or in Pashto. The man called Yaqub nodded again and laughed uncomprehendingly, looking at each of them in turn. His features were the gentlest of the three.

—I'm sure that's not the case, she said. —Please tell your brother that.

—Your Arabic is beautiful, the man said, ignoring her comment. —You speak it very sweetly. As if reading from a poem.

As he said this a question or a doubt crossed her mind and she glanced at Decker, hoping for some sign, but Decker's face and eyes were closed to her. She understood now what had changed him. The arrival of these men. The one called Altaf watched her slyly and his brother bobbed his heavy head behind him. They might have been grinning at the way she wore her clothes or at her pronunciation of Arabic or simply at the paleness of her skin. They might have been grinning at nothing. She looked from Altaf back to Decker and saw no resemblance there.

—You are a favored student here, the one called Altaf said. —Uniquely favored. I'm told you have a whole room to yourself. His grin shifted subtly. —Perhaps this is why your Arabic is still so pure.

—You studied here, with Mu'allim Hayat?

Altaf shrugged.

—When was that?

—Perhaps six years ago or seven.

—How long did it take?

—How long?

—To learn the Recitation. She sat forward with her elbows on her knees, as she'd seen the men doing the evening before. —I hope to have it learned within the year.

Altaf's expression clouded. Decker said something to him but he gave a quick hard laugh and shook his head. Again she'd committed some error.

—I failed to learn the Recitation, Altaf told her. He said it carelessly, as if the fact were of no consequence. —To commit the Book to memory, Brother Suleyman, one has to keep one's distance from the troubles of this world.

—Of course, Decker put in. —Just look who runs this place.

—I disappointed the mu'allim. I broke off my course of studies.

She apologized and did her best to cover her confusion. She had known that the compound was open to people from the village and to travelers as well but she had no recollection of either Altaf or his brother at the first or second prayer. It seemed a grievous sin to use the school for any other purpose.

—The mu'allim must not be displeased with you, Brother Altaf, she said. —After all, he's received you into his house.

Altaf shook his head. —We're not here for the old man, he said. —We came to see our cousin. Your good friend.

—My mistake, she heard herself mumble. —I thought—

—Our cousin has grown into a man, Brother Suleyman, as you can see. Altaf took Decker fondly by the collar. —You yourself, who are still a child, have much to discover before you can follow his lead.

—I do, she said, looking down at the gravel.

—What's that?

—I do. I have much to discover.

—And you shall, if God wills it. He rested a hand on her shoulder. —Apply yourself, little brother, that you may follow soon.

With that the two men rose and moved unhurriedly along the shaded wall of the courtyard and up the concrete steps into the house. They greeted no one and returned no one's greeting. Decker kept his eyes on them until they had passed out of sight.

—Who are those men, Decker?

—I told you. My cousins.

—Do you want to explain to me what the hell is going on?

—Brother Suleyman! I thought you'd given up cursing. I must have misunderstood.

—I'm going to ask you one more time.

—And then what?

—And then I guess you stand to lose a friend.

He said nothing to that, tugging idly at the hem of his kameez. She took in breath in steady pulls and waited for his answer. She felt far from things but calm and wide awake.

—One of them is, he said at last. —My cousin, I mean. Yaqub's father was the one who hooked us up with this madrasa. He's my father's older brother. He lives a few towns over.

—He didn't look anything like you. Or like your father either.

—Can't help you there, Sawyer.

—What do they want from us?

He gave her no answer. Across the courtyard the others were

getting to their feet and brushing the dust from their shirtfronts. She willed herself to speak softly.

—Why didn't you introduce us yesterday?

—I told you already. They didn't feel comfortable. They're kind of twitchy.

Again she sat back and waited. It didn't take long.

—They're hiding out, said Decker.

—Who from?

—Come on, Sawyer. They're not going to tell me that. If they did they'd have to shoot me or something.

—It almost sounds like that would make your day.

His face took on an air of gravity. —I probably shouldn't have told you this much, even. They don't trust you yet.

—They don't have to trust me. I came here for school.

—I guess I'll have to take your word on that.

—Decker, you'd better tell me—

—You know exactly what I mean. We could have stopped in Karachi if you wanted to study. We could have gone to the Emirates, like your mom and dad and everybody thinks. We might as well have stayed in Santa Rosa.

—But you have family here. That's the reason we came. You just told me your uncle—

—Don't bullshit a bullshitter, Sawyer. That won't cut it with me.

She leaned back and worked her palms into the gravel. —No way could I have stayed in Santa Rosa, she said finally. —You know what it was like.

—I'm just saying—

—I was a freak in Santa Rosa. A goddamn freak to everyone in town.

—Take a look around, Sawyer. Are you trying to tell me that you aren't one here?

The next day at noon she was first to the courtyard and took a place under the windows of the recitation hall. A bolt of red faux-velvet cloth had been unrolled in the shade and bowls of dhal and plastic plates of naan arranged in tidy rows along it. She sat near a pitcher of tea with a tortoiseshell handle and the others found places for themselves around her and began to eat and drink without delay. Talk sprang up slowly, hesitantly it seemed. The men beside her spoke to no one and the boy who sat across from her hummed a sad droning air between mouthfuls of bread. A clean-shaven man next to the boy passed her his cup.

—If you would be so kind, brother, the man said in English.

She filled the man's cup from the pitcher. —I'd like to speak in Arabic, if you don't mind. I could do with the practice.

—You don't get enough practice inside? Out here we may speak any language we choose. And about any topic.

—God is not unmindful of what you do, Ibra, someone called out.

The man heaved a sigh. Past him an older man shook his shorn head. He wore the long-suffering look of an adult compelled to spend his days in the company of children and he muttered loudly as he sipped his tea. The clean-shaven man gave an affable shrug.

—Please take no offense, brother. He means well, though you might not guess it.

She smiled. —I can't take offense. I don't know what he's saying.

The meal came to an end and the dishes and teacups were carried away. She'd barely spoken after that first clumsy exchange, other than to ask for bread or dhal, but it was clear to her that some shift had occurred. She'd become visible. More than once she'd glanced up from her plate to find the younger students staring at her boldly.

—My name is Ibrahim Shah, said the clean-shaven man as they got to their feet. —My father's name is Shah Qutub Mohammed.

She took his hand in both of hers, as seemed to be the custom. —Suleyman Al-Na'ama, she said. —And is this gentleman your father?

The man laughed. —In his way he is a father to us all, Suleyman, and a mother also. Abu Omar is the cook and cleaner here.

—I'm sorry. I misunderstood—

—And you must please forgive him his manners. He's an old soldier, with no good feelings for *khariji*. To him all foreigners are godless apes.

—I understand.

—Do you, Suleyman? That is our hope.

They went up the concrete steps and passed into the cool and twilit hallway. Ibrahim paused at the door to the recitation hall. —We are pleased to have you with us, Suleyman. You do our school credit. And in any case, what Abu Omar said was of no great offense.

—That's all right. What did he say?

—Please! It was nothing. He said you hold your teacup like a girl.

She awoke in the night to find Decker beside her. She needed no light to know who he was or to guess his intention. She'd have known him by his smell alone, or by his silhouette, or by the nervous way he had of rocking on his heels.

—Wake up, Sawyer.

It was quiet enough in the room that she could hear him pass his tongue along his teeth. He reached out a hand and brought it down against the whorl of cropped hair at the crown of her head. He seemed to think that she was still asleep. He brought his hand back to his mouth and breathed in deeply. Then he lay down next to her and spoke her name.

—Come on, Aden. You can't still be out.

—I'm awake.

—All right, then. He hesitated. —All right. Good.

—I just don't answer to that name. Not anymore.

—You'll answer to whatever name I want. You'll answer to Aden or Dipshit or the Shah of Iran.

She propped herself up on her elbows and waited.

—I want to get out of here, Sawyer. I can't stand this place.

She said nothing to that. He was staring at the ceiling and gritting his teeth.

—Are you even listening? Don't fall back asleep.

—I'm listening. She sat up and watched him. —I'm just wondering what you expected.

—Is this what you wanted? This box of mud and shit and bricks? Beans and backwash for dinner? The same prayers we were already sick of back in Santa Rosa?

—You were sick of them maybe. You don't speak for me.

—Aren't you even a little disgusted? Look at me. Aren't you bored?

She let her head sink slowly back onto her folded arms. It was cold in the room and she was grateful for the heat from Decker's body. She could almost see him steaming in the dark.

—The food could be better, she said finally.

—No shit it could. How about some salt just for starters. Some damn cheese. Some pepper.

—I'd love a cheeseburger. Do they have cheeseburgers here?

—Yesterday I got a look at the butter they use. It comes in a tin box with Russian words on it.

She turned her head to see him better. —Russian lettering? Cyrillic?

—That's right, partner. We're eating disco-era butter.

They lay together on their backs for an empty interval of time. A rooster somewhere nearby gave a single inconsolable cry.

—It's not even midnight, he said. —Even their chickens are ignorant.

—Go to sleep, Decker.

—You really think that you can keep this up?

—I hope so.

—What do you figure is going to happen if you can't?

She rolled onto her side and said nothing.

—Someone's going to catch you squatting behind a bush one of these days. Have you thought about that?

—Everyone squats over here. She smiled into the dark. —That's one of my favorite things about this country.

—Not like you. Girls do it different. You do it different.

—I piss just like you do. You're just making things up.

—They'll get used to you, Sawyer. They'll wonder why you don't shave. They'll start to notice when you're on the rag.

She let out a sigh. —We've talked about this. It stops by itself if you're skinny enough. And I've got pills to help with that part anyway.

—They'll find the pills.

—Not unless you tell them.

He cursed and turned his body toward her. —What about your tits, Sawyer? You plan to keep that bandage on for the rest of your life? You're not about to win any swimsuit contests, I know, but that thing must get painful. Or itchy at least.

—Never mind about that.

—Sawyer—

—I keep them wrapped all the time now. Even when I'm asleep.

—You're lying, he said, slipping a hand up her shirt.

What she felt was not surprise or shock but just a sudden chill. The cold was electric and ran through her and forced her mouth shut. She'd hoped so much to fall asleep beside him.

—I almost forgot what you feel like, he said. —You feel good.

Her teeth seemed to chatter.

—What was that?

—We can't do this Decker. Not here.

—It's a room with a door. It's the best place we'll find.

—We can't.

—Shut up and move over.

—It's that time, she told him, her voice simpering and thin.

—What?

—You heard me. It's that time. I can't mess up these clothes.

—You've got pills. You just said.

—I'm not taking the pills yet. I'm saving them up.

He stared down at her. She could see his teeth now and the whites of his eyes. He glanced back toward the door, then out the window at the empty square.

—Lying's a sin, Sawyer. Are you a sinner?

—Please Decker. I can't. I've just told you.

—You promised. He brought himself so close to her that his face began to blur. One hand was braced against her rib cage and the other held her wrist. —You promised me. You said you'd find a way to make this right.

She held her breath and made her thoughts go still and asked herself if she could do it. A line from that morning's recitation made the circuit of her mind: It is God who created you from dust, then from a sperm, then from a clot of blood. She took slow and careful stock of the act itself and held it up against the sin of mortal failure. She had done it before, after all: she'd agreed each time he'd asked her and had shared in his pleasure. It was only afterward that she'd felt shame. And in the judgment of the righteous she was already a sinner in her every word and deed. She looked up at Decker. He was weak, perhaps, and covetous, but he was not unkind. He was faithful to her. How mild was his desire against the sin that she embodied.

—I will, she said. —I will, okay? But not tonight. Not now.

—You listen to me, he hissed at her, straddling her hips. —I've had enough—

She brought her palm up hard beneath his chin the way her father had once taught her. How strange that he should come to mind just then. Her father of all people. She caught Decker's sleeve as he reared back and pulled him to the right with all her strength. His body tensed as it fell. Footsteps carried down the hallway as he cursed and groaned and struggled to his feet. It was likely a student on his way to the latrine but the noise froze both of them in place until the echoes faded. It was good to see Decker so frightened. His arm had been raised to strike her but he dropped it now and staggered to the door.

—Did I hurt you?

He winced at that and coughed into his sleeve. So graceless. So boyish. He stood in the middle of that small bare room with his arms half extended, as though the fall had affected his balance. Then he nodded once and stepped into the hall.

When she went to Hayat the next morning she found him sitting with a rumpled and water-stained magazine beside him on the floor. Coming nearer she saw that it was a copy of *Scientific American* from the previous year, one she'd seen on the kitchen table in her father's new house, opened to an article entitled "Staying Sane in Space—Is the Right Stuff Enough?" and in her surprise forgot even to greet him.

—Pressurization, Hayat pronounced slowly.

—Pardon me, mu'allim?

—Pressurization, he said again. —It seems to pose a problem. The weight of the air.

—I wouldn't know about that, mu'allim.

—Did you not feel this yourself, in your passage on the plane?

—I didn't, mu'allim. She sat down beside him. —I think I was too excited to feel anything.

—Of course. He smiled. —And it appears that you're excited still.

—I'm worried.

His smile faded. —What regarding, Suleyman?

—My friend Ali.

He waited. —Yes?

—We had a kind of fight.

—A fight. I see.

—But it's not our fight that worries me. Not really.

—No, child? What then?

—I guess I can't tell whether he was right.

He sat forward. —You'll have to explain. What was the issue over which you disagreed?

—Sin, mu'allim.

—A worthy topic of discussion. He regarded her a moment. —Which sin?

The air seemed to clot in her lungs. —The sin of falsehood, mu'allim.

—What manner of falsehood?

—Bearing false witness, she managed to answer. —Coming to a consecrated place—to a mosque, for example, or a school—

—Yes?

—Under circumstances that might not be fully honest.

—I see. Hayat made a gesture she couldn't interpret. —And is Ali himself guilty of a sin of this nature? Has he told a lie to gain admission here?

—No, mu'allim, she said hoarsely. —Not so far as I know.

She saw that he didn't believe her. —What was it that Ali said to you, my child?

—Anyone can come here to study, can't they? She hesitated. —Anyone at all, if their desire is sincere? No matter who they are, or who they were before?

—Anyone of sincere faith is welcome in this house.

He would ask her now. She was sure of it. He would ask and she would answer him and that would be the end.

—The weight of the air, he said, taking up the magazine.

—Yes, mu'allim?

He frowned slightly. —Was there something further?

—No, mu'allim.

—Then I bless you, child. You may return to your studies.

Two days later she took sick and was excused from recitation. She passed the vacant hours sequestered in the mullah's sunlit office, listening to the sounds of barter and gossip in the square outside and studying the play of light and dust across the ceiling. No one visited her there, not even Decker. By evening she'd begun to recover and she slipped in her bare feet out into the corridor. Her fever seemed to have broken and the floor felt delightfully cool. The others were still in the courtyard and the house was more quiet than it ever was by daylight. She felt steadier now but she had to see Decker. To see him and ask his forgiveness. She had a memory or a vision of him kneeling on the floor beside her bed.

The door to the dormitory hung open but the space beyond was cluttered and obscure. She stood for a time with her toes at the threshold, gauging the depth of the darkness before her, listening for evidence of life. The room smelled of paint and the bodies of men and something else she tried and failed to name. She had never set foot in that place and its maleness resisted her entry now as though the air inside were at a higher pressure. What light there was seeped dimly through the heavy vinyl blinds and she imagined herself swimming forward through that twilight like a diver. Of all the floors in all the rooms of the madrasa this alone was carpeted and her footsteps made no sound that she could hear. Some comforters lay fastidiously folded; some lay crumpled where they'd fallen when the call to prayer had sounded. The sour musk of unwashed clothes assailed her. She moved cautiously forward, taking shuffling steps, searching the rows to either side for Decker's duffel. On the far wall a banner in English read

GUIDE US TO THE STRAIGHT PATH
THE PATH OF THOSE ON WHOM
YOUR GRACE ABOUNDS
NOT THOSE UPON WHOM ANGER FALLS
NOR THOSE WHO ARE LOST

She found Decker's bedroll and his duffel in the farthest left-hand corner. Beside it a small boy lay sleeping under a fleece Superman blanket and she held her breath and got down on all fours. The boy did not stir. She slipped a hand inside Decker's bedroll and felt or imagined that it was still warm and fought the urge to hide herself inside it. The boy was whistling softly in his sleep. Decker's duffel sat open and a coverless book lay half hidden under his clothes. *Defense of the Muslim Lands* by Sheikh Abdullah Azzam. She leafed through it slowly, noting the passages he'd underlined in pencil.

She sat for a time with the book in her hands listening to the boy's steady breathing and when she was sure he was asleep she pulled the duffel closer. Decker's clean and dirty clothes were bunched indifferently together with his notebooks, damp and curling at their edges from neglect. A dated Fodor's guide to Pakistan. A copy of *Vibe* magazine from the airport in Dubai. *The Autobiography of Malcolm X.* The sleeping boy whimpered. She brought out a notebook and opened it at random, straining to decipher Decker's effortful Arabic scrawl. She remembered him on the airport bus, mouthing conjugations with a pen between his teeth. Then she thought of him in the courtyard with Altaf and Yaqub, sitting sullenly and slackly on his heels.

A commotion sounded in the corridor and she slid the notebook hurriedly back into the duffel as the first men returned to the room. They watched her as she passed but made no comment. She resolved to look for Decker outside and was nearly to the courtyard steps when she heard Hayat behind her. He asked in his soft contented voice where she was going.

—To talk to Brother Ali, mu'allim. Is that permitted?

—You are not a prisoner in this house, Suleyman. After last prayer we are all of us at liberty.

She waited for him to go on. —Is there something else, mu'allim?

—Night is coming, child, and you are without your shoes. He put a hand on her arm. —Your skin is hot to the touch. Even through the cloth of your kameez.

—I feel much better, mu'allim. Honestly.

—It delights me to hear it. He let go of her arm. —But you should be in your quarters. I'll have a pot of tea brought to you. Perhaps some bread as well.

She kept silent, wavering on the balls of her bare feet. The evening sky shone redly through the doorframe.

—In any case, Brother Ali is not outside. He is making a family visit with his cousins.

—He went with them? she stammered. —With Yaqub and Altaf?

—If that is how they are called.

She let the mullah guide her down the corridor. —Altaf studied here, mu'allim. Six or seven years past. Weren't you here at that time?

—Dear child! This school began with me. He smiled. —On occasion I permit myself to believe, in my vanity, that it will vanish with me also.

—Pardon me, mu'allim. You can't be expected to remember the names of all the boys who've come and gone. I'm sorry.

Her legs were buckling underneath her and she braced herself against the wall as she moved forward. Hayat said nothing more.

—Why are you smiling, mu'allim?

—Ah! Suleyman. You are young and strong in faith. And also somewhat foolish.

—What do you mean?

—Those men were never students at this school.

The next day as she stepped into the recitation hall she caught sight of Decker by himself in the last row. A seasick feeling gripped her. He waved to her sweetly and gestured to the empty place beside him. The hall was less than half full and the declaimer was chatting idly with Hayat. Decker yawned when she reached him and asked how she was feeling, for all the world as if he'd never been away.

—I've had a fever for days. Since the morning you left.

He nodded and glanced toward the door. —You seem pretty good now.

She opened her Qur'an and started reading.

—Don't sulk on me, Sawyer. I wanted to tell you but Altaf said I couldn't. These homeboys do not fuck around.

—Just go if you're planning to go. Never mind about me.

—I was worried about you, Sawyer. I still am.

She said nothing to that.

—Anyway, I had to come back.

—What for?

—To tell you about the crazy shit I saw.

The declaimer shut the door to the corridor and took his place under the great colored window. She watched for any sign that he was aware of her absence from the foremost row of students but as usual he seemed to notice nothing. Decker arched his back and eased his body forward.

—They took me across the border, Sawyer. What do you think of that?

She faced the declaimer and gave no reply.

—It wasn't even dark when we went. It was like going on a hike. Might as well have been no border there at all.

The room fell silent as the declaimer inclined toward the Book. The bare-walled space she sat in could not have been more different from her high school homeroom back in Santa Rosa but the creaking of the forty-odd bookrests was the same reluctant sound that she remembered. Let us begin. The declaimer laid the Book down flat and turned a single page.

—The fifty-sixth sura, he intoned. —That Which Is Coming.

—That Which Is Coming, they answered.

When that which is coming arrives—and no soul shall then deny its coming—some shall be abased. Others shall be exalted.

When the earth shakes and quivers and the mountains crumble away and scatter abroad into dust, you shall be divided into three multitudes. Those on the right—blessed shall be those on the right. Those on the left—damned shall be those on the left. And those to the fore—foremost of all shall be those. Such are they that shall be brought near to their Lord in the gardens of delight: a whole multitude from the men of old, but only a handful from those who came after.

They shall recline on jeweled couches face-to-face, and there shall wait upon them immortal youths with bowls and ewers and a cup of purest wine, that will neither pain their heads nor take away their reason; with fruits of their own choice and flesh of fowls they relish. And theirs shall be the dark-eyed maidens, chaste as virgin pearls: a reward for the deeds they have done.

There they shall hear no idle talk, no sinful speech, but only the greeting: Peace! Peace!

—Sawyer, Decker whispered. —Sawyer. Listen.

She shook her head and brought her voice to bear more fully on the Recitation. His left hand found the hollow of her back.

—Listen to me. Are you listening? I'm going there again.

As for those of the left hand—wretched shall be those of the left hand!—they shall dwell amidst scorching winds and seething water, in the shade of black smoke, neither cool nor refreshing. For they have lived in comfort and persisted in heinous sin, saying: When we are once dead and turned to dust and bones, shall we be raised to life?

At the next pause in the Recitation she rose from her place and pushed past the men and the children alike. Decker made no move to follow. With each step the mass of bodies tightened and it took all her strength to keep from shouting at them to get out of her way. The memory of Altaf's half-closed eyes as he praised her Arabic ran together with the face of the man in Karachi and with Decker's own expression as he pressed against her in the bookshop in Dubai. Why those three images assailed her now was beyond her understanding but she knew enough to take it as a warning. Each one of them had wanted something from her.

The declaimer's precise and girlish voice carried out into the courtyard:

We it was who apportioned death among you. And we shall not be forestalled from replacing you by others like yourselves. Or re-creating you in a form you do not recognize.

That afternoon she was lying on her bedroll with the door shut and bolted when a tapping sounded on its lacquered frame. She drew back the bolt and found Hayat outside with the little harelipped boy. She started to beg his forgiveness for her truancy and for locking him out of his study but the mullah took her hands in his and shook his head. The boy eased his feral body past them both and set about sorting her possessions and moving them into the corner farthest from the mullah's desk. Her first thought was that she was being expelled from the madrasa and for an instant she felt something akin to relief. But Hayat simply gestured toward her shawl where it lay in a heap beside her duffel and asked her whether she felt well enough to join him on a stroll.

Ibrahim Shah was waiting at the gate of the compound with the mullah's own shawl and ashplant in his hands. He nodded to her in his wry and courtly manner, touching a finger lightly to his lips, and she guessed that the idea to invite her had not been Hayat's. He arranged the shawl fussily about the mullah's shoulders and led the way across the rutted empty square. In the sunlight Hayat seemed older than he had inside the compound: his slippers dragged across the ground like runners on a sleigh, leaving tracings in the dust, and his ashplant knocked against his knee with every halting step. She drew alongside him and asked where they were going and he muttered something through his teeth that she couldn't decipher. It dawned on her at last that he was cursing.

—We're going to a farm, said Ibrahim Shah. —The family have a son who is ill. A simple family but pious. They are patrons and supporters of our school.

She resisted the urge to ask how a family of simple farmers could be patrons of anything and took the mullah's arm in hers instead. There was little traffic on the road at that hour but what few men they met murmured greetings to the mullah as they passed. For his part he seemed too short of breath to answer. When they reached the western gate of the village she asked if they might rest briefly, on account of her recent fever, and Ibrahim Shah smiled at her from behind the old man's line of sight and said that they certainly had time for a respite from the sun.

They sat facing north toward the mountains in the shade of the arch with the tilework cool as water underneath them. Ibrahim Shah said that many people took their ease there and watched their friends and rivals and relations bustling past. He said that it was like television for them and she smiled in acknowledgment of his joke. He asked in his considered English which television programs were her favorites and showed great surprise when she replied that she couldn't think of any that she liked. Hayat sat grimly between them, gray-faced and wheezing, grudgingly acknowledging the salutations of the passersby. After the gloom of the madrasa the blue plain rising toward the border seemed electrically lit. She supposed that every house she could see must be as dark as their own, with few if any windows to the godless world outside, and that darkness was the price of safety in that ravaged country. Ibrahim Shah sighed in answer when she asked if this was true.

When Hayat had recovered he leaned stiffly forward and asked how she felt. She thanked him and said she was greatly improved. They got to their feet and picked their way along a footpath that followed what had once been a sewage or an irrigation ditch but was nothing now but an incision in the fractured yellow earth. They were forced to proceed in single file and when Ibrahim Shah attempted to support the mullah's elbow the old man drew himself up with great dignity and announced that he was not yet a cadaver. Soon perhaps but not yet. She walked a few steps ahead of them, pointing out uneven ground, and Hayat said happily that each step was easier than the one before, since the farmer's wife's cooking was drawing him on. He claimed to smell sheep's milk simmering in a cast-iron pot, and to hear a kettle boiling, and to taste the oil of their hostess's pilau upon his tongue.

They must have been seen approaching along the footpath because when they reached the farmstead a man in a headscarf and eight children stood assembled to receive them. The man pressed a palm to his chest and greeted each of them in turn. He said that his sons were at work in a barley field seven miles distant and that he himself was little more now than a minder for their children. Hayat answered that this was a reward justly earned and the man smiled and confessed himself delighted with the arrangement. They spoke measuredly in Urdu, pausing often to regard each other, and Ibrahim Shah translated for her in his elegant Arabic. Their host showed only a polite interest in his foreign visitor but the children studied her with grave determination. The youngest was a girl of four who took her by the thumb.

After this welcome their host led them through the gate and across a wide flagstoned courtyard to a low and shuttered room gone blue inside with smoke. A young man lay on a rope bed at its center and watched the people gathered at the footboard without any sign of interest. The lids of his half-closed eyes shone as if they'd been painted and she thought at first that he was wearing kohl. When his father spoke to him he turned his loose-skinned and birdlike face away and she understood that he was close to death.

A stool was brought to the bedside and Hayat lowered himself carefully onto it and spoke in a hoarse uneven whisper to the son. Though everyone kept silent the mullah's words were plainly for the dying man alone. At times she imagined that he was speaking Arabic but it was possible that he was speaking Urdu or Pashto or some local language she had never heard. After a time he turned to Ibrahim Shah and made a small urgent gesture and Ibrahim Shah took her hand and guided her back out into the light. She felt the son's eyes on her as she stepped across the threshold but she told herself that the son's eyes were already focused on the other world. And in fact as she stood blinking in the daylight a sudden keening sprang up in the house behind her. She fought the urge to look over her shoulder.

The children had been waiting for her in the courtyard and in a few short steps she found herself surrounded. They seemed to take no notice of the keening. The elder among them held their siblings at bay but still they managed to catch at the tails of her shirt as they jockeyed among themselves for her attention. Her right hand was commandeered once again by the girl in the yellow kameez. Ibrahim Shah interpreted each volley of questions and the answers she gave without the least impatience. He seemed as eager as the children were to hear what she would say.

—You drink milk in America? Milk with chocolate powder?

—Sometimes, she said. —When the weather is cold.

—And on holidays, one of the older boys added. —And when you have rupees.

—And a cow for the milk, said another.

—That's right. But not so many Americans have cows.

The boy nodded sympathetically. Even in Pakistan, he informed her, many families had no livestock of their own. Then he turned to Ibrahim Shah and announced that he himself had eaten chocolate: he had been to Peshawar the year before, for Ramadan. A gaunt girl behind him asked Aden what had happened to her skin. Ibrahim Shah answered sharply in Urdu.

—Beg pardon, the girl said, reddening.

—That's all right.

—How did you get your hair to turn black?

—I was born with dark hair. Many people there have hair like mine.

—Have you made many children, said a grinning, lisping boy.

She shook her head. —No family. No wife.

—No wife *yet*, said Ibrahim Shah, smiling at her over their heads.

—That's right. No wife yet.

There followed more questions about food and English and air travel and football and videocassette recorders and she answered each as accurately as she could. It occurred to her that they were striving as much to make sense of the world of adults as of the faraway place of which she was an emissary and this lent a private sweetness to the game. It was obvious that Ibrahim Shah was embellishing her answers and she felt grateful to him for it. She had never had a gift for public speaking.

—You are here for jihad? said the boy who'd asked about the chocolate milk.

—Brother Suleyman has come to us to study, said Ibrahim Shah. He said it quickly, both in Urdu and in English. —His jihad has been his journey to the Faith. His jihad has been his pilgrimage to us. To make his *safar*.

—I don't know that word, said Aden. —What is that?

—*Safar*, said Ibrahim Shah, nodding. —The word means 'journey.' Among other things.

The boy watched her closely. —*Safar?* he said. He squinted at her. —*Mujahid?*

As she made to answer she heard a bellowing sound and Ibrahim Shah took her by the shoulder. A man of perhaps thirty staggered out of the house, dragging his right foot, beating at the air as if pursued by wasps. He stopped short with a jerk when he noticed the children, then howled again and forced his body forward. It was a great and stooping body and reluctant to obey. He looked enough like the man on the bed to be his twin but for his eyes which were pale blue and wide-set and staring. They rolled back in their sockets when he caught sight of her like the eyes of a terrified calf. The children covered their mouths with their hands as he shouldered his way past them and brought his flushed face close to hers. Ibrahim Shah's grip on her shoulder tightened.

—You have no cause to fear, Suleyman. Keep quite still.

The man's eyes were so blue as to look almost white, to seem flat and occluded and blind, and as they widened she could see her cropped dark head reflected. His breath was a cow's breath, grass-smelling and damp. He let out a soft cascade of moans as he observed her. The children had fallen silent and were waiting for some wonder to transpire. The idiot shut his foam-flecked lips and stopped his moaning, wavering on his feet, bobbing his head as if in time to music. Then he pressed a heavy palm against her breast.

—He means no insult, Suleyman. You are something new to him. He means no harm to you.

She clenched her fists to keep herself from cowering and stared into those shallow panicked eyes. Her chest was firmly bound beneath the cloth of her kameez but there was knowledge in the way his great hand gripped her. She'd almost forgotten that she had a body. She saw herself now as she looked to the children, how the two of them must look in their unnatural embrace, and though the blood rushed to her temples she felt calm and unafraid. What set her apart from him, from all of them, was also her protection. She was hidden by her clear and perfect strangeness. Her strangeness was itself a burqa that withheld her likeness from them.

Ibrahim Shah was pulling her gently free when Hayat and the farmer emerged from the house. Others soon followed—far more than the smoke-filled room had held. A cloth was spread over the paving stones and food and tea were laid out by two young men with downy beards who made her think of Decker. The children remained whispering raptly together but no place was set for them or for the old man either. Hayat ate hurriedly, immodestly, barely answering the questions of their host. The farmer sat very straight with his hands in his lap and watched the mullah eat. She wondered what his family would have for dinner that night, or the next night, or the rest of the week. Surely not pilau with almonds and raisins and tender chunks of slow-cooked lamb.

She sat with Ibrahim Shah at a small remove from the older men and ate with great deliberation, taking care to savor each succulent morsel, mindful of the weeks of bread and dhal to come. It seemed shameful to her to be eating so well not ten steps from the sickroom but perhaps it was the custom. She was frightened of asking. She did as Ibrahim Shah did, taking fistfuls of pilau into her palm. She made a game of it. She took rice whenever he did and she drank each time he drank. He seemed not to notice. Between mouthfuls he asked how she'd come to know Brother Ali.

—Mu'allim Hayat asked me the same question.

—And how did you answer?

—We met on the street in the town next to mine. I was wearing shalwar kameez and he came up to me and asked me why.

—Ah! said Ibrahim Shah. —I was told that you met in a mosque.

—Who told you that?

—I don't seem to recall. Perhaps Ali himself.

She said nothing to that.

—Ali told me there was an engagement.

—A what?

He sipped from his teacup. —Ali has said there was an engagement between you, Suleyman, and a member of his family. At times these are difficult matters.

She set her plate down carefully on the multicolored cloth. —I still don't understand.

—You changed in your feeling. You devoted yourself to your studies.

—Ali is mistaken. There was no engagement.

—I see, said Ibrahim Shah. —I have misunderstood.

He bent forward and scooped up a fistful of rice. She watched him contemplate the food in his hand, as if weighing its merits, then raise it to his lips. This seemed to demand the whole of his attention.

—It was a mistake to let him bring me here, she said. —I know that now. I should have come alone.

He ate in silence for a moment, his expression abstracted. —It is true that of our students, Brother Ali is not among the most devoted. He has his thoughts, you might say, fixed on other pursuits. Especially since the arrival of his friends. He dreams about the fight across the border.

—He and I are different people.

—Of course, Suleyman. That is perfectly clear.

She slept heavily that night on account of the meal and arrived late to prayers the next morning. She felt her way blindly out into the yard, finding a place to kneel just past the concrete steps. The ash-colored sky to the east gave off just enough light to disclose the grid of bowed and huddled bodies. She had the sense of something massive rushing toward her, something heavenly and final, and felt serene and wide awake and filled with faith. Morning prayer had always been dearest to her and she knelt and touched her forehead to the night-cooled ground and listened to the imam call the whole world into being. She brought her attention to bear on the noises around her. The coughing and sighing and heavy-voiced chanting. The rustling of garments and creaking of bones. She took in the noises and asked God's forgiveness. She mustered her courage. When at last her eyes came open it was day.

Altaf and Yaqub sat not ten places from her and a man she'd never seen before knelt gracefully between them. Though his eyes were blue or green his face and neck were darkly weathered and his thick un-parted hair was darker still. She stopped praying and watched him. He was older than Altaf, perhaps twice Decker's age. He kept his gaze on the mullah and his hands at his sides. She had never seen Yaqub or Altaf before the midday meal and she noted the newfound dignity with which they said their prayers. They gave the kneeling man as much space as the crowded yard permitted. His hands shook very slightly. When the prayer was done he was the first to rise.

At midday she found the man sitting where she herself had sat two days before, under the windows of the recitation hall. The same bolt of plastic-backed cloth had been unrolled along the wall and he was pouring cups of tea from the pitcher with the tortoiseshell handle. She watched for a time from the top of the steps. He seemed to know many of the students and he greeted Ibrahim Shah courteously when he walked by. Decker sat directly across from the man, shoulders slouched, barely touching his food.

Altaf rose and beckoned to her as she came down the steps.

—Brother Suleyman! Come sit with us.

—There's no room.

—We will find room, he said, taking her by the arm. —You may sit in my place. I have eaten.

She let herself be pulled forward, averting her eyes, as bashful and demure as any virgin. The empty place was next to Decker and she glanced at him as Altaf steered her downward. His hands lay folded in his lap and his expression was one that she seemed to remember. He was either exhilarated or afraid.

—This is the boy, said Altaf, crouching just behind her. —Suleyman Al-Na'ama, from California. His father is a mullah in that country.

Even now Decker refused to look at her. He'd seemed almost a man when they'd first met in Santa Rosa, one year and seven thousand miles from the baking gravel yard where they now squatted. It was hard to imagine. He fidgeted and chewed his lip and blinked down at the cloth beneath his feet. God alone knew what else he might have told them.

—California is not a country, Brother Altaf, said the man.

She glanced up to find his eyes on her. She'd mistaken their color: they were like two chips of sandstone. The urge to look away was overpowering but she was not a timid child like Decker was. A coward might look away, or a girl, or a person with something they hoped to keep hidden. She kept straight-backed and still and returned the man's stare. She studied him as she was being studied.

She was dimly aware, as she sat thus observed, of Altaf protesting that he knew perfectly well what California was. It was a portion of the United States of America. The portion to the south, against the sea.

—Is this so, Brother Suleyman? the man said to her.

—Near enough, she heard a voice reply. Her own voice or the voice of the boy she pretended to be. To her relief it sounded confident.

—Tell us more about your country, brother. We hear many things, of course, but most of it is little more than gossip. None of us have the privilege of visiting, you see. To us you are something like a merchant—a very young merchant, and a brave one—come back from the empty places on the map.

Her Arabic was not so good that she could pinpoint his accent but she knew that it was different from the rest. If not for his eyes the face would have been unremarkable. The eyes of a sniper, unblinking and sure. When he raised his cup she saw that two of his fingers ended at the second joint.

—Some children asked me the same thing yesterday, she said. —We had a discussion about chocolate milk.

—You take chocolate with milk? said Altaf. —In suspension?

—Ah! said the man. —We're no better than children ourselves, Suleyman, as you see. You come thousands of miles and we ask about milk.

For a time no one spoke. She tried to make sense of Altaf's obvious excitement and of Decker's sheepish silence and failed on both counts. But she guessed that the man was the reason for both.

—Brother Ali can tell you everything you want to know about our country, she said finally. —He's older than I am.

The man shook his head. —We want to hear your answers, little brother, not those of your friend. We hope you won't deny us.

—I'd consider it a privilege to answer your questions, she said. —But first I'd be honored to know who you are.

The man raised his eyebrows. —Have these colleagues of mine made no mention of me? My name is Ziar Khan. I was born in this village.

She nodded gravely, with a thoughtful air, as she'd seen the others do at introductions. —Ziar Khan, she repeated. —And what is the name of your father?

—You know his name already. He smiled. —My father is the master of this school.

Ziar Khan was the mullah's firstborn and sole surviving child and the woman who had borne him was long since dead and seemingly forgotten. He'd been sent to Yemen after his mother's death to be fostered by a relative whose husband was a kindly and God-fearing man, a scholar of scripture and an engineer. At the age of fourteen he'd been brought back to the madrasa, from one day to the next, to learn the Recitation from his father. He'd begged to be allowed to stay in Yemen but the mullah had insisted. He often dreamed, even now, of his foster parents and the yellow room he'd slept in. His clothing and his manner and even his way of speaking Arabic served to emphasize the breach between his father and himself.

All this Ziar told her, in fragments and snatches, in Arabic and English, over the course of the eight days that followed. His curiosity about her seemed boundless, inexhaustible, and the fictions she invented were as much to please him as to keep the truth obscured. Never had she been listened to so closely. She told him about childhood fights and football games and girls she'd tried to kiss under the bleachers. She availed herself of every possible preconception and cliché. He accepted all she said without suspicion, shaking his head in innocent delight, and with each detail her story became more real. This was the first gift he gave her: to bring the character named Suleyman to life. More than his authority or his grace it was his belief in her that held her so beguiled. In spite of all the lies she told—because of them, she sometimes thought—she felt herself becoming understood.

Each morning she reminded herself of the risk. It was rare that he answered her questions directly, at least when she first asked them, and she took careful note of each of his evasions. She never learned why he was sent away or how he came to be called home a decade after. He never spoke of motives. He showed none of the distrust that Altaf had shown, certainly not toward her, but he was secretive by temperament and custom. He would walk away abruptly in the middle of their talks, often before she'd finished speaking, and be gone for the remainder of the day. But the next morning he'd repeat the things she'd told him word for word.

He carried a cellophane-wrapped picture of his mother in a plastic frame, the precise size of his inner jacket pocket, and on the fifth day brought it out for her to see. Its subject stood by the roadside, in the shade of a cypress, staring straight into the camera. She was light-skinned and slender and the smile on her thin lips was cautious, the smile of some-one who smiled only rarely.

Ziar allowed her to hold the photograph for the space of a few breaths, rubbing his fingers together nervously, then took it back.

—At one time I was dying, he told her in English. —And I prayed to this woman. This girl. He smiled to himself. —Which is maybe a sin. I hoped not to die, which is also a sin. Maybe so. I was thinking this girl, she must be high in Heaven.

—High in Heaven?

He nodded. —Maybe even at the ear of God.

She had looked for Decker more than once to tell him what was hap-pening but now Decker was rarely by himself. He kept his distance from her, or was kept at a distance: she couldn't tell which. She had tried to talk to him regardless, first in English and then in Arabic, and he'd told her in a wooden voice to answer Ziar's questions. By then she'd come to understand that the answers she gave were being checked against those that Decker himself had given but somehow this knowledge caused her no alarm. He seemed more frightened than ever but she had no in-terest in sharing his fear. Not with regard to Ziar. She answered every question that was put to her.

On the eighth day Ziar asked her to walk with him out to the west-ern gate. The evening meal had ended and the yard was being swept. —Too much sitting is a poison to the spirit, he said in Arabic, cradling her right elbow lightly in his palm. —No matter what my worthy father says.

She got to her feet feeling weightless and clumsy. Altaf smiled at them and wished them happy walking. Decker stared at the ground and said nothing.

They met Ibrahim Shah at the gate of the compound. He was re-turning from the bazaar in Sadda with a handcart laden to the height of a man with Tyvek sacks of flour and Chinese tea and other goods that she could only guess at. He greeted Ziar with cool formality and his manner toward her now was much the same.

—Greetings to you, brothers. A fine day for an outing.

—We're walking to the mosque, by way of the western gate, Ziar told him. —You may report this to the mu'allim, if he asks.

—Ah! said Ibrahim Shah. —Our village mosque is no great sight, I fear, to such a traveler of the world.

—You're right about that, brother. But one must walk somewhere in this backwater, and the mosque is as good a destination as any.

If Ibrahim Shah was shocked by this way of speaking he gave no sign of it. —I said much the same thing to Brother Suleyman myself, he said politely. —Your studies will not run away from you, I told him, if you should choose to stray. They will be here for you when you return. Do you remember, brother?

—I remember, she murmured.

—It is kind of you to say so. As always you do us great honor. He pushed the handcart past them. —May you both enjoy a sweet and restful hour.

They thanked him and walked with measured steps across the square. —Ibrahim Shah is a worthy man, Ziar said. —In my absence he's been as a son to my father. He will duly attain to mullah at his death.

—Why should that be, Brother Ziar?

—What curious questions you ask, Suleyman. Did I not just say he was a worthy man?

She felt herself redden. —But why not you?

—You're a boy yet, little brother, sharp-witted though you may be. These matters are difficult to understand.

—I don't like it when people tell me that. I'm not a child.

—No indeed. You are not that. He smiled. —I've sometimes asked myself, during these talks of ours, exactly what you are.

They walked past the cracked mud-walled cistern and the new concrete well drilled with American funds to the bazaar and the mosque, then farther to the west. When they had passed the gate she'd sat beneath with Ibrahim Shah and the mullah she asked him to tell her the story of his mother's photograph. He replied without a moment's hesitation.

———

—I was sixteen when I left this school to fight across the border. Not a man yet, Suleyman, in anyone's opinion but my own. I told my sisters I'd come back in six months with a belt made from the hair of Russian soldiers. They laughed at me, as I deserved, and I cautioned them not to laugh, for I would surely die a martyr. This life rarely defers to our notions of it, little brother, though I was too unworldly to have known that then. I returned after a year and a half, in the best of health, to find both of my sisters in the ground.

By then my home was in the camps, not here. In the camps and in the hope they represented. The camps were beautiful in the years of the Russian war, little brother, nothing like the chicken pens we're left with now. Money came from all points of the compass—from Karachi, from the Saudis, from Morocco, even from your own country. In my childhood men had carried arms, of course—belt knives, or pistols, or even Kalashnikovs, if they were men of means—but those had been trophies only. At the camp called the Mountain I trained with Makarovs and Kalashnikovs and M16s and Stingers and explosives, both plastique and homemade. There was a course in ballistics taught by a professor from Lahore, a man of genius. The Mountain was a university to me. Childish though the idea was—and sinful—I prayed that I would never have to leave.

These prayers went unanswered, of course. My new life started on my first day at the front. We were climbing a pass from one line to another when the boy before me seemed to whistle, then to give a kind of laugh. Everyone fell to the ground—the boy and I were the only ones left on our feet. His cap hung strangely and I tugged on it to ask him what had happened. It came off in my hands, little brother, and his head came off with it: the top of his skull from the crown to the ears. He was shot twice more before he hit the ground.

God's design is not for us to know, but I was a young man, and I tried to understand why this boy had been killed when I was spared. He'd been a comrade to me at the Mountain, a dear one, and we'd asked to be sent into the war together. He had black hair and a pale and earnest face: not unlike your own face, little brother, come to think of it. At the camp we'd called him Abu Mushkil, Father of Trouble, because he'd shown no talent for the training. But his given name was Sangar. Sangar Kost.

As the weeks passed it grew evident that God preferred to spare me. I became accustomed to this idea, I accepted it as a fact, and this acceptance lent me the appearance of courage. But I was not courageous, Suleyman: only complacent. I felt myself to be untouchable, sequestered, set apart for some future purpose. What fear I felt was for my brothers only. They endeavored to fight as close to me as possible, imagining God's love for me might shield them. They should have learned from Sangar's example, but self-interest clouded their judgment. I watched the men and boys around me fall like chaff.

It was a full year before God saw fit to lift his sheltering hand. It happened noiselessly, invisibly, in the course of one late winter afternoon. Our strategy had been a sound one for a small group such as ours—to keep to country known to us, to valleys too narrow for air support, and to confine ourselves to nighttime operations—but we'd come to feel too clever, Suleyman, or possibly too proud. Humility is a virtue, after all, even in war. We drew too much attention to ourselves.

The helicopters—Black Sharks, they were called—were the one thing our entire unit dreaded. I'd observed them from a distance and I'd seen what they could do. Five times they'd flown overhead, within easy striking distance, and five times passed us by. I'd been close enough the last time to see the pilot's features through the glass. He looked laughably young, younger even than I was—but the Russians' hairless faces always made it hard to guess. He saw me, I'm sure, but he held to his course. One half-grown mujahid was not worth the petrol, I imagine, or the ammunition, or the time. Perhaps he was tired. Or perhaps this was God's warning and I failed to understand.

We were bathing in the river when a Black Shark squadron found us. Two flights of six in arrowhead formation—more at one time than I'd ever seen. We'd grown proud, as I've said. No cover for a hundred strides and most of us still hip-deep in the water. They flew in low from the east, keeping the sun behind them: their shadows reached us twenty seconds before the first came into range. I got slowly to my feet in that shadow, wet and naked to the waist, and watched those great black sunspots dropping toward me. It was useless to make for cover, useless to reach for my rifle, useless even to speak. We might have been targets made of mud for them to hit.

Their first pass was high, which is what saved my life. I'd raised my right arm for no reason I can explain: it must have looked to them like a gesture of welcome. I felt a shock, I remember, as though my hand had been slapped. The only pain I felt was in my shoulder. I looked at my fingers and saw two were gone. That set me to running at last, though I had little hope of cover and even less thought of escape. I saw the men around me shouting but I heard no sound at all.

They made seven full passes, all twelve machines firing, and none of our party was spared. Some of us were hit by bullets from the PKMs and some by shards of sandstone from the bluffs or from the boulders. A brother bound my hand and led me up the creekbed. He was bleeding from what seemed a shallow cut above his knee. Once we'd reached shelter he drew his coat around himself and when I looked at him soon afterward I saw that he was dead.

I rolled onto my side then and asked God to aid me. I whimpered and pleaded and stammered His praises. We lay in a thin stand of tamarisks not far from the water and the sound of dying rose up all around us. Have you ever heard that sound, little brother, when young men are dying? The noises they make are not noble, as the actors and poets would have us believe. Fourteen boys lay below me, shrieking and losing consciousness and waking in terror and shrieking again. The Russians had ground troops deployed in the area and I was certain that a sweep patrol was coming. The pain was spectacular by then but I found I could stand without fainting. I searched my brother's body and found a Makarov PM and a cartridge in his belt. I laid stones from the river at his head and his feet and took the pistol and checked that the cartridge was full. Then I went back to the others and sent each of them to God.

The caves in that valley are ancient and their walls are inscribed in many places with verses in Arabic and in older alphabets now lost to us. I passed that night and the following day in a hole in the sandstone barely wider than my shoulders. From its mouth where I lay sweating and shivering by turns I watched the Soviet sweepers do their work. There was little use they could make of my brothers now but they amused themselves as well as they were able. They stayed a long while, an entire platoon, joking in Russian and defiling the bodies and washing themselves in the river where my brothers had bathed not six hours before. It was a judgment upon me but in my anger I could make no sense of it. When they'd finally gone my teeth were buzzing in my skull and I was dizzy from thirst and the sandstone pressed against me like a living, breathing thing.

It was cold that next morning, bitterly cold, and I heard the life departing from my body: a thin, steady hissing, like steam from a kettle. My hand had bled through its binding and was frozen by blood to the floor of the cave. It came away with a sound like tearing paper but I felt no more pain. Life was leaving me quickly.

It was then that I thought of the portrait.

The photograph was wrapped in cellophane from a packet of cigarettes, just as it is now, and tucked into the pocket of my Red Army coat. If I were one of those poets, I'd tell you that I always kept it there, against my heart—but the truth is that I'd put it there by chance. It was spotted and filthy from months of hard travel and I could hardly make out her features. I tried to peel the cellophane away but could not do it. I slid the picture up to my lips and licked it clean. I kept it between my teeth for a time, like the bit to a bridle, until I started to shiver. There are tooth marks on it still: here, Suleyman, in the bottom left-hand corner. Do you see?

I prayed to my young mother then, instead of God—or perhaps it was a form of conversation. Perhaps it was no mortal sin. Conversation with the dead, one-sided though it may be, is not the same as prayer. My mother had no great influence with Him: if she had, I'd not have been abandoned in that cave. But then I thought: it could be she's forgotten me. It's been more than ten years, after all. Perhaps the dead forget their lives in the calm of the Garden of Heaven. Perhaps that forgetting is itself what Heaven is.

I was delirious, you see, and thinking thoughts that bordered on apostasy. I was indeed a blasphemer in those hours in the cave. With each breath I took the walls embraced me more tightly and my thirst and fever mounted and on the second day I crawled or imagined I crawled deeper into the dark and found that the tunnel opened up into a chamber. I lay on my back for I know not how long, sobbing and laughing and speaking aloud. I've been hurt, little mother. I'm flat on my back on the floor of a cave. I see you so vividly, looking out from the shade of a cypress by the roadside. Smiling from the safety of its shadow at the man holding the camera, the man with the blue eyes who is not your husband. It's the first photograph ever taken of you and you have no sense of how to behave. You want to please this man, to do as he's asked, so you raise your chin and draw aside your veil. You are not thinking of this photograph as evidence. You are not thinking of this photograph at all, only of the man behind the camera. Your husband's second cousin from Karachi, well traveled and courtly, who has quietly asked you to take off your veil. Although you are a virtuous and respectable woman, newly married to his cousin. No one else will see this picture until you are dead. This portrait is for your admirer only. But I myself have seen it, little mother, and I've held it in my teeth. It's proof to me that you were once alive. It served as evidence to your husband, as well—a remembrance to him that you cared for another. And it's evidence to me, here in this cave, that I exist.

That same evening after last prayers she found Ibrahim Shah waiting in her quarters. He sat cross-legged on one of the two cushions, arms fastidiously folded, and greeted her as genially as ever. Her chest was aching and she wanted desperately to undo the bandage and lie down and rest. She had always felt kindly toward Ibrahim Shah but his unannounced presence there at the end of the day, and on that day especially, put her on guard at once. His posture was perfect, his voice self-assured. The reproach behind his manner was as clear as winter air.

—How was your walk this evening, Suleyman? Do you find yourself refreshed?

—It was a walk, that's all. You've taken walks.

—I have, little brother. I've even been so honored as to take a walk with you. He pursed his lips. —But Brother Ziar and I, it saddens me to say, have never walked together.

—You should try it. You might learn some things.

—Ah! What about?

—About the fight across the border.

—The fight across the border, Ibrahim Shah repeated.

—That's right.

He nodded for a moment. —Let me tell you something.

—I'm listening.

—I was twelve years of age when I came to this house. My family hails from a village ten miles westward of Kabul. The name does not matter, not any longer, because the place itself has been expunged. This was done in three steps. First the Federal Army came, then the Soviets, and finally God's own mujahideen.

Of these occupying forces I can tell you, Suleyman, that the mujahideen were by no means the most temperate. My father and my sister were burned alive in our home for selling cigarettes to Russian soldiers. My mother died soon after in a manner I prefer not to describe. I passed the next eighteen months alone, arriving finally in Peshawar's refugee quarter, and by the grace of God was taken to this place. I have lived here since, little brother, and I will not leave until I myself am dead. What occurs across the border is of no interest to me. I have this house, I have my faith, and that is all.

Silence fell when Ibrahim Shah had finished. His affable expression had not changed.

—Forgive me, she said finally. —I'm very sorry for your loss. I didn't know.

—Of course you did not know. I did not say.

—But you've told it to me now, Brother Shah. I'm not sure I know why.

—Perhaps you do know.

—Please tell me what it is you came to tell me.

He nodded again. —You will think I feel hatred for armed jihad on account of this story, he said. —Of course you will think so. But I do not confuse the men who burned my house with the group now called the Taliban, or in fact with any other group of Pashtuns. My family's murderers, if they still live, likely fight for the north, as do many former mujahideen. They are fighting for reprisal, or for money, or simply to fight.

She nodded. —Ziar says the same thing. That's why all genuine believers—

Ibrahim Shah raised a hand. —Please allow me to finish. The Taliban have taken up arms, against an army of the godless, to found a righteous Muslim state. Of that I have no doubt.

—Then why—

—I oppose the jihad of the Kalashnikov, little brother, because the God I follow is the God of mercy. *Merciful to all. Compassionate to each.* For me these are the greatest words in all the Holy Book. They are repeated more often than any others. Perhaps you recollect this passage?

She stared at him. —Of course I know those words, she said at last.

—I do not doubt it, because no one could forget them. He brought his hands together. —The faith I follow is one that raises humility above all other virtues, Suleyman. And there is no humility in the righteous self-love of the mujahid. There is no modesty in it, no denial of desire, no compassion, no restraint. He sighed. —But of course such virtues hold no attraction for the young. Especially those for whom war is but a fairy story. To such young men inaction is the greatest of sins. To others—like Ziar Khan, perhaps—it would appear to be the only sin there is.

—Thank you for your counsel, she said. —I'd like to sleep now.

—Of course. May God sweeten your slumbers. He considered her a moment longer, then rose from the floor. —Petition Him, little brother, that you may wake up enlightened.

———

When Ziar failed to appear at the morning prayer she allowed herself to imagine that he'd been called away on business and she applied herself to the Recitation with an abandon that brought a smile to the declaimer's mirthless face. But he was missing from second prayers as well, and so was Decker, and as soon as prayers were over she went looking for Hayat. She found him in his office, within arm's reach of her bedroll, paging through an instruction manual for a Zenith color television. She stepped inside and shut the door behind her.

—Brother Suleyman! he said, dog-earing a page of the manual and setting it aside. —Are you not attending the afternoon reading from scripture? I selected the passage myself, with you in mind.

—I beg your pardon, mu'allim. I was looking for—

—What is it, Suleyman? Are you feeling poorly?

—No, mu'allim.

He waited for a moment. —Then what ails you, child?

—Are they gone?

—I'm an old man, Suleyman. Old and befuddled. I need more in the way of specifics.

—You know exactly what I'm asking you.

She'd spoken the words without thinking and she expected him to show surprise at her impertinence, perhaps even anger, but his expression remained kindly and composed. Nothing she said or did could trouble him, apparently. Not him, not Ibrahim Shah, not anyone else under that roof. She was suddenly sick of all their smiling faces.

—Sit down, said the mullah, gesturing toward the cushions. She sat on the floor with her feet on the kilim. He raised the glazed yellow lid of the teapot on his desk and looked momentarily aggrieved to find it empty. He clucked to himself and shook his head and set the pot aside. She sat with her arms around her knees and watched his small unhurried movements and asked herself what they might signify.

—Do you remember, Suleyman, when you first sat with me here?

—I do, mu'allim. I was just thinking of it.

—On that day I asked you why you'd come to us. You said that you had come to us to learn.

—I did, she said.

—And you have been a fine student. He pursed his lips slightly, exactly as Ibrahim Shah had done the previous night. —But what you have learned in your brief time with us could fit into a fold of your kameez.

—I'd be grateful if you'd tell me where they've gone.

—Whom do you mean? Your traveling companion? The boy called Ali?

She managed to nod.

—Your friend has crossed the border with my son.

Though she was already sitting on the floor she felt herself list sideways. She braced her palms against the kilim until her dizziness had passed. Hayat watched with interest.

—You are discomfited by this news, he said. —You are asking yourself why you were not informed.

—Did they tell you when they might be coming back?

The mullah made a peculiar downward gesture with his chin. It made no sense to her. Somewhere nearby a motorbike sputtered and failed. A long moment later it started again.

—My understanding, he said finally, —is that your friend has gone to war.

She felt herself flinch.

—Is this your understanding, Suleyman?

—I don't know anything about it.

—I see. He smoothed down his shirtfront, moving idly as if to provoke her. He called for more tea.

—My son visits this madrasa only rarely, Suleyman, and never for reasons of study. He comes to rest, or to hide, or to seek medical attention in Sadda. Most often he comes looking for recruits.

—You have no objection to armed jihad. You told me that.

The boy with the harelip entered the room and Hayat sat back to let him take the tray. —I told you something else, he said. —I told you it was a waste of many gifted boys.

—Not everyone can sit here and recite all day. Not when a sovereign Muslim state is under siege.

—By other Muslims.

—The warlords? You can't be serious, mu'allim. Those men are Muslims in name only. Sometimes not even that.

Hayat's smile returned. —I see that my son's time with you has not been wasted.

—You wouldn't let him stay here if you thought that he was wrong. You wouldn't even let him through the gate.

—Bless you, Suleyman! the mullah said. —What price an old man wouldn't pay to see the world so plainly. He coughed into his fist. —The nearer you approach God's throne, my child, the stranger He appears. He is no more simple than this world that He has fashioned. His face, you'll find as you draw near, is not a human face at all. He coughed again. —You're wondering what I mean by this. Should you choose to remain in this house you may learn.

—God was simple to the Messenger, she said, pressing her palms into the kilim. —He wasn't strange to the Prophet. Not at all.

—The Prophet was God's chosen herald, Suleyman, and His particular delight. He shook his head. —You and I, I fear, are less than specks of pollen in a corner of His eye.

He was squinting at her now, rocking slowly back and forth, like a student focused on his recitation. A question was forming in his mind. Though she knew how she must look she could only remain as she was, slouching red-cheeked before him with her palms on the floor like the most abject sinner. She wished to God that the harelipped boy would come. If he would come then she could get away.

—It saddens me that you are not at today's reading, Suleyman. It will sadden Brother Ibrahim as well.

Hayat took a Qur'an from a pile on the desktop. —I gave instructions for a specific passage to be featured, as I've already mentioned. Perhaps you'll let me read it to you now.

When she gave him no answer he put on his glasses and opened the Book. —From the ninth sura, he said formally, as though a hall of eager students sat before him. —The title of this sura is Repentance.

He cleared his throat softly and held up a hand.

—Had they wanted to march out, they would have made preparations for it, but God was averse to their joining the expedition. So He slackened them, and it was said to them: Stay behind with those who stay behind.

—Mu'allim, I don't—

—Had they gone out with you, they would only have added to your difficulties, hastening between your ranks and intending to spread discord among you, while some of you would have lent them an ear. But God knows full well who the wrongdoers are. They had once intended to sow discord, and had turned matters topsy-turvy for you, until the truth was at hand and the command of God won the day, even though they detested it.

—Is that what I am to you, mu'allim? A wrongdoer?

—Not at all, Suleyman. He shook his head patiently, indulgently, as she'd seen her father do times without number. —But if you had gone off with my son, you might have been.

The boy returned at last and set the pot between them. He remained at the mullah's left shoulder, arms loosely folded, silently taking her measure. Hayat made a gesture and he disappeared at once.

—Noor is a fine child, he said. —He had difficulties when he first arrived, as many do. He was restless and cried for his mother. He was headstrong, as small boys will be, and distrustful. But he is learning to submit. The mullah took her teacup and filled it. —Do not lose hope, Suleyman. This may also prove to be the case with you.

—Tell me where they've gone, mu'allim. I'll submit to whatever you want. This is the only thing I'll ask of you. I swear.

As they sat in that sunlit room in utter silence the sound of footfalls carried to them through the wall. Labored steps, shuffling and circumspect, as of someone very old or very tired. She thought of the caretaker, Abu Omar, and pictured him on his changeless daily rounds. The image was a balm to her and she thanked Heaven for it. Then she remembered how the old man had stared that first day in the yard, the contemptuous look he'd given her, and what he'd said to Ibrahim Shah about her girlishness. She set down her cup without tasting the tea.

—We are discussing the ninth sura, Suleyman, said the mullah. —Not any other subject. I have nothing more to tell you in the matter of my son.

She nodded at the floor.

—Have you nothing to say with regard to the passage I read?

After a moment she nodded again.

—I am waiting to hear it.

—O Prophet, she said woodenly. —Urge the believers on to the fight. If there are twenty steadfast among you they will overcome two hundred. If there are a hundred of you they will overcome a thousand unbelievers. For they are a people of no understanding.

His mouth twitched at its corners. —That is from the eighth sura, Suleyman. We are discussing the ninth.

—Hypocrites, male and female, are alike. They command what is forbidden and forbid what is virtuous. They clench tight their hands.

—Take great care, Suleyman. You bring distinction to this house but we are not beholden to you. We may close our door to you at any time.

—Why did they go without me? I'm asking you to help me understand. She took a breath. —I beg you, mu'allim.

The mullah made as if to speak, then stopped himself. —They went suddenly, he said at last. —In the middle of the night. Such is the custom.

—He never tried to recruit me, she heard herself stammer. —He never asked me, not once. Am I so worthless to the cause? Am I so weak?

—You said you had no interest in fighting, Suleyman. You swore to me, in this very room, that my suspicions were mistaken.

For a time she said nothing. —I didn't, she said finally.

—What does that mean?

—What I told you was the truth.

—Stop mumbling, child. I can barely hear you.

—I'm sorry, mu'allim.

—I have no use for your apology. I do not hold you accountable. He looked past her and sighed. —I know perfectly well that my son has seduced you.

—Please, mu'allim. Why would he do that? Why would he do that and leave me behind?

The mullah turned his teacup back and forth.

—What is it?

—I asked that he not take you, he said. —I asked of my son that he leave you in my care.

—What did you say? Tears were welling in her eyes now and she struggled to speak clearly. —You did what?

—You've shown such devotion, Suleyman. Such faith. We have lofty hopes for you.

She raised her head. —You told him not to take me. You decided this.

—Your purpose lies in study, little brother. In Sunna and Recitation. Armed jihad is not for children. Believe me when I say that both of us prefer you here.

The mullah's voice was sympathetic now, affectionate, even honeyed. She pressed the knuckles of her fists against her eyes.

—Do you understand, child? Are these reasons sufficient?

—I understand, she said under her breath.

When I first got here Teacher I made a mistake.

I thought they could see me and guess what I was. Everybody
I met. I told myself they couldn't but it seemed as if they could
and even maybe see right through my clothes. X-ray vision or
something like that. Mystic sight. It felt crazy to be here. Like
they were waiting for me to do just one wrong thing. I was
so frightened Teacher. I wrote you a letter and threw it
away.

One thing in that letter was I asked what you thought of me when
I converted. When you finally believed it. You thought I was
making fun of you at first do you remember? You said I was
pretending. But I left the door of my room open so you'd see me
praying there when you walked by.

My next mistake was I should have sent that letter. You owe
me an answer. How you took it when you realized I'd made
My Own Decision. That no way was I joking. That it was
real for me in ways that it was never real for you. I knew
what Mom thought loud and clear but all you did was
you got quiet. You got quieter and quieter. And then you
disappeared.

When I finally got my visa did I tell you what she said? She said
I bet he feels fulfilled and justified. She thinks I did it to impress
you but I know that you know better. I did it to erase you. And it
worked all right Teacher. I forgot what you taught me and that

I was your daughter and I even forgot the place where I was born. That made things easier.

My friend Ibrahim Shah said something when I told him about my family. Your father was like a god to you Suleyman he said. Now you know there is no god but God.

2

Three days later she walked into a low stucco building a stone's throw from the University of Peshawar's brick-and-terra-cotta gate. The room she entered was floored in white tile and had once been a pharmacy or some kind of clinic. Lines of glue ran along the walls where shelves of cosmetics and skin cream and medicine had hung in some lost age when such extravagances could still be found for purchase. Now the color of the floor could barely be guessed at through the litter and the dust.

The room was empty save for a man in a skullcap hunched over a desk. A green apothecary's cross showed faintly on the wall above him through a wash of yellow paint. A slogan had been scrawled below it in Arabic but she couldn't make sense of the script. She stopped before the desk and waited. The man was taking apart a handheld transistor radio of the kind her mother might once have taken to the beach. He gave no sign of having seen or heard her.

—As-salaamu alaikum, she said.

The man turned the radio over. —Wa-alaikum as-salaam.

—I've come here from Sadda. From the madrasa there.

The man shrugged his shoulders.

—I've learned the first sixteen suras, she said, forcing herself to speak slowly. —Nearly half of the Book. And I'll return there, God willing, once I've fulfilled my obligation.

He looked up at her without interest.

—My obligation to go to the Mountain, she said. —The promise that I made to Ziar Khan.

The man pushed the radio aside and brought his elbows down to lean against the desktop. —Ziar Khan, he repeated. His voice was thick and wet and strangely garbled. When he smiled at her she saw that half his lower jaw was gone.

—That's right, she said. —I think you know the name.

The man said nothing for a time, grinning in his hostile slack-mouthed way. Then he answered her in Pashto and reached underneath the desk.

—*Nenet Pashto*, she said, raising both her arms. —*Nenet Pashto. Suk Arabi. Suk Arabi.* Ziar Khan.

He straightened in his chair, looking back and forth between her and the clutter on his desk. The radio, a hunting knife, two rolls of duct tape and a snarl of copper wire. For a moment all was quiet. Then a door behind him opened and he got reluctantly to his feet and a man in tinted glasses took his place behind the desk.

—You speak no Pashto, the man in the glasses said in English. —And no Urdu either. What do you speak.

—I speak the language of the Messenger. I speak the language of the Most Holy Qur'an.

—That is praiseworthy. But this is Peshawar, not paradise.

She lowered her eyes and nodded.

—Not paradise, he said again. —Not some tucked-away madrasa. Not a cool and shaded garden underneath which rivers flow.

—I can get there on my own. Just tell me the way.

—The way? He raised his eyebrows. —To where, little brother?

She hesitated only for an instant. —To the Mountain.

—We have no end of mountains here. You may visit whichever you like. How you choose to spend your holiday is no concern of ours.

—I'm here at the request of Ziar Khan. He came to my madrasa and he summoned us to arms. I was to go to the Mountain as soon as possible. I gave him my word.

—As soon as possible. At Ziar Khan's request.

—That's right, she said. —As soon as I could get away.

—You are lying, said the man.

She took a step backward. A truck passed outside and the room seemed to darken. The slack-mouthed man was standing close behind her.

—Come with me, said the smaller man, pushing his chair back and closing a drawer of the desk.

She nodded and reached for her duffel but the slack-mouthed man took it and ushered her forward. —Never mind your baggage, the smaller man said in a reasonable voice. —You won't have need of it.

They led her into a windowless low-ceilinged chamber that looked to have once been a safe room. The walls were cinder block and slick with condensation. To her left a padded metal apparatus hung between cantilevered rails, as if for the support or the confinement of a body. They steered her toward it and a sob of fear escaped her. A moment later she recognized it as an exercise machine.

The two men left her there and locked the door behind them. She guessed that they were searching her duffel and sat down on the floor and tried to think of all the things that it contained. Among the T-shirts and the boxers were the panties she'd been wearing on the flight from California. That and the little silver wheel of pills. It was possible she'd thrown away the panties but she somehow couldn't manage to remember. Her chest was aching in its binding and her bowels began to cramp. Thus far her anger had sustained her but she could feel that it would carry her no further. It was childish indignation, childish righteousness. From now on it would only bring her pain.

The thing she feared most was being asked to explain her decision to leave the madrasa. She had no explanation that could stand their scrutiny. She had her knowledge of scripture and her concern for Decker's safety and that was all she had, or almost all. She had her resentment of the mullah's interference. She had the memory of Ziar's voice as he described his mother's picture.

It seemed to her now in that windowless room that she'd had no reason for anything she'd said or done since leaving Santa Rosa: no reason and no alternative. Her life was a smooth line, an unbroken wire, too slender and too dark for her to see. She closed her eyes and sensed it quivering before her.

Much later the man in the tinted glasses was sitting close beside her on a stool. Her duffel lay open on the floor between them.

—Why go to the Mountain, said the man.

—I told you before, she answered. —I want to serve.

—To serve, he repeated. —Serve who. Ziar Khan?

—To serve God, she said. —To obey Him and obey His chosen servants.

—But you are a liar. He smiled at her. —Therefore you should fear God and the men who do His bidding.

—I do fear God, she said.

He reached into her duffel. —What is this now, he asked her. He brought out the wheel of pills.

—Medication.

—What?

—Medication, she said slowly. —Without it I couldn't be here.

He hummed to himself as he frowned at the pills, to suppress a shout of outrage, possibly, or perhaps only a yawn. Eventually he dropped them back into her duffel. He took out a pair of boxer shorts and held them to the light. They seemed to intrigue him.

—Where is your passport.

—I don't have a passport.

—You are *khariji*. You are Israeli or British or French. Of course you have a passport.

—I'm American.

He sucked in a deep breath and nodded.

—I'll tell you what you want to know, she said. —I came to you, remember? All you have to do is ask.

—Where is your passport.

—I threw it away.

A single-piston scooter started up out in the street. *Pok pok pok*. The man eased himself forward. —But why did you do this?

—I don't need it.

For the first time his face showed surprise. —You certainly need it. You need it for going away.

She said nothing to that.

—You are a fool, said the man. —Where is this place, where you have no need of your passport? Is it Sadda? Is it paradise? Is it prison?

Again she gave him no answer. He turned and spoke in Pashto to the taller man, who let out an unamused laugh.

—You won't get to this place, the man said. —I am sorry.

—I'll get there. If you won't help me, sir, I'll get there on my own.

He shook his head slowly and bent down and zipped up her duffel. His expression was solemn. He motioned to someone standing just outside the door.

—Ask Ziar Khan about me, she said quickly. —Just ask him.

—This person you mention is well-known to us, the man said as he watched her being hoisted to her feet. —You are very mistaken. He is famous in this country as a liar and a thief.

—I don't believe you, she said, feeling her legs lock beneath her.

—You are too young a boy, said the man. —Young and beardless and stupid. Do you hear what I say? You are stupid to travel in a place for which you have no understanding. You will dishonor yourself. You will bring yourself shame.

—I'm not afraid of you, she shouted as she felt herself pulled backward. Tears were running down her cheeks.

—Why do you go to the Mountain, said the man. As he spoke the words a burlap hood was pulled over her head.

—I told you. To keep my promise—

—Why do you go to the Mountain.

She fought for air and felt the fabric work itself between her teeth.

—Please. If you don't think I'm worthy—

—I'll tell you the answer. You go there to die.

They kept the hood on for what seemed countless hours and when she asked for water they raised it just enough that she could drink. She couldn't think what the hood was for unless they meant to kill her but she knew there was no glory in it for them. They were waiting for something.

When the reinforced door shuddered open and she felt them beside her she got to her feet at once and let them guide her forward by her sleeves. A second layer of cloth was pulled over the first, falling almost to the floor, and she guessed from the sound it made as she walked that it must be a burqa. The cloth was maddening against her eyelashes and her lips and the brick floor seemed to vibrate underneath her. The hand at her back was immense and impatient. There was no glory for them and no profit. She felt the coolness of the evening now and the cobbles of the street under her feet. Women's voices in passing. An idling engine. A car door creaked open and small hands pulled her urgently inside. Women's hands, she decided. Other doors were jerked open and slammed closed again and the engine was put into gear. The air stank of transmission fluid and tobacco. She wondered that she could smell or breathe at all through the spit-heavy cloth. People sat on either side of her, their elbows and shoulders wedged hard against hers, no differently than during recitation. She tried to keep calm by remembering her suras. The other passengers' breathing was as shallow as her own and their bodies fidgeted beside her. They began whispering to one another in Pashto, almost too softly to hear, and she realized that they were only children.

After an hour of halting progress through the city and then over rough country roads and then over what must have been no road at all they came to a stop so abrupt that it lifted her out of her seat. She heard the sound of rapid conversation between men, slightly muffled by the glass, and a woman's voice beside her hissing what could only be a warning. Once the car had started moving again she understood that they'd been at a checkpoint. She tried to picture what she must have looked like to the men who'd stopped the car, slumped forward in a burqa with burlap where her features should have been. Perhaps this was a common sight in this part of the country. Perhaps no one had bothered to look.

She was still trying to get the image into focus when the children left the car, suddenly and wordlessly, as though they had been abducted in their turn. The car was moving again but the children were gone and all at once the car had pulled up and its doors had come open and she was being told to get out with her hands at her sides. Her underclothes and shirt were soaked in sweat. The urge to vomit overcame her and she took the sodden cloth between her teeth and bit down hard. She wondered if there had ever been children beside her. She was out of the car now and being pushed forward. The image came to her unbidden of a figure in a cheap and rumpled burqa listing drunkenly over uneven ground in the dark and she felt a surge of pity at the sight. She fell and was dragged to her feet and pushed forward. Men were speaking in businesslike murmurs and she heard a sound as of a bullet being slid into a chamber. She could picture the pistol and the stone-faced man who held it and her own sad huddled body from the back. Then the sound came again and the smell of smoke reached her and a harsh voice said in Arabic to get the boy in off the street.

Some manner of gate swung open and she entered it and heard it latch behind her. One set of hands restrained her and another removed the burqa in a single practiced motion. She understood the voices but this brought her little comfort. Someone told her sharply to keep still: a foreign accent, Saudi or Yemeni. She was taking in air to say that she was standing still already when the hood was pulled away and she could see.

She found herself in starlit darkness with a group of men behind her. One demanded her name and she stammered an answer. They seemed to know that she spoke Arabic. She was led through a doorway and then through another and finally across a gravel courtyard. They left her in an L-shaped room with travel posters thumbtacked to the walls and a dozen men arrayed on threadbare kilims on the floor. No one seemed surprised to see her. She managed a greeting and they answered softly and in unison and made a place for her among their number.

She sank onto her knees and looked around her. Her body was still shaking. Most of the men were young, so young that their jawlines were plain to see beneath their downy beards, but their bearing was that of fatigued and worldly travelers. Some were dressed in jeans and T-shirts or in shoddy-looking tracksuits and as they spoke she thought of Decker and the joke he'd made about American Express. With the exception of a single Pashtun who said not a word they were Arabs who'd come from Yemen and Oman and the Saudi lands to train at the camps and fight across the border. They questioned her politely, almost never interrupting, and hid their curiosity as best they could. As she answered them her terror slowly faded. They told her nothing about themselves but the countries they came from and the names they'd chosen to be called by in the camps. The word *jihad* was often used but never in the sense of inner struggle. *Jihad* for these men had one meaning only.

At an hour so late that the sky had gone pale she was led across the courtyard to a narrow vaulted hall. A man with a beautiful white beard streaked with henna sat alone there, elegant and straight-backed, on a platform made of Nestlé packing crates. He asked her the same questions the Arabs had asked, and like them he showed no amazement at her story, or her nationality, or her presence in that starkly lit and air-conditioned room. He barely seemed to hear her answers but she knew that he was listening to them closely. He was listening for points of contradiction. He asked about the United States—about the living conditions of the poor, whether the people there could be said to have a sense of right and wrong, whether any could be said to live by faith—and when she'd answered him he asked her to recite from the Qur'an. He seemed infinitely patient and to have no need of sleep. When she herself had grown so weary that her Arabic began to falter he asked her the names of the men she'd met at the madrasa.

—Altaf Rahimi and Yaqub Yesharraf, mu'allim, she said. —And Ziar Khan.

—I am not a mullah, the man said amiably, winding the red tip of his beard around his thumb. —I am not a wise man, sadly, nor am I a man of letters. There is no call to use that honorific.

—I beg your pardon.

—Not at all. I am pleased by your error. He brought his hands together. —Do you care for this country, Suleyman Al-Na'ama? Have you been treated well?

She glanced up at him. —Treated well?

—With the courtesy and indulgence due a traveler from the far side of the world.

—I've been treated so well. Better than I deserve. And I do care for this country.

—You do not know this country.

She bowed her head and said nothing.

—Your family are people of the Book, you have told me. And yet the book you refer to is not the Most Holy Qur'an.

—No, sir. It isn't.

He appraised her a moment. —Tell me now. What was it that brought you to the Prophet? What was it that caused you to leave your place of birth?

—There is no god but God, she said. —And Mohammed is His messenger.

—That is a fact, said the man. —That is not a reason.

Suddenly she felt wide awake again. —I've been asked that same question for a year and a half now, she said. —Over and over. I was asked it at school and in my parents' house and every other place I went. I was asked it before I'd ever even stepped inside a mosque. I never expected to be asked that question here.

—You are angry, the man said mildly. —And of course you are afraid.

—I'm just tired.

—Clear your head now, Suleyman Al-Na'ama. Think of those other questionings, each one of them, as rehearsals for your visit to this room.

She sat cross-legged on the polished floor and gave the man no answer. It was quieter than anywhere else she'd been in all that country. Its stillness reminded her of the courtyard in Sadda before first light. She thought she heard men somewhere arguing in Urdu but that might have been the radio and the language they were arguing in could have been any language on earth. She thought of Hayat Khan and of Ibrahim Shah and how different they were from the man who now watched her through attentive half-closed eyes. At that hour in their mud-walled madrasa she'd likely have been the only one awake. The only one not sleeping the sleep of the righteous. Soon it would be time for prayers in the yard with the low hills assembling themselves out of nothing and the night sky showing the first faint bruise of dawn along its rim.

—Things are beautiful in this world, she murmured. —Some things are. I don't know why God makes some things perfect and some things just wrong. Why He makes some things empty and other things full. Full and perfect. Can you tell me why?

She waited for the man to speak but he said nothing. She looked above her at the vaulted whitewashed brick.

—I've felt like that most of my life. Not alone and not frightened. Just empty. She looked down at her hands. —Then I went to a mosque with my father. A little ugly mosque in a storefront. It wasn't anything close to beautiful but it wasn't empty either. It was the opposite of empty. It was filled with believers. There was hardly room to stand.

—Yes, said the man.

—I still don't know why he took me. But I remember what he said after. He laughed at them. He told me that they barely knew their prayers.

—Yes, my child.

—I went again without telling my father. I knew what he'd say so I kept it a secret. I went every day for a month. Then I met my friend Decker. And then I felt full.

The man gave no reaction. He seemed to think that she had more to tell.

—I know it sounds stupid, she said. —Way too simple. Like eating dinner or something.

His eyes never wavered. Amber colored and deliberate as a cat's.

—Full, he said, working his lips subtly after he'd spoken, as if the word or the idea were new to him. —No longer empty.

She nodded.

—And tired, he said.

She felt his eyes on her. The courtyard in Sadda. The gray before sunrise.

—Yes, she answered.

—Very tired. And also afraid.

She wanted to look past him then, at the windows set high in the chalk-white brickwork, but something about his hands held her attention. They were pale and liver-spotted and gracefully tapered. At last she told the old man he was right.

—Of course I am right. You think it was bravery that brought you to me, or high spirits, or the beauty and importance of our cause. But it is fear that moves men to take action. Particularly action that is foolish. It is fear.

She watched his hands and said nothing. They kept perfectly still.

—You have a quality about you, Suleyman. Some attribute I can't yet put a name to. I regret you won't be staying with us longer.

It took her a moment to answer. —Why not?

—I beg your pardon?

—Why won't I be staying?

His eyes widened. —But of course you know why, little brother. You are going to the camps.

As if down an echoing corridor she heard herself laughing and stammering her thanks. The old man's smile faded. Her gratitude was of no use to him.

—I'll tell you one thing further, he said softly.

She assured him she would listen to whatever he might say. He bent forward and reached for her hand. His palm was loose-skinned and dry.

—In Kandahar, where I was born, there is a tradition. An ancient tradition and a hateful one. The shame of every Muslim. Boys are taken from their mothers, many among them less than ten years old, and kept and raised and trained to serve men's pleasure. Dancing boys they are called, and in truth their dancing is a thing of wonder. But these are boys in name only. They are beautiful and skilled and greatly prized but they have forgotten their families and their boyhoods and the names their fathers gave them. They are lost to all virtue. They eat and sleep and die in Heaven's shadow. Are you attending to me, Suleyman Al-Na'ama?

She fought the urge to pull her hand away. —I'm not sure what you mean. Are you saying—

—I say only this. His yellow cat's eyes closed as he released her. —Do not, under any circumstances, go to Kandahar.

The camp called the Mountain was in fact a loose cluster of cinderblock buildings on the outskirts of the town of Mansehra, a stone's throw from the border to Kashmir. She rode there in a flatbed with the Arabs she'd met in the night and she began to hear echoes of gunfire even before the truck had left the eastern suburbs. No one they passed on the street seemed to notice the shooting. If not for the shock and delight on the faces of her companions she'd have been tempted to doubt her own senses.

The youngest of the Arabs spent the last few kilometers with tears in his eyes, whether of joy or dread or carsickness it was difficult to tell. He was mumbling some kind of prayer, attempting to keep his thin voice manly, and she wondered as she watched him whether hers might sound the same. Her breasts were tender and her throat was raw and she felt close to tears herself. The gunfire grew louder, then dimmer, then all at once so loud that she could feel it in her teeth. Then the camp appeared before them with its white gate open wide.

The boy was called Abu Intiqam. He explained in faltering English, with a warrior's dignity, that his name meant Father of Vengeance. In spite of the risk she felt a sudden urge to take him like a child into her arms. She told him that his name was very grand and asked if he'd chosen it himself and he assured her that he had. Then he hung his head and groaned into his shirtsleeves and said nothing more until the truck had stopped.

They were led by men in skullcaps to a shack whose corrugated tin roof seemed to writhe and buckle in the midday heat. The grounds of the compound were rough and ungraded and its buildings rode the sloping hill like fishing buoys riding out a swell. Everything looked arrested in mid-motion. Men lay slackly in the shade, laid out seemingly at random, as though some act of violence had only just occurred. But their clothing was immaculate and bright.

She and the Arabs entered the shack one by one, for no reason she could determine, with their hands crossed before them like prisoners of war. The office they stepped into smelled of kerosene and sweat. She'd expected another round of questioning but was asked only her age and her fighting name and whether she was bringing any money. The man who asked these perfunctory questions was handsome but joyless and kept his sight fixed on his typewriter. It seemed to be giving him trouble. He looked up only once, when she told him that she hadn't brought a bedroll, and asked her in a weary voice whether she had lice or complications of the skin.

—No English, the man said loudly, in English. —No American. Yes? We speak no English here.

—Yes, brother, she said in Arabic.

—Yes what?

She blinked at him uncertainly. —We speak no English here.

In fact she found over the following weeks that a good amount of her training was conducted in her native language, even in that place where English was synonymous with godlessness and greed. The photocopied manual on ballistics was in English and the mimeographed first-aid pamphlet was in English and the primer on techniques of urban warfare had been printed by the Langley Tactical Press in Alexandria, Virginia. There were no other Americans at the camp and no Europeans either and it seemed possible that there had never been. Once again she was set apart from the others and given privileged attention. At mealtimes she was often asked to interpret between the Pakistanis and the Arabs and a place was set for her at the instructors' table. She would have preferred to sit with the Arabs she'd arrived with but she was careful to seem grateful for the honor. This much she'd learned since coming to the country.

The evening meal was the only occasion at which the whole of the camp ate together and that first night she barely touched her food.

She sat mute and still with her eyes on the entrance and waited to catch sight of Ziar Khan. It was hard to imagine Decker in that place but she was sure that he was coming. The Arab boy, Abu Intiqam, asked why she wasn't eating and she told him she was happy and he asked her nothing more. Her answer was appropriate and he was satisfied. The food was long-grained pilau with carrot shavings and yellow raisins and dark chunks of beef, far better food than she was used to, and she willed herself to force a mouthful down.

All that evening she felt girlish and exposed in her excitement. Her breasts still ached under the bandage and she longed to loosen it or better yet to take it off completely and she wondered for a moment if she could. A man across the table explained that the food they were eating was unusually lavish and that she and her Arab friends should take great care to fill their stomachs. Another man compared that evening's feast to a pavilion in the orchard of paradise and the camp's customary fare to the latrine of an animal hospital and everyone laughed. She bowed to the man and took a second helping of garlic flatbread and refilled her cup and turned back toward the door.

After what seemed an hour of sleep she awoke to the sound of bare feet shuffling past her in the dark. For the first time in a year she found it hard to rouse herself for morning prayer. She slapped her cheeks lightly and adjusted the bandage and took a pill from the crumpled package in her duffel. The others were already out and gone. She made her ablutions alone in the shallow creek that ran steeply behind the canteen, mindful that no one was watching, and reached the camp's tar-roofed mosque just as prayer was beginning. The mosque was papered from floor to ceiling with posters for Harkat-ul-Mujahideen and lit only by whatever meager daylight crossed its threshold. Some of the men prayed ardently with their brows pressed to the floor while others yawned and scratched their heads and gossiped. The lack of discipline unnerved her. The memory returned of her father outside the little storefront mosque in Santa Rosa, fiddling idly with his cell phone, ignoring the imam and his modest congregation. Waiting on word from someone. From a woman. She heard her father's conde-scending laugh.

When prayers were done a few of the men lit hand-rolled cigarettes and she went and stood unobtrusively among them, glad for the reprieve their smoke afforded her from the sour smell of sweat and unwashed clothes. A quarter of an hour later they waited assembled in loose columns on a square of hard-packed clay between the mosque and the canteen. A gray haze hung over the lowlands and she watched her breath combine with the breath of the others as day crept hesitantly up the slope. It put her in mind of dawn in the courtyard in Sadda but it wasn't the same. Not at all. The man who had led them in prayer now called out numbers from a lectern and they stretched and pumped their fists and ran in place.

She was assigned with twelve other recruits, all but one of them Arab, to a trainer who called himself Abu Imam. He was slender and dark-skinned and every mistake his students made afforded him the same shy amusement. His English was excellent but he spoke English rarely. He was Eritrean and just shy of thirty and he'd learned his trade in the Rift Valley fighting the Ethiopian occupation. He had the carriage of the runner he'd once aspired to be and they spent their first morning running relay drills and sprinting up the sawgrass-covered bluff above the compound. The sky was dead white and the heat was terrific. Her only shoes were the sandals she'd bought in Peshawar and within hours both her feet were chapped and bleeding. Others were in worse shape, vomiting or soiling themselves, entreating the trainer for mercy, but this brought her precious little consolation. Her sight was darkening from exhaustion when they stopped for third prayers and hobbled to the canteen for dried flatbread and tea. She sat sprawled in the shade and mumbled a heartfelt thanks to God that it was over. Then Abu Imam issued each of them a Kalashnikov minus its magazine and they got to their feet and fell in line and ran the drills again.

Over the six weeks that followed she ran drills by daylight and by darkness and swam bearing loads in the river and learned to disassemble her rifle and clean it with motor oil and put it back together without opening her eyes. After the first week they ran barefoot and she learned to move over sand and scree and gravel with speed and with economy and to shape her heel and instep to the contours of each stone. She learned how to target instinctively, without using the Kalashnikov's sight, and how to communicate by Morse and semaphore. She learned how to throttle a man using a wire, or a drawstring, or a strip of silk torn from a shawl.

In the evenings she lay on her bedroll faint from thirst and from exertion and before the light had faded she was lost to all the world. Her own body soon became as rank as the others' and she prayed to God that her sweat would smell no different. Often now when she started awake in the icy predawn twilight she would struggle to remember where she was and for what reason. She awoke each day to pain and bafflement and wondered what catastrophe had found her. But she was the first to the tar-roofed mosque now, not the last.

She was squatting under cover of a line of oil barrels behind the munitions shed one afternoon when Abu Intiqam discovered her. He was too young for the Mountain, younger even than the boys who cleaned the instructors' quarters and attended them at meals, and he'd taken to following her from place to place with anxious subservient eyes. But now his eyes were wide and hard and shining. She crouched contemptibly before him. He was staring at the gap between her lowered pants and her upraised kameez.

—As-salaamu alaikum, she willed herself to say.

—Wa-alaikum as-salaam, he murmured.

Her hunger and exhaustion were a blessing in that instant. She felt at a great distance from her body as it squatted there forlornly in the filth. The fourth call to prayer sounded as she pulled her pants up and got to her feet. Abu Intiqam stood staring with his hands bunched into fists. He was waiting for her to explain.

—I'm different from you, she said, smoothing down her kameez. —You can see that yourself.

He bobbed his head, still staring at her hips.

She compelled herself to wait, to move unhurriedly, to keep her expression composed. As if this moment were a solemn rite of passage for the boy. Her body felt as strange to her as it must have seemed to him: as alien, as bewildering, as defenseless.

—I'm different from you, she repeated.

When he gave no reply she took a step toward him and laid her right hand lightly on his shoulder. Her arm was shaking.

—Abu Intiqam, can you tell me why that is?

His color seemed to deepen. —I can't.

—Because you're afraid? she said gently. —Or because you don't know?

To her great relief he confessed that both were true. She knelt down beside him. —Then I'll tell you, little brother. You're a warrior of the Mountain now. You've earned the right to hear.

—To hear what, Brother Suleyman?

—This is not my first jihad.

For a time he said nothing. —I don't understand.

—I come from the other side of the world, she said, in a voice she barely recognized as hers. —A place where believers are hated. I lost my friends when I came to the faith, all of them, and my family decided that I'd gone insane. I was told I was too young to know my own mind, that I was a danger to myself. That bad things would happen and that I would deserve them. My mother and father turned their backs on me. And worst of all, little brother: what they told me turned out to be true. Bad things did happen. She tightened her hold on his shoulder. —I tell you this, Abu Intiqam, that you may learn from my example.

He nodded and started sucking on the knuckle of his thumb. The call to prayer sounded again. The temptation to abandon him to his confusion was enormous. If I go right now, she thought, then I'll have told him nothing wrong.

—Forgive me, Brother Suleyman, he said. —I still don't see—

—They cut me, she heard herself whisper. —They cut me, little brother. With a knife.

He let out a whimper at that and she knew he believed her. It was possible he'd never seen a woman naked, not even in a photograph. —Forgive me, Brother Suleyman, he said to her again.

She smiled at him and took his hand and walked him down the hill. It caused her pain to see him so bewildered. It was happening now, just as Decker had warned her: the lie she'd become had been spoken aloud. Some small frontier had shifted. Abu Intiqam was weeping and she kissed him on the forehead. The late sun was blinding. For the first time since she'd left her home she knew that she was lost.

That night the Prophet came to her and drew the bedding from her shoulders. He had her mother's smoke-stained fingertips and her father's graying stubble but his eyes and skin and voice were Ziar Khan's. His body cast no shadow. Perhaps he was a demon sent to tempt her. He requested that she follow him and helped her to her feet.

They stepped over the sleeping bodies of her brothers and even over some who were awake and staring blankly at the ceiling. Even over some who were at prayer. The Prophet moved wearily, as if he'd come a great distance to find her, and he assured her that he had. She wanted to ask him why but lacked the courage. She wanted more than anything not to offend. His manner toward her was casual, even familiar. Though he was attentive he was strangely melancholy. Mankind had disappointed him, even the faithful. The faithful perhaps most of all. His disappointment had aged him and turned his hair gray but he was a young man still and beautiful and proud. His orange tracksuit was threadbare and discolored but he wore it like a robe of beaten silk.

As they climbed the escarpment in the cold and the starshine she explained to him what had brought her to the camp. She told the Prophet that she knew it must seem strange that a girl of barely eighteen should travel so far and take such risks but that there had been no other option. She told him that it was the believers who had drawn her to the One True Faith, the believers above all, and that if she had stayed in her mother's ruined house with only God's word and her own thoughts for company she would soon have lost her mind. She explained to him how her father had deceived her and betrayed her. She described her mother's beatings. The Prophet walked close beside her, panting slightly from the climb, nodding thoughtfully as she spoke. He knew all that she was telling him but it felt glorious to tell it. She had never talked so much in all her life. The escarpment rose before her and her breath aspired toward Heaven and the world in all its failings lay behind her on the plain. She asked the Prophet if he would punish her and he raised his tired bloodshot eyes to Heaven. She asked if God would punish her and the night sky poured into her open mouth.

The next day the tactical training began. She learned how to stage an ambush in the mountains and the desert. She was taught how to use camouflage to draw near to a mark. A specialist instructed the group on how to improvise medical assistance to brothers in the field, and how to carry them to safety with a minimum of strain. She learned to stanch blood flow. She learned how to storm a house and how to hold it from counterattack. She learned how to sow cover for advancing infantry, how to coordinate a kidnapping, how to evaluate a building as a target for a bomb.

One afternoon Abu Imam led them to a newly built structure behind the admissions shed whose whitewashed walls were already beginning to flake. The day was dry and windless. The mood among the Arabs and a group of Chechens recently arrived from the north was restless and playful, the high spirits of schoolboys before a holiday assembly. An instructor fanned the room with a flattened cardboard box in an absurd attempt to cut the stifling heat. Folding chairs had been arranged in four precise rows and a television was wheeled with elaborate pomp out of an alcove. Abu Imam was uncharacteristically somber. He gave them to understand that what they would see over the next hour was more important even than their marksmanship or orienteering drills, and that he was grateful to count himself among their number. The video had been sent by a benefactor of the Mountain, a man of great learning and personal means. Those with Arabic were called upon to translate for their neighbors.

—What's it saying, little brother? a red-haired Chechen asked in English as the tape began to play.

—Nothing yet, she said, straining to hear through the hiss.

He gripped her seatback with his sunburned fingers. —How nothing? I hear someone talking.

—O believers, she said quietly. —Retaliation for the slain is ordained upon you.

—Very good, little brother. But what does it mean?

—It's a passage from the Book. From the second holy sura.

—Is that all? sighed the Chechen, sitting back in his seat.

The film that followed had been copied and recopied times without number and its color had been all but leached away. A silver veil of static billowed over the screen and the robed figures behind it appeared to be hemorrhaging light. An elderly man addressed the viewer from a divan set beneath a keyhole arch. His speech was barely audible. The veil shuddered, then lifted, then lowered again. Airplanes flew in tight formation over cities being rendered into ash. Palestine was mentioned, then Chechnya, then Bosnia, then Kashmir, then regions still unknown to her. The airplanes crossed from right to left and schools and housing grids and mosques were geometrically erased. Every soul shall taste death. The footage bled white. This present life is but the rapture of delusion. The camera tracked at shoulder height through trauma wards past mutilated children. Dates of air strikes were intoned in litany. A keening arose in the smothering dark. She felt her hands trembling. Every soul shall taste death. Behind her the Chechen was weeping into his shirtsleeves like a child.

O believers, bear in patience, be steadfast in the fight, keep to your battle stations and fear God. Perhaps you will prevail.

After the video had ended and the antediluvian TV had been returned to its alcove one of the brothers approached her. Of the camp's many Pashtuns he alone spoke fluent English and possessed some hard-won knowledge of geography and world events but this fact had not inclined him in her favor. She had just left the shed when he fell in beside her, breathing heavily and mumbling to himself. The expression on his face was bemused, almost bashful, but she was careful to keep an arm's length between them. She had seen that dazed look on his face before.

—What is it, brother? Did I make a mistake?

—You say the Qur'an perfect. Beautiful. His voice had gone thick. —I can hear that you went to madrasa.

She thanked him and kept moving. The others had branched off or fallen behind. She looked about her for Abu Imam.

—Those aeroplanes, brother.

Abu Suhail had stopped walking and she stopped now as well, careful not to let him get behind her. —What airplanes? The ones in the movie?

—I see those are your aeroplanes, he said. —Your bombers.

—America's you mean. The United States.

—Yours, said Abu Suhail. He met someone's eye behind her but she didn't turn to look. She heard a muffled click, dull and metallic, as if a soda can were being opened.

—Abu Suhail, she said, facing him squarely, raising her voice so the others would hear. —The place where I was born is not my country. I don't have a passport. I don't have a family. We surrendered these things, all of us, when we came to this place. Am I right in saying so? We let them go to take up our jihad.

—I surrendered no family, he said tonelessly. —My family are murdered in the bombings.

—Brother, if you'll only—

—Tell me again about these planes. About your planes.

—Not my planes, she stammered. —Not America's either. You weren't listening in our ballistics course. Those were Neshers, made in Israel. Those were Israeli Air Force fighters.

He blinked at her with great effort, as if he were drunk. —Planes from Israel.

—That's right.

—But Israel, he said slowly. —Israel is yours.

He was almost touching her now and she could feel each word he spoke against her skin. Though he was no more than twenty his breath was an old man's and it made her stomach clench to smell it. Perhaps her own breath smelled no better. She turned her head and saw the Chechens watching from the shade of the canteen.

—Tell me your name, said Abu Suhail. —Yours and that of your father.

—Have you forgotten where we are? This is the Mountain, brother. I have no name here but the one I chose.

—Tell me your name, he repeated, catching her by the arm. —Your American name.

As she started to answer a horn sounded behind her, once and then three times in swift succession, and she heard the metal pull-gates screeching open. She twisted out of Abu Suhail's grip and turned in time to see a plume of dust unfurling in the slanting yellow light. Two pickups with flatbed trailers hitched to them clattered over the barrier and jackknifed to a stop between the mosque and the canteen. The trailers were stacked with Tyvek sacks of lentils and there were men in homespun coats and headscarves sprawled across the sacks. The driver of the first truck was the Talib who had questioned her in the pharmacy in Peshawar. The driver of the second truck was Ziar Khan.

She took a handful of steps toward the trucks and the men, feeling her way across the sloping ground without lowering her eyes. Abu Suhail and the others had forgotten her. The wind was rising and the cinched mouths of the sacks snapped and fluttered in the flatbeds and she stood with her arms held out to either side in case she lost her balance. The sky above the compound seemed to darken. She watched the men laughing and calling out greetings and tossing the sacks two at a time from the trailers. She felt dizzy with fear and had no idea why. It held her in place like a pole driven into the ground.

Someone must have mentioned her in passing, an American teen with antiquated Arabic and no passport, because when she came to Ziar's table at the evening meal he showed not the slightest surprise. He set his teacup down unhurriedly and waited for her to speak. Her voice failed her when she tried to say his name.

—Suleyman Al-Na'ama, he said fondly. —I should have had the good sense not to leave you in Sadda. I should have known that it would serve no purpose.

—Your father said he made you promise not to take me.

—Did he? I don't remember. He waved to someone at another table. —I've made my father many promises I didn't mean to keep. Shame on my ungrateful head for that.

—There's no shame, she said quickly. —I made my own decision.

—He's not likely to see it that way.

—I don't care how he sees it.

—Of course not. He nodded. —But you aren't his son.

The din of the hall receded as she returned Ziar's smile. A dome of light and calm seemed to enclose them. In his expression she saw that her future at the Mountain was still undecided, and she told herself that she was willing to submit to his judgment: to Ziar Khan's and no one else's.

—Who was that man you came with?

—Which man, little brother?

—The driver of the other truck.

He raised his eyebrows. —In this camp his name is Abu Shakt. Why do you ask?

—I've met him before.

—So I understand.

—He said you were a liar and a thief.

Ziar nodded and rose from the table, taking hold of her forearm to help himself up. His grip was less gentle than she remembered. —Brother Suleyman! You almost sound as if you disbelieved him.

—Is he a comrade of yours? Did you fight the Russians together?

—Come for a walk, he said, guiding her out of the hall. —Back in Sadda, as I remember it, you asked fewer questions.

—In Sadda I had fewer problems.

He laughed. He was a silhouette now with the first stars behind him.

—That can mean only one thing, Suleyman Al-Na'ama.

—What's that?

—You're becoming a man.

They walked past the mosque and the munitions hut and the ditch of the latrines to the beginning of the escarpment, exactly as had happened in her dream. Her fear had long since vanished and her body seemed to float inside her clothes. There were clouds to the south, rolling in from the lowlands, and the lights of Mansehra turned them a bilious green. She tried to concentrate on what Ziar was telling her. She fought the urge to take him by the hand.

—When we left the madrasa I was tempted to wake you, little brother, but I'm a better son than that, praise be to God. Your friend Ali urged me to do it. You mustn't think badly of him. He said more than once that you'd make a better fighter than he would. Ziar shook his head. —Within a few days I believed him.

—He's right, she said. —I would, Ziar. I will.

He paused a moment, looking back the way they'd come. —We crossed the border on foot, as is the custom. There is a camp there, a small one, not three hours into tribal territory. But your friend Ali had told me fairy stories. He claimed to have fired small arms, and to know how to care for a rifle, and his cousin Yaqub abetted him in these falsehoods. Yaqub is a well-intentioned man and a dependable soldier, Suleyman, but he is easily misled. They caused me no small embarrassment in that place, the two of them. No small measure of trouble.

—Trouble? she said.

—I chose to hold Brother Altaf accountable, which I still consider just. He was the most deceitful of the three. He told no end of lies when I confronted him, Suleyman, not least about you. You won't be sharing the midday meal with him again, I'm sad to say. Or with his brother.

—Why is that?

—Because they are no longer of our party.

A thin rain began falling as they clambered up the slope. She was certain now that Ziar was pleased to see her and she barely felt the burning in her legs. She told herself that she had his confidence, that he would never have spoken so unguardedly with the earnest bearded men who shared his table, and the joy this notion brought her made the night go very still. She felt no fatigue. She could have kept on for hours. It was only after they'd reached the crest of the escarpment and begun to descend that she realized she'd barely thought of Decker.

—What about Ali?

—What about him?

She hesitated. —Did you leave him there too? Or did you send him home?

—Home to where, little brother?

She stepped past him so he couldn't see her face. —I'm sure whatever you chose to do was right.

—And I am duly honored by your trust.

—I'm only asking—

—I did less to him, Suleyman Al-Na'ama, than a liar deserves.

She opened her mouth but said nothing.

—Suleyman.

—Yes?

—He's been in the infirmary since we arrived. The water here does not agree with him.

She felt herself shiver. —He's here? At the Mountain?

—Go to him, little brother. Go to him and keep him company. Perhaps you'll find a chance to teach him how to aim a rifle.

—Ali's not a liar, she mumbled. —Not really. He just thinks a thing is true if he says it enough.

—I see. And how do you know this?

—I just do, that's all. She started downhill, sliding over the scree. —Maybe sometimes I feel that way myself.

—Go to him, Ziar called after her. —But bear in mind, Suleyman, what the Prophet has told us.

—What's that?

—For all you know, you may love something, and it is harmful to you.

She found Decker asleep in the infirmary with a white enamel bucket within arm's reach of his cot. The bucket's rim was chipped and encrusted with age-blackened filth and she pushed it away with the sole of her foot and bent down beside him. The violence of her happiness amazed her. After a while he shifted and sighed to himself, almost too faintly to hear, and she sat down on the cot and spoke his name.

—For fuck's sake, Sawyer, he said without opening his eyes. —Tell me you're not really sitting there.

She laid a hand on his shoulder. It felt wasted and cool. —I'll tell you anything you want to hear.

—All right then. He let out a breath. —Say I'm back in Santa Rosa. Tell me I'm as fat as Biggie Smalls and watching Kathie Lee Gifford on TV. Tell me my shit doesn't look like dirty Pepsi.

—All true, she said. —Except for that last part. I can't help you there.

—I always had a crush on Kathie Lee. At last it can be told.

—I don't believe that for a second.

—Believe it, pilgrim. She had that hot-mom thing going on. Like first she'd bake you a big tray of brownies, then she'd take you somewhere, like into the laundry room, maybe, and—

—Are they taking care of you? Is there some kind of a doctor?

—Look around, Sawyer. He laughed. —They dump you in here and see if you can make it back out. If you're lucky they give you a bucket.

—Can I ask you something?

—I thought I was the one asking the questions around here.

—Ziar told me something happened to Altaf.

Decker lay back on the folded towel that served him as a pillow. —You never liked him anyway.

—What happened?

He stared up at the ceiling for a time before he answered.

—It all just went down the crapper. I mean right away, Sawyer. Before we'd even crossed the border. I'm a goddamn idiot. I'm lucky I'm not facedown in some ditch.

She smiled at him. —You smell as if you are.

—They killed him, Sawyer. They took him out and shot him in the head.

A tapping carried to them through the wall behind the cot. The admissions office was on the other side and she heard the clatter of the old electric Remington and the mournful droning of the air conditioner. The floor beneath her was bisected by a dark and ancient stain. She touched a palm to the wall and it came away wet.

—Who's they? she said finally.

He seemed not to hear. —I was ten feet away when they did it. Maybe not even that. They didn't even have the decency to take him off somewhere.

—Would that have been better?

—What do you mean?

—Would it have been better if they'd done it somewhere else?

—Fuck you, Sawyer, he said, turning his face to the wall. —You didn't have to see it. You weren't there.

—That's true, she said. —I wasn't. You left me behind.

He made a small choked noise that could have had any meaning she chose to assign it and curled up again and lay still. —I want to go home, he whispered.

It took her a moment to answer. —You should go home, Decker. You should go home as soon as you can.

—They've got my passport and everything. They've got all my money.

—We'll figure it out, she said. —I'll talk to them.

She sat beside him on the cot and ran her fingers through his hair. The tapping of the Remington continued without pause and she asked herself what manner of report or decree or manifesto was being drafted on the far side of the wall. It dawned on her that she had no way of knowing, no way even to guess, and the thought brought tears of panic to her eyes. She stared at the thin cold thread of light beneath the door, willing herself to see the truth for which the rituals of the camp were merely symbols. God was in that place, or the submission to God's will, or perhaps only the desire to submit, which was the highest form of love that she could give. Not the submission itself but the desire. She listened to the pull and sigh of Decker's breathing. It didn't matter what was happening on the far side of the wall. Her duty was clear to her at last, or clear enough. She had no other family, no other love, no other calling. He was the only person in the world who knew her. Her duty was to keep him safe from harm.

All that week she devoted herself to her training with a fervor that caused even Abu Imam to sing her praises. She learned to set land mines and to lay trip wires for IEDs and to dismantle them in such a way that they could be wrapped in squares of thick gray felt and used again. Her fingers were smaller than the others', more nimble and precise, and she was given the task of checking the shearing pin and resetting the safety on the plastic antitank mines that had proven so effective in the fight against the Russians. She practiced marksmanship and tracking and began to study Pashto. Each day after fourth prayers she visited Decker in the infirmary and told him what she'd learned, and eventually he began to pay attention. At times his former bluster would flicker to life, especially when he asked about the mines and IEDs, and by the end of the week he was treating her with good-natured contempt whenever anyone was near. She offered solemn thanks to God for this small mercy. Within a fortnight Decker was able to get to his feet without her help, and the next day he left the infirmary. He made no further mention of escape.

The following Juma'a at dawn prayer she caught sight of Ziar at the entrance to the mosque, silhouetted by first light, watching Decker with a look of steady interest. His half-smile might have been meant for her, or for Decker, or even for the red-bearded Chechen who was leading the prayer, and she thought to herself that this was one of the qualities that made him a leader of men: his smile applied to everyone and no one. And still she knew in her most secret self that what bound her to him now was theirs alone. She looked at Decker beside her, mumbling intently along with the Chechen's clumsy Arabic, then turned her head again, not caring who might see her, to return Ziar's smile. But now Ziar was nowhere to be seen.

Within a few days Decker was well enough to begin his formal training and her standing with Abu Imam was such that she was able to persuade him, after a lengthy discussion, to admit Decker into his group. She vouched for his probity and his zeal as a Muslim and promised that she'd keep him out of trouble. She hadn't laid Abu Imam's doubts to rest, not fully, but that made no difference. All that mattered was that he'd agreed.

Decker was faltering and awkward at first, as Ziar had described, but he showed a grim resolve that she could never have foreseen. His illness had changed him. He rarely spoke now, not even to her, and forced himself to eat the rancid rations that the others barely touched. Although he was excused from the midmorning run up the escarpment he insisted on climbing as high as he could and spent the rest of the hour sheltering from the wind, blue-lipped and shaking from exhaustion, cleaning the antiquated rifle he'd been issued. It was a Degtyarev DP, a Russian light machine gun from the first half of the century, but he seemed not to notice its age or its weight or the Kalashnikovs that everyone else carried. Abu Imam began to tease Ziar, in the evenings, with anecdotes of Brother Ali's boldness and devotion to jihad. Ziar nodded cheerfully and wished him all the best.

They were laying antipersonnel mines along the bluff above the compound when she caught sight of two elderly men in kaftans struggling slowly up the slope. Ziar followed just behind them, dressed all in white, as if for the Day of Assembly. Some form of premonition or foreboding brought her up onto her feet. Ziar made a gesture and Abu Imam brought his cupped hands together and called out her name. It was happening too quickly. She watched them as if she were watching the news. Abu Imam frowned and called to her again. The foreboding grew stronger. She looked over her shoulder at Decker. He raised his head for a moment, stared down the slope blankly, then turned back to the channel he was cutting in the clay.

—You've done well in the course, little brother, said Abu Imam when she reached him. —You've distinguished yourself. It is for this reason that these gentlemen are here.

—I know that, Abu Imam. And I thank you.

—You know this? The smile left his lips. —What else do you imagine that you know, Suleyman Al-Na'ama?

—Only what you've taught me, she said distractedly, bringing her hand to her heart. She was picturing Decker behind her. Abu Imam seemed about to say something further, perhaps even to embrace her, but instead he stepped aside to let her pass.

Ziar and the men in the kaftans were waiting on a ledge of level ground. The men gave their names as Abu Bakhsh and Abu Hamza and she knew as they began questioning her in their dignified, weary voices that her time with Abu Imam was at an end. They asked about her tenure at the Mountain, her understanding of scripture, the extent of her familiarity with explosives and small arms. The sun was behind her and they bobbed their heads in unison and squinted as though she was hard to see. Ziar kept his distance, observing the proceedings with an air of amused detachment, like a precocious young merchant waiting for his elders to review a bill of sale.

When the men were done Ziar thanked them and led her with a flourish away from the mine course to a bend in the road where a battered blue pickup stood idling. A Pashtun boy she seemed to recognize sat slumped behind the wheel. He awoke with a start when Ziar rapped on the windshield and stammered an apology and skittered up the road and disappeared. She was glad to see him go.

She stood with Ziar by the clattering hood and they looked westward together down the long narrow curve of the valley. No one else was in sight. The day was exceptionally clear and she saw or imagined the spires of a city at the margins of her vision, past the far northern summits, where there wasn't and could never be a city. The truck coughed and grumbled. A line of pockmarks edged the wheelwell where a spray of bullet holes had been patched over. The putty was cracked and discolored and collared with rust. She counted seven rounds in all. She ran her fingertips lightly along them.

—They tried their best, those two grandfathers, Ziar said with mock solemnity. —But you outplayed them, Suleyman. Congratulations.

—I didn't know we were playing.

—Didn't you?

The need to please him in that moment was as urgent as a cramp.
—I'm sorry, she heard herself answer. —I think I'm confused.

—You're a child still, he said. He glanced back toward the compound. —This makes your case difficult. To those graybeards you seem practically a baby.

—There are plenty of boys up here younger than me, she said quickly.

—Such is the case, Suleyman. There are many young boys. But none have yet been brought across the border.

She took her tongue between her teeth. He expected no answer. He was in a patient frame of mind and she gave thanks for the reprieve.

—Most in this camp are of the opinion that my faith in you is misplaced, he said. —Abu Imam is the only exception.

—What are they saying about me?

His smile was almost sheepish. —Some have told me that I am besotted, that my thinking is troubled. As if you were a dancing boy from Kandahar, little brother, and I were a wrinkled old degenerate, taking opium with my tea. He reached past her and grasped the door handle. —Am I an opium eater, Suleyman? Tell me truthfully. Are you a dancing boy?

She held her hand over the engine block and felt the heat run smoothly up her arm into her chest. She kept it there as long as she could stand it.

—No, she told him finally. —I'm not a dancing boy.

—I'm grateful to you for saying so, said Ziar, pulling open the door. —Now get in.

They rode in silence down the valley until the crushed clay of the roadway turned to tar. Never had she seen or heard or felt with such precision. Her body was a girl's body still and it felt far too much but that mattered only if she chose to listen. She looked out the window and watched the hills passing. They meant more to her than her frail body did. Her forgettable body. They were fractured and dark and they fluttered like wings.

The hills fell away and the suburbs enclosed them. The speed of it dazed her. At a nondescript turn on an avenue of stucco-fronted houses Ziar rolled to a stop and sat back and braced his palms against the dash. She waited for him to look at her but his attention was devoted to the street. It was paved in fitted concrete slabs and graded at its edges and its curbs and trees and sidewalks all looked lovingly maintained. Aside from a fine yellow film on the windshield there was no trace of the dust they'd driven through. They might have been in some sleepy California suburb. The whitewashed houses shone so brilliantly it almost hurt to look.

Ziar killed the engine. —We're low on petrol, he said. —I'll tell you something, little brother.

—What's that?

—We may not have enough for the drive back.

She glanced at the fuel gauge and saw it was broken. Ziar's attention was fixed on her now, not on the street. His fingertips drummed on the dashboard. She was ready for the future but the future lay in shadow. Her clarity of foresight was gone and in its place was a shortness of breath and an impatience for the next ordained event. The next sudden turning. She had no idea what would happen and she needed it to happen. She needed the doubt she felt to disappear.

Ziar took her hand. He looked pleased that she'd given no answer. He seemed to take it as a gesture of good faith.

—Do you see that house, little brother? The one with the half-open gate?

She followed his gesture. —I see it.

—A man lives there alone, with no women or children. An importer from India. A man who calls himself a patron of our cause.

—A rich man, she said.

—A man who made pledges. Who promised us money. A man who speaks with one side of his mouth to our people and with the other to the ISI.

—The ISI?

He made a gesture of impatience. —The ISI, he repeated. —The intelligence service in this place. The night police.

She looked across that wide street at the house and the gate and the car parked behind it. A gray sedan without a number plate. A low columned breezeway. A ceiling fan turning behind a bay window. The flicker of a countertop TV.

—What are we here to do?

—We're here to get petrol. That's all, little brother.

—All right.

Her readiness surprised him. —Look behind your seat, he said. —There's a canister and a length of plastic hose. You've taken petrol from a car before?

She nodded. —Abu Imam showed us the first week.

—Of course. He turned and reached behind her. His face was closer to hers than it had ever been and she felt his breath against her collarbone and neck. He passed her the hose and the canister. —Get what you can, he said. He pushed the door open.

She felt lightheaded as she stepped onto the curb. When she reached the gate she stopped short and gripped the ironwork and fought briefly for air. There was rust around its hinges where the yellow paint had buckled and she scratched the flakes away and counted slowly down from twenty. Then she stood up straight and forced her body forward.

The yard was bare and paved in hexagons of multicolored tile. The sedan was a Mercedes and a child's plastic wading pool sat empty and inverted just beyond its right front tire. Again it seemed to her that she might be in California. It occurred to her as she knelt beside the car and lifted the tank guard and unthreaded the cap that the owner of the house was supposedly childless and she asked herself what the wading pool was for. She set the cap down on the tiles and fed the hose into the tank. Her head was clear again and she was wide awake. She thought about the flickering light behind the bay window and imagined how she might look from the interior of the house: a hunched form on the tiled ground in an attitude of prayer. She felt the hose touch bottom and brought the near end to her lips. She sucked until she tasted gas and dropped the hose into the can. The taste was vicious, less a taste at all than a sensation of pain, and she pressed her shirtsleeve to her teeth and sucked on it to keep herself from heaving. The light glimmered bluely. The canister rattled. She pulled the hose free and got up to close the tank. A shirtless man was standing in the window. Three shotgun shells lay brightly on the hood of the sedan.

By the time the house door opened she was running and his features were a blur along the margin of her sight. A heavyset man with a high outraged voice. She looked back and saw that he was barefoot and held something curved and dark in his right hand. Then she was out the gate with the canister in her arms like an infant and stumbling headlong up the street toward Ziar's truck. It was a different color than she remembered and its windows appeared to be tinted and she was almost there before she saw that it was not his truck at all. She passed it without slowing and understood as she heard voices and footfalls behind her that she was forsaken in that place and that she'd been brought down from the Mountain as some form of sacrifice. Ziar must have driven off while she was busy with the tank. Her confusion made her clumsy and gas was spilling from the canister onto her fingers and her sleeve. As she turned to let it fall a white stone like a hen's egg struck her just above the ear. The ground met her skull and her right elbow in the same instant and she heard the sound of the canister striking the pavement and the smell of gas grew stronger. She heard what must have been curses in some idiom unknown to her and somehow found her footing and began to run again. Tires screeched in the distance and she asked herself in a measured deliberate voice whether they meant to run her over. She stumbled again and rolled onto her back and the man was above her and she saw now that the object in his right hand was a knife for cleaving meat. A group of young men stood behind him and they looked down at her with expressions of disgust and incredulity. The first man raged and gestured with the cleaver. When he reached for her she kicked upward with all her strength and rolled away from him and staggered to her feet. They caught her in less than a dozen steps and someone seized her by the collar and forced her head back. She'd already sunk to her knees and surrendered to Providence when the tires screeched again and the man hit the pavement beside her with a sound like a sackful of gravel thrown off a roof. A hand pulled her up by the hair and people were running toward or alongside her and suddenly she was in Ziar's pickup looking back over her shoulder at a body in the street. One boy was still running after them but he was fat and bowlegged and she saw that his heart wasn't in it. Before long he planted his feet and bent over and waved to the truck as if giving it permission to go on without him. The hand he used to wave with held a Makarov PM.

They were halfway to the Mountain before Ziar looked at her. He was shaking with anger. He reached past her and opened the glove compartment and took out a handkerchief and pressed it to her temple.

—Take this, he said. —Hold it firm. Sit up now and keep your eyes open.

She did as she was told. Her thoughts refused to come to order. —I'm sorry, she said.

—What are you sorry for?

—I don't know. She felt herself tipping sideways. —For dropping the canister.

The laugh he gave sounded angrier still. —Dropping the canister, brother? It's under your feet.

She looked down and saw it resting on its side between her shins. Somehow she hadn't smelled the gas. The pain was worse and sweat was beading on her nape and on her forehead. Suleyman, came a voice.

—Suleyman? Do you hear me?

She noticed that her forehead was now pressed against the dash. Ideas came and went. She was certain that they hadn't stopped to fill the pickup's tank.

—Do we need to pull over?

—Why?

—To fill up the tank.

—Open your eyes, Ziar said. His voice was oddly muffled. —Open your eyes and sit up straight. We'll soon be at camp.

—No, she said, pushing back from the dash.

She felt the truck slowing. —What did you say?

—I want to know why you're angry. I want to know what I did wrong.

—You've done nothing, Suleyman. You've shown courage. He laughed again. —If I'm angry then I'm angry at myself.

—What for?

—For my weakness, he said. —For placing the opinion of a clutch of old men with dye in their beards above my own judgment. Do you understand?

She nodded. —You're telling me that we weren't out of gas.

Instead of answering he pulled over to the shoulder and reached between her knees for the canister and went out and filled the tank. As he poured he kept his back against the truck and scanned the road in both directions. There was nothing to see. She watched him and knew that his caution was a reflex, conditioned behavior, the consequence of experience no training camp or manual could give. He spoke to her now in the voice she knew best, certain and impersonal and calm.

—We'll take you to the infirmary. You can have the bed that Ali slept in. You'll like that, I think.

—You hate him, she murmured. —I wish I knew why.

—Listen to what I tell you now, he said. —In Mansehra or in Sadda it is no great offense to claim to be a thing that you are not. Even at the Mountain, or in the recruitment office of Harkat-ul-Mujahideen, it is no mortal crime. But across the border this is not the case. Brothers die there if you cannot do a thing that you have said. They die, little brother. Does this answer your question?

—But you saw him every day at the madrasa. You must have known he wasn't any fighter. You couldn't have believed what he was saying.

He stared at her a moment. —Of course I believed him, he said. —Ali is a Muslim. He knows it's a sin to deceive.

When she gave him no answer he climbed back in and drove her slowly up the rutted valley road. The Mountain's gate was opening before he spoke again.

—Pay attention now, Suleyman. I have no feelings against Brother Ali. I'll see that no harm comes to him.

She leaned back against the headrest. —Thank you for that.

—But I'll tell you something further, little brother. Your friendship with Ali will do you no credit. Not where you'll be going.

—Where will that be?

Ziar didn't answer.

—But he has enemies there? Her teeth seemed to be chattering. —Why is that, Ziar? Did he do something bad?

—What Ali did makes no difference. He eased the truck forward. —I tell you this as a caution. Nothing more.

As she looked at him her vision became clouded. It was true about Decker. He was no credit to her. He was a risk and an embarrassment. No one else in all that country knew the girl she'd been before.

—No, she said. —I'm not taking him anywhere he'll get in trouble. I'd rather not go.

He blinked at her. —Have you not understood me, Suleyman? It seems that you haven't. Ali will not be coming.

—He won't? Her voice sounded petulant, almost wheedling. —What will happen to him, then? Where will he go?

Ziar shook his head. —Your friend has no future, he said gently. —Not with us.

Decker came to see her in the infirmary that same afternoon. —The last will become first, he said, grinning. —Or something like that.

She lay back in the dark. —How was your day?

—My day? My day was badass, thanks. She felt him lower himself gingerly onto the cot. —My day was radical.

—What did Abu Imam have you doing? Did you lay some more mines?

—Laid 'em down. Dug 'em up. Stuck 'em back in again. Not sure what the percentage is in that, but maybe that's just me.

—The percentage is you don't die. That's the percentage.

—If that's the point then why lay mines at all?

—You don't have to.

—I know that. He smiled down at her. —I can head back to the States any old time I want. Then you can finally kick back and relax.

—I heard something happened, she said. —When you were in the mountains with Ziar.

—I'll bet you heard that. I'll just bet. And I don't have to think too hard who told you.

He sat framed by the doorway and she saw him for a moment as a cut-paper cameo, the kind travelers carried with them in lockets in centuries past. As if she'd already left him behind.

—What happened, Decker?

—Lots of things happened. He shifted on the cot. —I already told you how they did Altaf.

—That's true, she said. —You told me that.

—I fucked up, that's all. You need particulars?

—I need to know what we might be getting into.

—We're not getting into anything. I'm not exactly top of the roster around here, in case you forgot. I'm a half notch up from licking the latrines.

He seemed to expect a reply but she felt too weak to answer. Finally he gave a sort of cough. —What did he say?

—Who?

—Don't fuck with me, Sawyer.

She rolled onto her side. —He said I'm leaving soon.

—He can't decide that. He can ask you, that's all. And you can tell him no.

She stared at the wall. There were cracks in it she hadn't seen before. Faint hairline cracks. One ran up to the rafters.

—You can't just ditch me, Sawyer. Not like this.

—Not like what exactly, Decker? Like how you ditched me?

—That's right, he said slowly. —Like how I ditched you.

He lay down next to her and she made room as best she could. His body was tense and his eyes were wide open. It was too much to look at.

—This is my fault, she whispered. —I think that this is maybe all my fault.

—It doesn't matter whose damn fault it is. We're here.

—Oh God, she said.

—Maybe it's not a bad thing. We fucked up but we've made it this far. We just have to keep going.

—Why?

—Are you dumb enough to think they'll let us leave?

—Listen, she told him. Her mouth was dry as sawdust. —Decker, listen. I think you should try.

He went silent again.

—Did you hear what I said? I think—

—So you can be with him? Is that why? Just the two of you together?

—Decker, don't—

—I think that's why, Sawyer. I wish I didn't but I think that's fucking why. So you can be alone with him and no one here to tell.

She pushed herself upright or as near as she could manage and stared back at him. It was easier now. Under her grief was a new feeling, a coldness or a hollowness, a numbness where her trust in him had been. It was almost a relief to find it gone.

—I never thought of it that way, she said.

—Whatever you say, Sawyer.

—I never thought of it that way because I knew you wouldn't tell.

—Well I've got news for you, Brother Suleyman Al-Na'ama. I'll tell every last secret you've got.

The pain in her temples was worse than before but she held herself steady. —What happened to you, Decker?

—Nothing happened, he said evenly. —I've always been the same. I'm not going to be dicked around by Ziar Khan or the rest of these toothless old bastards or Hayat or you or anybody else. I'm done with all that. I'm not going to sit around here shoveling donkey shit while you grandstand like God's gift to the faithful. You're a sinner and a liar and if I keep quiet I'm a liar too.

—I don't believe you, she said. —You wouldn't do that.

—Is that right, Sawyer? Why the hell not?

—Because we take care of each other.

He went still for a time. —Try me, he said finally. —Run away with Ziar Khan and see.

She reached toward him and he put up no resistance. He refused to look at her but he let her take his hand in both of hers and bring it to her chest. She realized as his shoulders began heaving that she'd always thought of him as younger than she was. Even when they'd lain together naked on his narrow single bed. Even when he'd made her laugh and gasp and curse in shock and pleasure.

By the end of the week she was recovered enough to walk without dizziness and Abu Imam permitted her to accompany the group as an observer. They were practicing with large-scale explosives now, placing ordnance such as dynamite and plastique in a slate-walled ravine an hour north of camp. It was cool in the mornings and the blue sky above them looked just out of reach, like the roof of a tent. From time to time an airplane passed over. She sat swaddled in a kaftan there and watched the others working.

She hadn't forgotten what Ziar had told her about Decker and she looked for some sign that he was held back, set apart from the rest—but if anything he seemed exceptionally favored. He'd ingratiated himself with Abu Imam in the time she'd been gone, that much was evident, and he was proving to have a talent for explosives: he was often asked to run the wires now and set the charges. She had no idea what to hope for as far as Decker was concerned. Not if he chose to stay. She decided for the moment not to hope or think at all.

She was sitting with the Arabs at the evening meal when Abu Intiqam came and stood expectantly beside her. They had spoken many times since their encounter behind the munitions shed but something in his manner put her on her guard at once. He was looking at her thoughtfully, rubbing his small palms together. She was still thinking how to address him when he touched her sleeve and spoke in a high formal voice.

—Brother Khan wishes to speak with you, Brother Suleyman. Come back to the instructors' table.

She nodded and got to her feet. Her unease would not leave her. Decker was sitting with Abu Suhail at a table of Pashtuns and he set his cup down and watched her as she crossed the room. She had never seen him in Abu Suhail's company before. He muttered something as she passed their table and a number of them laughed.

—Brother Suleyman! said Ziar when she reached him. —You remember Abu Bakhsh and Abu Hamza.

She nodded and told him she did.

—Sit with us, said Abu Imam, making room for her.

—No, brother, Ziar said fondly. —Let our little mujahid sit next to me.

Abu Imam smiled and inclined his head politely. The old men ran their prunelike fingers through their beards in perfect concert. She rounded the table and sat across from them, at Ziar's right hand.

—How is your injury, Suleyman Al-Na'ama? said the older of the two. She tried to remember whether he was Abu Bakhsh or Abu Hamza. The one who hadn't spoken cupped his left hand to his ear.

—I feel well, father, she said. —It was just a little cut.

—A little cut? He appeared to be smiling.

—Yes, mu'allim. And a bruise above my ear.

—We visited you, Suleyman. In the infirmary.

—You did?

—Shall I tell you what you said to us there?

She was quiet a moment. —In the infirmary?

—He doesn't recall, said the thicker-set man. The man who'd spoken first looked troubled.

—He's made a fine recovery, Ziar put in. —Abu Imam has told you—

—Yes yes, Brother Khan. Let our mujahid speak for himself.

She turned from one to the other, still unsteady on her feet, trying as she so often did to guess what was expected. It seemed that Ziar was being taken to task for what had happened in Mansehra but she couldn't say for certain. In her desperation she looked to Abu Imam in hope of reassurance. He nodded to her subtly.

—He doesn't recall, the thickset man repeated.

—You told us to keep our hands to ourselves, said the first man.

—You warned us that you were a soldier of God. You threatened us with damnation if we tried to take your clothes.

She slid her hands under the table's edge and gripped the bench beneath her. Their laughter shook her worse than any censure could have done. She found herself bowing and mumbling an apology that went unheeded in the sudden crush of voices. She wondered how close the two of them had come. She wondered where exactly they had touched her. She thought of the night she'd spent in that vaulted room in Peshawar's refugee quarter and what the yellow-eyed man had told her as he held her hand in his. She willed herself to glance at Ziar and return his easy smile. Then she saw Decker standing behind her.

—Seems like good times over here, he said in English.

Already the laughter had fallen away. Ziar said something in Pashto but Decker ignored him.

—What are we celebrating, Sawyer?

—Brother Ali, she said. —Brother Khan called me over—

—Don't talk to me in Arabic. Talk to me in English.

—Decker, she hissed at him. —Have you gone crazy? We can talk—

—I'm wondering what you think you're doing, Aden Sawyer. I'm wondering if you remember what I told you.

—Decker for God's sake sit down.

In the hush that had fallen her whispering seemed to echo off the walls. Decker gave no reaction. Ziar was leaning past her, squinting intently, as if the bareheaded boy standing at her left shoulder were difficult for him to see.

—As-salaamu alaikum, Brother Ali.

Decker nodded absently. —Wa-alaikum as-salaam.

—Were you sent for, little brother? Do you bring us news?

He shook his head, looking only at her.

—Tell us what you've come to tell us, then. Don't dawdle like a child.

—I didn't come to tell you anything. I'm talking with my friend.

The silence was more perfect now. The hall seemed draped in coarse and heavy cloth. A bolt of felt had been thrown over them, smothering their voices and fixing their bodies in place. Only Ziar was moving. He was reaching his right arm toward Decker.

—Return to your seat, little brother, and keep your own counsel. We have neither the time nor the patience for your sulking. Or do you see your father and your mother here among us at this table?

—Be seated, fool, someone called out behind him. —Do you hear?

Decker looked away from her now, past Ziar, past the old men, down the table at Abu Imam. Abu Imam got to his feet and came toward him.

—I do bring news, said Decker.

—Hush, little brother, said Abu Imam.

—I will not, said Decker, his voice going shrill. —You'll be happy to hear it. What you do afterward is up to you, but I'm going to—

He'd turned back to Ziar, raising both arms for quiet, so that Abu Imam's hand when it met his jaw sent him spinning away from the table as if in an attempted pirouette. It seemed to her that there was grace of a kind in the way that he fell, a grace she'd never seen in him before. He fell quickly and smoothly and without a trace of anger or surprise. Abu Imam had already returned to his place at the table. Ziar considered the scene for the briefest of instants, his head half turned, his face expressionless, then reached for the teapot and refilled his cup. Talk resumed at once, while Decker was still on all fours, as if the interruption had not been of the slightest consequence. She sat frozen in place, expecting Decker to speak, to get to his feet and bear witness against her in a voice too righteous to ignore, but he sat where he'd fallen, frowning thoughtfully down at the floor. Sometime later he stood and walked quietly out of the hall.

———

She awoke before daylight to find Ziar above her with a pistol in his hands. It was of a make she didn't recognize and it seemed to her that she could smell the cordite from its muzzle, as if it had recently been fired. No one else was awake. She sat up and forced herself to pay attention. Something must have happened. She looked from the gun to Ziar's face and back again.

—We leave tomorrow, Suleyman.

—What did you do?

—Did you hear me? We leave tomorrow. Tomorrow at this hour.

—You told me you'd watch out for him. You promised me that he'd be left alone.

For the first time since Sadda he seemed to return her look without affection. He studied her as if they'd had a delicate and unspoken understanding that the panic in her voice called into question. She felt a surge of hatred toward him as he watched her.

—Answer me, she said. —Why won't you answer?

—I have faith in my judgment, he said slowly, as if to himself. —In the judgment God gave me. I have no great discernment or learning, much to my regret, but I believe myself to be an able judge of men.

—I don't understand.

He drew himself up proudly, much as Decker himself had done the day before. —Your friend Ali is well, Suleyman. As well as our Lord in His wisdom has seen fit to make him. That he is a child in a man's body, a fool with less sense for his own welfare than a toddler might have, is apparent to you best of all. This too I understand. It must be why you ask such foolish questions.

—You mean—

—Though I may come to regret the oath I swore regarding him, I'm not at liberty to break it. I remain a Muslim, Suleyman, by God's unending mercy and His grace.

—I'm sorry, she said, getting to her feet. —I shouldn't have said that. I'm still half asleep.

To her relief he simply shook his head. —My foster father in Yemen had a saying: Every man is an ass before his first cup of tea. He grinned at her. —Some men, of course, remain so after drinking the whole pot.

—Thank you, she said, catching hold of his hand.

He stood as motionless now as when her eyes had first come open. The holding of hands was not uncommon among brothers in the camp but she had never seen Ziar touched in this way. He kept himself at a remove from both the trainees and the teachers. He was a Pashtun, after all, and not a Chechen or an Arab bound for fighting in Kashmir. She had touched him without thinking and now it was too late to reconsider. His hands were dry and warm and seemed to tremble. She felt the smooth skin where his damaged fingers ended. She noticed for the first time that the remaining fingernails were badly bitten. He took in a breath.

—Come along now, little brother. We mustn't miss the call to prayer on our last day.

She spent that morning as she'd spent all the previous week, placing and arming and disassembling mines, and after the midday meal she went with Abu Imam's group to the ravine. Its boulder-choked bed was the only line of shade at that hour and they huddled there and tried to think and speak and breathe despite the heat. It was the last day of the incendiaries course and the trainees' mood was festive. They were finally going to work with combat-grade explosives, full wartime payloads, blast zones of a hundred feet or more. She sat back in the dwindling shade and listened to their chatter. She was treated no differently from the others, not even by Abu Imam, and there were moments when she questioned whether Ziar's dawn visit had happened at all.

She hadn't expected to find Decker among the group, given all that had happened, but he was first in line and boisterous as ever. He showed no abashedness, no humility, not even with Abu Imam. She herself was now the deferential one. As if she and no one else were in disgrace.

After the five o'clock prayer she caught Decker's eye and he gave her a bashful smile and waved her closer. He waited to speak until the rest were out of earshot.

—You're leaving tomorrow, he said.

—Who told you that?

—Those two old beard-pullers. Abu Bakhsh and Abu Hamza. They came to see me after morning prayers.

—I don't believe you, she heard herself saying. —Why would they do that, Decker?

—They liked the guts I showed last night. They liked my initiative. He hummed to himself. —And they don't seem to have much love for Ziar Khan.

—That doesn't make sense. I don't—

—They told me to prepare for my departure. That's a direct quote. And they brought me Ziar's apologies, if you can believe it. For what happened last night.

—His apologies? she murmured. All at once it was terribly bright.

—That's right, Sawyer. He was grinning again and rocking on his heels. —He wished me safe travels.

—Safe travels? she echoed.

—What's the matter with you, Sawyer? You look like you're about to lose your lunch.

—Listen to me, Decker. Please listen. You need to go to them, right now, and say you'll be good. You need to promise them—

He put a hand on her shoulder and gave it a shake. —Hey there, Sawyer. Aden! Look up here at me.

She recovered her balance and lifted her head. The slate beneath her was cool but the far side of the creekbed twitched and rippled in the heat. Abu Imam and the others stood arranged there with the sun-lit rock behind them like apostles on an icon. He was instructing them in the handling of Semtex and its use as a detonating agent for TNT. He brought out a thimbleful for them to admire, handling it with careful practiced movements. Day was leaving the ravine and it seemed strange that they were staying so late and working with such unprece-dented payloads. It confused her.

—Ziar thinks of me as dead weight, Decker was saying. —But this isn't his camp. He's here on a guest pass. Those two old boys run the show, it turns out, and they don't see things his way. Abu Imam told them how good I am at setting charges. You've seen it yourself. I'm the only one in this unit who can calculate a blast zone. I'm the only one who can prime a detonator.

She felt herself nodding. —That's probably true.

—I'm going to Kashmir with the Chechens. Something big's in the works there. I'm guessing a bridge.

—A bridge? What do you mean?

He gave a nervous laugh. —What do you think?

She sat up straight and forced herself to see him as he was. The matted hair. The restless mouth. A tic above his eyebrow that she hadn't seen before. His teeth as beautiful and white as she remembered.

—Please don't do this, Decker. You're not ready. It's too soon.

He got to his feet. —All right, then. Fuck you, Sawyer.

She caught at his pant leg but he kicked it free. Abu Imam and the rest paid them no mind.

—There's a reason I didn't tell them last night. About you, I mean. Do you want to know why?

—Decker, she said. —Please just—

—You don't matter to me anymore. I've got something that I'm better at than anybody here. If I told them it would only hold me back.

—Brother Ali, came a voice. —Please advise us in setting the charges.

He turned without another word and stepped into the sun. She watched as he took his place at Abu Imam's side and held his hand out proudly for the Semtex. Abu Imam said something too quietly for her to catch, paused very briefly, then placed it like an eggshell into Decker's upturned palm.

She reached the circle around Decker just as he was pressing the remote charge into the Semtex. The men held their breath as he worked it with a sure hand into the palm-warmed plastique and attached the Semtex in turn to a twenty-kilo load of TNT. Abu Imam was talking softly in his sepia-colored voice. A landslide had sent a tank-sized boulder into the creekbed, obstructing the current, and the charge must be correctly placed to clear it. Twenty kilograms was more than required, perhaps, but it was time for the group to witness a high-payload detonation. They were rehearsing for warfare, after all, and an RPG might have a blast zone greater than the ravine's entire width. They would need to grow accustomed to the shock wave and the noise of the report. He instructed the men not to cover their ears.

Once the charge was laid and the detonator attached, Decker made a leisurely gesture to Abu Imam and a wheel of snarled and corroded-looking cable was brought from a small cave that the group used as a depot. She wondered absently as she watched him attach the free end of the cable to the detonator key whether the cave was a new one or centuries old. A sensation of timelessness stole over her with the weight of a drug and made the scene before her seem arbitrary and unreal. She'd spent less than half a week in the infirmary but in those few days everything had changed. The camp itself had changed. She'd driven down to Mansehra assured of her place in the order of things and now there seemed to be no order. None at all. She barely recognized her brothers' faces.

Even in that last hour of daylight the sun was ferocious and she felt its spiteful heat against her neck and through her clothes. The heavy wooden spool that held the cable was being wheeled up the creekbed by the two youngest Arabs and Abu Imam and Decker were walking beside them with considered steps, hands clasped identically behind their backs, like scholars on a contemplative stroll. Abu Imam himself looked unfamiliar to her, a slender dark-skinned man in an immaculate kameez, unrelated to the person she remembered. She felt the group's excitement as a pulsing in her skull. One of the Pashtuns was known for his terror of thunder and he mumbled to himself and pressed his fists against his sides. She told him in the few words of Pashto she'd learned that there was no cause for fear, that Abu Imam would let no harm come to him, and he groaned and shook his gray face at the ground.

Thirty paces up the wash was the next heavy rockslide and Abu Imam announced that they would place the hellbox there. The slide would serve to shelter them, he explained, from volatile debris. A car battery was unwrapped from a frayed square of oilcloth and eased into the hellbox and attached to the cable with extravagant care. It was Decker, not Abu Imam, who oversaw the assembly of the triggering mechanism by the two Arab boys. She could hardly believe it. She heard Abu Imam's voice behind her, murmuring assurances to the terrified Pashtun. The payload was three times the weight of any charge she'd seen a trainee lay before. She moved back until she could see the entire group clustered around Decker where he squatted on the ground. This is an entertainment to them, she thought. A fireworks display. The sense of unreality intensified and now she seemed to understand its meaning.

Abu Imam held up a hand and stepped clear of the group to scan the ground between them and the payload. When he was satisfied that all was in order he nodded to Decker and gave the command. The rubble sheltering them was in shadow but the boulder sat high and massive in the sunlight. The older of the boys at Decker's feet murmured an entreaty to God and began to turn the crank of the hellbox to muster the charge. The smaller boy held his friend by the collar and whispered encouragements into his ear. She could see the boy's lips form the words and hear the quavering of his eager high-pitched voice. He was saying that their endeavor was blessed and their cause even more so and that God would either annihilate the obstruction or preserve it as He saw fit in His boundless providence. The older boy mumbled a prayer, looked skyward for a moment, then arched his back and rammed the handle home. The gray-faced Pashtun fell flat on the ground and the men to each side of him clapped their hands over their ears as if the walls of the ravine had already been sundered by the fist of the Almighty but the boulder remained exactly as it was. The only sound aside from the shouting and clapping and crying to Heaven was a delicate toylike clicking as the hellbox spring unwound.

—Well, brothers, Abu Imam said after a time. —Who among you is ready to be called home to God?

—It must be the crank, the older boy stammered, tipping the box on its side.

—Leave it, said Decker. —It isn't the crank.

—How could you know that, brother?

Abu Imam stepped forward. —Perhaps there is a problem with the detonation key.

—There must be, said Decker.

—Not necessarily. It may have been improperly assembled.

—I assembled it myself. There was nothing improper.

—Only the Unseen is infallible, Brother Ali. We are all of us subject to error.

Decker squinted at the hellbox and said nothing.

—What did you mean, Abu Imam? the younger boy asked.

—About what, little brother?

He looked down at his feet. —About going to God.

Abu Imam nodded to himself for a time before he answered. —We shall need to disassemble the relay in the order in which it was assembled. We'll begin at the payload and work in reverse.

—Of course, the boy said. —But then we'd have to—

—I'll do it, said Decker.

She watched the understanding ripple outward through the circle to the Pashtun lying huddled on the ground. He pushed himself up, shook his head for a moment, then managed to stand. —Abu Imam, he called. —Make use of me. I'm ready.

Abu Imam glanced at Decker, who seemed to hesitate. But even as she called his name he raised his voice so everyone could hear.

—You don't know what you're doing, he said to the Pashtun. —You wouldn't be of any use at all.

—Brother Ali, murmured Abu Imam.

She took his reply as a caution to Decker, a plea to reconsider, but by the time she reached the circle she could see how wrong she was. The crowd drew back as Decker stood and brushed the sand from his kameez, the one he'd bought in Peshawar in some spectral former life. She saw him as he'd been on that faraway morning, moving from stall to stall in his tangerine tracksuit, blustering and haggling in his cheerful anxious voice. Abu Imam and the others receded and she and Decker were alone in all that wilderness of dust and splintered slate. She moved clumsily toward him. She heard him clear his throat and ask the brothers for their blessing. She spoke his name again but he ignored her. He seemed not to care for any blessing she could give.

—As-salaamu alaikum, said Decker.

—Wa-alaikum as-salaam, they answered in chorus. —May the peace and the benedictions and the mercy of God be upon you.

—Decker, she rasped. —Decker look here at me.

But it was Abu Imam who turned to her and told her to be still. Abu Imam who was normally so gracious. Decker righted the hellbox and clapped back the handle and said there shouldn't be a problem. He said it in English. The light had all but vanished and he seemed to stumble slightly as he stepped out of the circle. He followed the cable along the creekbed, keeping its coils to his right, crouching here and there to untangle a snarl. His lips were moving as he worked but she heard nothing but the booming of the blood behind her eyes. He seemed careworn and frail as he picked his way forward. He looked like a prematurely aged child.

—Suleyman, came a voice. It meant nothing to her. She went to follow Decker and a dark hand took her roughly by the wrist. He was standing at the payload with his feet set wide apart now and she called him using every name she knew. She freed herself and lost her balance and looked up to see him grinning in the sunlight with the cable in his hands. Her sight retained that image even as she felt herself thrown backward and the shock and the aftershock lifting her body. A sound so swift as to be memory before the mind can frame it. Her eyes were shut against the shock wave and her ears seemed stuffed with linen and his silhouette persisted like an electric light extinguished in a place of perfect dark.

Dear Teacher in this last lazy hour between fifth prayers and sleep someone said Why not write to your family. I said I'd tried twice and he just shook his head like No way. Unacceptable. Which I said to him I can't think what to say and he said Suleyman (my name now) it's best to start off with A Blessing on Your House. So this is it. A blessing on your house Professor Sawyer. End of blessing.

Here's something I could write about—you never asked me how it happened. In all the times you asked me Why you never asked me How. The light was on in your study so I just went in. I'd heard you take off in your busted-up Volvo. Very professorial. Very tweedy. Off to see your Esteemed Colleague. That's what I used to call her. And other things ok but they were less polite.

What was it you said that last day at your office? I was distracted Aden and I do regret that. That much my dear I truly do regret.

You were cheating so I looked at your computer. You were off with the EC. Mom didn't know about her yet but she was drinking like she did. I sat down at your desk. I felt like a detective. I sat in your six-hundred-dollar chair and frowned and touched my fingertips together. I got into your *worldview.* It wasn't hard Teacher. I tried to hate my wife and daughter and it wasn't hard at all.

IT IS NOT FITTING FOR A PROPHET TO BETRAY HIS TRUST. WHOSO BETRAYS HIS TRUST SHALL COME FACE-TO-FACE WITH WHAT HE BETRAYED ON THE DAY OF RESURRECTION. —3:163

You'd left Windows open. I just turned up the brightness. You
were researching a lecture. Remember it Teacher? On sharia.
Fundamentalist Islam. The rule of the faithful. Most of the pages
were in Arabic but a couple were in English. I didn't understand
much to be honest but there were Links for Further Reading.
I was trying to learn what was happening Teacher. That's how it
started. To figure out what you saw in her. Your exotic EC.
I wanted to know if what you'd done to us made any kind
of sense.

I got onto a chatroom. Sheikh Azzam. Harkat al-Jibbah. Three or
four in the morning. I thought I wouldn't understand a word but
everything was there. So simple and beautiful. The call. Good and
evil. The six requirements. Fighting Has Been Prescribed. You'd
have rolled your eyes at all of it and called it superstition. Magical
thinking. You'd have laughed at it like you laughed at the mosque.

GOOD AND EVIL DEEDS ARE NOT EQUAL. DRIVE
BACK EVIL WITH WHAT IS BETTER. THEN YOU
WILL SEE THAT ONE WHO ONCE WAS YOUR
ENEMY HAS BECOME YOUR DEAREST FRIEND.
—41:34

People will show up one day and ask about me and I bet you'll
know exactly what to tell them. You'll say Family troubles. You'll
say She was angry. You'll say She was bored. And I was bored
Professor Sawyer I was bored half to death. I was bored the way a
cat gets bored that's never let outside.

I can't explain Teacher. Not so you'd understand it. You probably
never believed one single thing in your whole life.

The mosque in the strip mall wasn't working anymore. I needed
something bigger. Something no one could laugh at. I'd only just
met Decker but I wrote down all the names and sites and

everything he mentioned. I even recognized some of them from the windows that you'd left open. I couldn't help but take that as a sign.

GOD STANDS WITH THE BELIEVERS. —8:19

So here I am Teacher. No one lies to me now. When they come and ask you questions you can say you never knew me. I'm giving it to you in writing. You can tell them in all honesty you never had a child.

Decker just came in to say first prayers are starting. He's having fun here too you wouldn't recognize him. Believe it or not. He says to tell you hi.

3

A fine dry snow was falling on the pass across the border. The guide told them that snow was a rare thing so late in the season, even high in the mountains, and a true and certain portent of God's favor. He was white-haired and toothless but in spite of his age he was nimbler by far than the men he was guiding. Most of them wore sandals of leather or plastic, flimsy and ill-suited to the country, and they cursed him as they struggled through the drifts. Though he sang the Prophet's praises without pause as he climbed, *La ilaha illa Allah, Muhammadun rasul Allah,* Ziar and the other Pashtuns kept their distance. When he announced for the fifth or sixth time that the snow was Heaven's blessing Ziar told him through clenched teeth to save his preaching for the mosque. The old man laughed and said the nearest mosque was two days' march away.

They climbed all that morning through washes of traprock and ash-colored scree fields and gorges down which streams of runoff fell. No grass grew there and she saw no living creature. The guide wore crepe-soled boots made in India or China and answered every complaint with lines imperfectly remembered from the Recitation. His most cherished passage was from the third sura and he leered at them when he spoke it, disclosing his tobacco-colored gums. This present life is but the rapture of delusion.

—Where are you taking us, father? one of the Pashtuns called out from the rear of the line. —Answer me if you can!

—To God belongs the east and the west, said the guide. —Wheresoever you turn, there is the face of God.

—What did the old babbler say?

—Didn't you hear? said another. —He has no idea.

There was scarcely room for all of them on the saddle of the ridge and the guide seated himself on a boulder and beamed down at them as they took their midday meal. He smoked a porcelain pipe packed with sweet-smelling shag and declaimed in a high whistling voice between sucks:

—We created man from thin clay, like earthenware, and We created djinn out of shimmering flame. We created man and We know what his soul murmurs to him. We are nearer to him than his jugular vein.

—Lord, who created man from clay, make that jackass shut his mouth, muttered Abu Suhail.

—Where did you learn your Qur'an, father? another called out. —In an opium house?

The guide gummed his pipestem. —God guides many, he intoned. —But the dissolute alone he leads astray. They who violate God's covenant, who sever what God commanded to be joined. They who sow discord on the earth. They are the losers.

—Well may that old degenerate talk about dissolution, Ziar said to her. They were sitting a few paces up the ridge from the others with their backs against a sun-warmed shelf of granite. Since the explosion in the ravine she'd avoided his company but now she was too tired to resist.

—What do you mean?

—He lusted after his cousin's firstborn. At an age when the girl still ran about bareheaded.

—How do you know this?

—He presented himself to the family and confessed his intentions. Ziar drew his coat closer about him. —His cousin has often taken me over this pass.

She said nothing for a moment. —What happened to her?

—To the daughter? Nothing at all, at the time. He spat onto the ground between his boots. —Three years later she became his wife.

She chewed her flatbread and stared up at the guide who sat serenely sucking on his pipe. When he had met them at the border south of Torkham two days earlier she'd taken comfort in his reedy old man's chatter: of all that company he had seemed the most benign. He caught her eye now and she looked away.

—Suleyman, said Ziar once they were underway again. —Suleyman! Hang back a moment.

—What is it, she said without slowing. They were descending the west-facing slope of the ridge and the scree lay slick and glittering in the sun. She heard Abu Suhail stumble behind her, then mutter a curse, then beg Ziar's pardon for cursing. Ziar ignored him.

—You're wondering about us now, little brother. I can see that you are. About this company and the cause that you have joined.

She pictured him a step or two behind her, moving loosely and surely, his handsome face chapped from the cold. She took her time answering.

—I've been wondering that for a while.

—Not at the Mountain. When I watched you there you showed no hesitation. You showed nothing but conviction and desire.

—A lot has happened since then, she murmured.

—What's that, Suleyman? I didn't hear.

—A lot of things have happened since you found me at the Mountain, she said, turning toward him at last. Tears were running freely from his crow's feet to his beard but she knew better than to think that he was weeping. It was only the wind. She bit back her grief and looked him in the eye.

—How can I bring you comfort? he said. —I'll do anything that lies within my power.

—You can tell me why they killed him.

—They did not kill him.

—You're lying.

He passed a hand across his brow. —You test my patience with this question, Suleyman. You test it severely.

—I'm going to keep on asking it. I'll ask until I get an honest answer.

—Do you think anyone at the Mountain would have hesitated to execute Ali, or even you yourself, had they been given cause? Do we seem wealthy, perhaps, to squander such a payload of explosives? Who would plan such a killing for so unimportant a boy?

She swung at him then and he let the blow fall. She felt the sharpness of his rib cage through the lining of his coat. His slightness surprised her. She drew back again.

—You are dear to me, Suleyman, he said as he restrained her. —Dear to us all. God has sent you to our mountains from the far side of the world. He held her tightly as the others shuffled past them. —I advise you now as your dear friend, as your brother, to recover your conviction. You will find your time here difficult without it.

—You've advised me before, she shouted. —You advised me to trust you. You promised me no harm would come to him.

—Attend to me closely, fool. Where we are going my good opinion counts for very little. This place is no madrasa. This place is the war. What marked you as special or exalted to your teachers and your mullah has no currency on this side of the border. Even Kashmiris are distrusted in this place.

She watched the others lurching down the slope. No one looked back at them.

—I understand you, she said finally. —You're saying I'm going to get myself shot.

—You're going to get us all shot, he answered, his hoarse voice nearly swallowed by the wind. —The persons you are soon to meet are Pashtuns first and Muslims only second. They have been invaded and exploited and left to rot in mass graves too many times to feel indulgent toward outsiders. Even I was seen as foreign when I first returned from Yemen. I'd become intricate to them, ambiguous, two things at once. Only combat simplified me in their eyes. He drew her closer. —And your case, little brother, is more intricate by far. You must take pains to be one thing to them only. Your faith alone will give them

faith in you. The faith that I myself have seen, in Sadda and in Mansehra. He took back his hand. —The alternative is a bullet in the skull.

—I don't care.

—That may well be, he said. —But is it possible, Suleyman, that
you don't care for me?

The others had reached the foot of the slope now and were looking
back to see what was the matter. Even from that distance she could make
out the guide's arms fluttering as he recited scripture. Past and below
him threads of snowmelt twined themselves into a creek and still farther down a wedge of turf glowed dimly. It was the first green she'd
seen since they'd left for the border.

—No, she said at last. —I care for you.

They walked all that night and the next day at noon they arrived at a
mud-brick enclosure from which wooden stakes rose to three times the
height of a man. Red and green and white banners hung slackly in the
windless air, sun-bleached and tattered, and at the base of each stake
lay a weathered slab of stone. The guide signaled a halt and drew himself
upright, smoothing down his kameez, as dignified and stately as a
mullah. The cemetery gate was made of raw oak posts with juniper
branches threaded through them in a lattice, like the gate to a sheep
pen, and he waited there until the stragglers reached him.

—Every soul shall taste death, he announced. —You will all be
paid your wages on the Day of Resurrection.

A stoop-shouldered Pashtun whose name she could never remember made clear to the guide that the past days had done much to prepare him for death. He was willing to collect his wage in full.

The old man made a chewing motion with his shriveled toothless
mouth. —Do you imagine that you will enter the Garden without undergoing that which befell those who came before you? He brought his
right hand elegantly to his heart. —O believers, bear in patience, be
steadfast in the fight, keep to your battle stations and fear God. Perhaps
you will prevail.

With that he turned and marched off down the pitted valley road.

A handful of the men began hobbling after him on their cracked and blistered feet but Ziar gave the order to remain. He slipped the pack from his shoulders and propped it against the cemetery wall and sat on it with his back to the crumbling sun-warmed brick and closed his eyes. She set her own pack down beside the gate and lifted its wooden handle and went in.

Though the walls barely reached to her shoulders there was peace of a kind inside them, the hush of buried bodies, and she walked to the precise midpoint of that imagined peace and sank gratefully onto her knees. Whenever it was quiet now she sensed Decker behind her, breathing with her as she breathed, witness to each misstep, each falsehood, each fool's bargain she struck. She knew better than to ask for his forgiveness. She bowed her head and listened to him in that otherworldly calm.

Sometime later the air seemed to whisper and she glanced up to find a magpie perched above her on the cemetery wall. In the bright mountain mist the white of its belly was painful to see and its head was the blackest black there ever was. She'd studied its picture in a green clothbound book of her father's and knew that its name in Pashto had once been Herald of Kings but none of this had prepared her for the creature sitting just beyond her reach. As she gazed up transfixed the mist seemed to part and the magpie's blue and emerald highlights iridesced like Heaven's mystery disclosed. She felt herself sobbing and took her shawl between her teeth to make no sound that might send that wondrous bird away from her. It let out a single disdainful cry and began to preen its flashing wings and there was nothing else of consequence on earth.

By the time Ziar came for her the magpie had flown and her tears were long since dried and she felt purified and gutted. He asked how she was feeling and she told him she felt well. He nodded to himself, considering her answer. Then he asked if she remembered what he'd told her on the ridge.

—Of course I remember.

—Even holy war is war, Suleyman. Are you listening to me? Do you follow?

—I'm not trying to follow.

He glanced toward the gate. —I've known young men to come

here, young Arabs especially, expecting to ride into battle on cloud-colored horses. But fighting always closes more doors than it opens, at least for the fighter. The first truth of jihad is disappointment. Accept that fact and you'll fight long and well.

—Why are you telling me this?

—Take care not to judge us, little brother, by our sins and errors only. However debased your comrades may appear, I swear this: our enemy is more debased by far.

She let her eyes close. —I've got no right to judge.

—You have every right. You're the best of us all, Suleyman, and the most radiant in God's sight.

She was taking in air to answer when a rumbling carried to them from the far side of the wall. Ziar stood up at once. She thought at first that a plane was approaching and had begun to look for cover when she saw him making calmly for the cemetery gate. By then the sound had divided into three competing phrases and she heard the bite of tire treads on gravel. She got to her feet and followed him outside.

There were three trucks in all, each one crowded with men carrying Kalashnikovs and Makarovs and strange long-barreled rifles, and the brown and black streamers trailing wildly from their fenders caught the light just as the magpie's tail had done. The streamers struck her as familiar and as the trucks came to a hard stop she saw why. They were made of tape torn out of videocassettes and unspooled reels of film.

—Taliban, Abu Suhail said, repeating the word like an invocation. —Taliban. Taliban. His voice was all but drowned out by the rattling of the trucks.

The driver of the foremost pickup leaped down lightly and went to the passenger door and helped a small black-bearded man out of the cab. The others remained in the idling convoy. The small man's beard was spade shaped and sparse and his heavy-lidded eyes were dark with kohl. His legs stuck out grotesquely behind him, as though his knees had been turned backward, and his forearms rested on aluminum canes with molded plastic braces. He addressed Ziar in a warbling voice, erratic and sluggish, like someone just woken from sleep. Try as she might she couldn't understand a word.

—What's he saying? she asked Abu Suhail.

He shook his head dazedly. —Brother, he said, —that is Abu Abdullah Nazir. He took her by the arm and began to sway lightly in place, keeping his eyes on the man with the backward-turned legs.

—Can you hear what he's saying?

Abu Suhail only laughed. —It doesn't matter.

After what seemed a great while Ziar nodded slightly and the man called Nazir made a sign to his driver and the engines were all killed at once. The sudden silence pressed itself against her ears.

—God's greetings to you, soldiers, Nazir said in Pashto. —May you never tire.

—Stand up, all of you, said Ziar. —Take up your packs.

—Leave them just as they are. It's you I want to see, brothers, not the burdens you carry.

As if at some hidden signal Nazir's men swarmed down from the flatbeds. He inched forward so totteringly that it seemed he might fall. She saw now that his eyelids and his brow were scarred and puckered. This man is not asleep, she told herself. Remember that, Aden. This man is not asleep.

He went to Abu Suhail first and bent so close to him that they seemed to be kissing. The smile left Abu Suhail's lips and his eyes rolled upward as if he might faint. Nazir spoke a word to him in Pashto that she'd never heard before. Then he was standing before her.

—*Khe chare*, mu'allim, she said. —As-salaamu alaikum.

Nazir inclined his head toward hers and took a ragged breath. The lower half of his body seemed to dangle from his crutches like a marionette's. She averted her eyes and waited for him to address her. When at last he did he spoke in faltering English.

—How can it be? he said. —And for what reason?

—Forgive me, mu'allim. What did you say?

—You do not speak.

He wavered before her, the plastic braces of his crutches squeaking. She stared down at the ground between her feet. He said something musically over his shoulder and she heard a voice repeating it and Ziar's own tired voice rising in agreement. Ziar said something else then, almost too quietly to hear, and a fourth voice assured him that all would be well.

She was told to raise her head and found the driver of the truck standing where Nazir had just been, holding a Makarov eight-shot toward her by the barrel. She took it and gripped it as if in a dream. One of the pickups was maneuvered so that its bed faced them and she let the driver push her forward and stood stiff-armed with the Makarov in her left hand while the driver worked the tailgate with both arms to get it open. Somewhere nearby a voice was singing praises, *La ilaha illa Allah, Muhammadun rasul Allah*, and she recognized that wheedling voice just as the tailgate dropped. The guide lay in the flatbed with his limbs hogtied with wire. A small curse escaped her. He stopped singing then and arched his back until his eyes met hers.

—Payment of wages, a voice said behind her.

In a dream she looked on as the guide was pulled backward and pitched to the ground at her feet. A circle of men closed around them. She looked for Ziar but couldn't find him. She thought of the magpie in the sunlight and the memory helped to calm her. She raised the pistol and the crowd fell back at once.

—Suleyman! came Ziar's voice. —The safety.

The pistol was one she'd trained with at the Mountain and she knew very well that its safety was off. Safety off and a round in the chamber.

—I want to know what he's done, she said, hefting the Makarov. Its weight was a comfort. She reset the safety.

Abu Suhail mumbled something in Pashto and reached for the pistol. She hadn't noticed him standing beside her. He met her eyes and stopped short. Someone started to laugh.

—You should fire, he whispered. —You should have already.

—Mu'allim Nazir?

—Yes, my child.

—I want to know what he's done.

The silence that fell seemed to give the guide hope. He pressed his forehead to the road and rolled himself onto his shoulder. Sand clung wetly to his lips and to the left side of his beard. He seemed unsurprised to see her above him, mute and expressionless as a dressmaker's doll, pressing the Makarov to her chest to keep it safe. He saw her for exactly what she was.

—God knows full well who the wicked are. You will find them, out of all mankind, those most attached to life.

—Suleyman, said Ziar. —Little brother.

—Unbeliever, Nazir said to her in English. —Unbeliever. Sisterfucker. ISI.

—Give it to me, said Abu Suhail. —Give it to me. I can fire.

—But if a brother is forgiven what is ordained, then gracious pardon must be offered. An act of leniency from your Lord and a mercy. Whoever commits aggression thereafter—

—Who's forgiven you? she asked, disengaging the safety.

Abu Suhail seized her wrist and tried to take the pistol from her. She spun away and freed her arm and swung it in a smooth arc as she fired. The old man's body seemed to shiver with excitement or surprise. She counted the rounds down from eight, *sab'a sitta khamsa arba'a*, and came to rest at *wahid* staring at the knot of wide-eyed men behind her. Ziar was first among them with his thin mouth hanging open. The driver's face was empty of expression. Nazir was already hobbling back to the trucks.

—I apologize, Abu Suhail was stammering, either to her or to the body on the ground. —I apologize to you, brother. Do you hear?

She thought of Hayat as she let the gun fall. She closed her eyes and saw herself lying on her bedroll in the corner room in Sadda, in the time of her illness, watching the play of light and dark across the ceiling. She thought of Ibrahim Shah and his reasonable voice. She saw herself reciting at dawn in the courtyard, then riding the bus from Karachi with Decker, then sitting in her father's warm and well-appointed office. The gun hit the gravel. She was lying on her bed in Santa Rosa, head tucked under the covers, feeling the whole house shaking as a plane passed overhead.

For seven weeks they lived and trained at Abdullah Nazir's camp, the Orchard, four days' march into the mountains from the fabled Torkham Gate. It lay on a wedge-shaped spit of land at the convergence of two great gorges and the ground was black and fertile and the camp itself was shaded by stands of holly oak and pine. It had been an experimental farm during the Soviet occupation and stumps of olive trees partitioned the field on which their tents were pitched. To the south and the east the gorge walls hid the sun but to the northwest the view was open to a great distance and in the evenings the Hindu Kush blazed blue and cold against the sky. It was said that the coming offensive would take them north over those ranges but whether this was true or hearsay none among them seemed to know. Even Ziar could only smile and shrug his shoulders.

The training they were given was taken largely from a Pakistani manual for the drilling of light infantry and involved a large amount of standing at attention and running in place. It was monotonous and mindless, and often in direct contradiction to what Abu Imam had taught them, but she welcomed any duty that might help the hours pass. She'd begun now with killing and could see no way clear of it and found herself impatient for the killing to resume. It was the waiting that she couldn't stand, that made her anxious and sick, not the killing itself. Shooting the guide had been quick. Decker still somehow persisted but she never said his name aloud or thought about her life before the camps. There was no way out for her but straight ahead.

The bed of one river was lined with smooth brown pebbles, the other's bed was lined with shards of yellow quartz, and in both of them the hulks of exploded bridges lay like the bones of dragons just beneath the surface. The trucks that supplied the camp drove straight into the water just downriver of the bridges, regardless of how many men or sacks of flour they were carrying, and when they stalled in midstream there was much imprecation and quotation of scripture and submission to the greater will of God. But over the ironwork the current was broken and shallow and a person on foot could pick his way across. It was hot now in the afternoons and blackberries and Persian roses thrived in the shade on the north-facing banks and she often found time to slip away unnoticed in the hour just before the evening meal. A short walk upstream along the quartz-bedded river lay a bend where the current doubled back into a pool and on days when her chest gave her trouble she'd pull her kameez over her head and unbind her rib cage and let the water do its work until the itching and the ache were washed away.

The tents they slept in were made of heavy sun-bleached nylon with UNICEF printed at intervals both inside and out and she shared hers, by a random stroke of fortune, with no one but a seven-year-old boy. He had come across the sea from Yemen by way of Iran with his three elder brothers, he told her, and his three elder brothers had left him behind. He spoke a beautiful and cultured Arabic and asked very few questions and aside from his sobbing each morning he gave her no cause to complain. Ziar was like a god to him and in the evenings when they spoke together in a flowing Yemeni dialect she would sometimes even catch him in a smile.

As the days and weeks passed she found herself venturing farther from camp, saying her prayers by the banks of the river, or in some clearing in the woods that she could never find again. She had no means of determining the hour except by the height of the shadows against the walls of the gorge and she would kneel and pray whenever the mood took her. She prayed for the man she had killed and the friend she had lost and petitioned God to grant her some small sign that He was near. She prayed to Him that her father might not condemn her for her ignorance and that her mother might forget her altogether. She begged on all fours to be freed from her doubt and restored to the purpose she'd found at Sadda. On those days she lost count of how often she prayed. On other days she never prayed at all.

Ziar was absent now for days at a time, often as much as a week, and ignored her when she asked him where he'd been. She began to wonder whether the killing of the guide had changed him as well, whether he might feel as she felt, but when she mentioned this he simply shrugged his shoulders. Soon afterward he began to bristle at her questioning and she learned to keep such notions to herself.

One Juma'a evening Ziar came to the tent, muttered a preoccupied greeting to the Yemeni boy, then took her hand and led her out into the twilight. Wild sorghum had grown up around the olive stumps and she thought about the Russians and whether they'd been pleased with their experiments and whether they were still alive or long since dead. They passed the tent of the Arabs, who called out to them both, and Ziar let go of her hand for a moment to return their salutations. By some system of barter too intricate for her to grasp the Arabs had acquired a water pipe and she could barely see their faces through the smoke. It was a beautiful pure white smoke and smelled of apples. Everything was beautiful now in the midsummer dusk. As they rounded the corner of the abandoned grain depot with its rusted doors stamped in Cyrillic she stopped and looked back and saw the smoke rising like steam from a laundry and a feeling she had no name for made her chest and throat go tight. A memory or perhaps a premonition. Ziar stood waiting where the footpath disappeared into the trees.

—How are you managing in this rest home, Suleyman? Have you expired yet from boredom?

—You ask me that on every walk we take.

He nodded. —Because I don't believe your answer.

—I'm not bored. I don't let myself be.

—You've been absent from meals, I've been told.

She glanced at him. —Who told you that? Abu Suhail?

—Also that you keep to yourself in your tent. And that you choose not to bathe with the others.

They walked in silence for a time. At last Ziar sighed.

—You must realize, brother, that your behavior here is not inconsequential.

—I shot a man for them already. What more do they want?

—You had no choice but to shoot him. That's how Nazir sees it.

She stopped walking. —Why give me the gun at all, then? Why not leave me alone?

—Because you were the one who gave them the most doubt.

—Aside from the old man, you mean.

—Which old man?

—The guide.

Ziar shook his head. —The guide was of no consequence at all.

They'd come to the fine spit of sand where the rivers rushed together with a low pauseless thrum like the spinning of heavy turbines underground. A stand of tamarisks hid them from camp and a flock of yellow mynas squabbled harshly in the trees. The rivers were differently colored, the western slightly muddy and the eastern blank as glass, but the difference was so subtle that she'd never truly seen it. Now she saw it plainly and Ziar commented on the strangeness of the billowing milky boundary and the stubbornness of the two competing streams. He spoke the names of each river and then the name of the river they were subsumed by in turn and she nodded and watched him and felt something change. Her breath had gone shallow. If he was aware of her excitement he gave not the slightest sign.

—Are you unhappy here, Suleyman? Tell me the truth. Are you forgetting all we taught you at the Mountain?

—If you'd been here you'd know.

—Am I not with you now?

She stared into the water.

—Forgive me, little brother. He ducked his head to catch her eye. —I've been here when I could.

—It wasn't enough.

—You're right, he said. —Not nearly enough. My spies tell me you've grown undisciplined and fat. He reached out suddenly and pinched her through the cloth of her kameez. She gave a cry and jerked herself away.

—Did I hurt you, Suleyman? He grinned. —Then you must not be as fat as I supposed.

She wavered there on the balls of her feet, her shoulders hunched forward, her arms held out toward him. A shudder ran through her.

—What is it you have on inside your kameez? It felt like a bandage.

—It is a bandage.

His expression changed. —Show me.

—Don't touch me, she told him in English.

He kept still for a moment, frowning ever so slightly, then lowered his arms.

—I'm pleased to see your courage hasn't left you.

—It's not courage.

He nodded. —That may be. But I choose to call it that.

—Why did you bring me down here, Brother Khan?

—Ah, Suleyman. He looked back toward camp. —When you call me that it feels like a reproach.

—Tell me.

—A company is being formed for the foreign trainees at the Orchard. All the *khariji*. The Arabs and the Moroccans and the Chechens and the Turks. And the Americans, of course. He winked at her. —Of which there is, at present, only one.

She studied his expression. —A new company.

—This is a particular honor, brother. A company called the Ansar. Nazir will have you brought to him tomorrow morning, to his offices, after second prayers.

—The Ansar, she repeated. —The Helpers.

—So it is to be called.

—Where will we go? To the front?

—That's for Nazir to decide. There may be other uses—

—It's not an honor, Ziar. He doesn't trust us. He doesn't want us in his army.

Ziar shook his head and turned back to the river.

—You're fighting already, she said slowly. —That's what you're not telling me, isn't it? That's where you've been going when you go away.

—Take care not to speak in this tone to Abu Nazir, Suleyman. Mind what questions you ask. Mind your voice and your manner.

A rush of contempt for him made her suddenly lightheaded. —I'm not speaking to Abu Nazir right now. I'm speaking to you.

He made a gesture of frustration, violent and quick. —I've cautioned you once already. You were a favorite at my father's madrasa, and even at the Mountain, but only on account of your novelty. Many of us had never spoken to an American in our lives, let alone a devout American, sworn to the faith. You were like the peacock in the rich man's garden. Do you know of this fable?

—I'm guessing that it doesn't turn out well.

—Don't make light of my words. Don't make Ali's mistake.

She closed her eyes. —Please don't say that, Ziar. Don't say that name to me.

—I'll say whatever name I choose. Is this an American custom, to ignore considered counsel? To play the fool when the opposite is called for? I myself told Ali—

—Let's go to him now.

—What?

—Let's go to Nazir. If he has doubts about me let him say so. I'll tell him anything I need to tell him.

—Anything you need—

—That's right. She took his hand in both of hers. —So I can stay with you.

She waited a long and breathless moment for him to reply. When he said nothing she let go of his hand and started back up the path. She willed herself to move loosely and mannishly, ignoring her lightheadedness, swinging her arms with each step. The walls of the depot were coming into view through the trees when she felt Ziar's hand on her shoulder.

—Don't go to him now, little brother. He has visitors. A delegation from Peshawar. Persons it is better not to meet.

—Tell me what I have to do to make him trust me.

—He won't ever trust you. You're *khariji* and American besides. These are not advantages for you. Not with Nazir.

—But you'll help me? She took a step and tried to bring him with her. —You'll tell me what to say?

—He wants to be rid of you, of this much I'm certain. You make him uneasy.

—Rid of me how?

—Your best hope is to convince him you're useless. Useless to him but of some modest use to me. Nazir is a cunning man, and an artful general, but he's never even been to Kabul. You're a mythical being to him, little brother, an unknown quantity, a complication in his mind. This is a man who loves simplicity and truth.

—That's not the sense I've got from him so far.

His grip tightened. —Exactly this, he said. —Exactly *this* is the thing that you must disavow. Abdullah Nazir is your general, your lord and master, and you must abase yourself before him. He is a god whom you must beg for clemency. Do you hear?

She waited for him to let her go before she answered. —There is no god but God, she said. —And Muhammad is His Messenger.

All the next morning she waited but no summons came. When at last her patience gave out she rose from her cot, her body heavy with foreboding, and walked back through the grove and across the parade ground, where even then a few recruits were trotting wretchedly in place. The stamped metal doors of the depot hung open and a colossus of a man with an Uzi tucked into his belt like a toy pistol stood between them with his huge arms loosely folded. He was well-known to her and she walked up to him and salaamed. The Uzi was roughly at the level of her shoulders and she imagined herself pulling it free before he could react, then jumping clear of his arms and disengaging its safety, but beyond that her imagination failed her. He smiled and returned her salaam.

—God's greetings, Ehsannullah Sattar. May you never tire.

He nodded to her amicably, as if to thank her for her visit, then recrossed his great arms. —God's greetings to you, Little Executioner.

—I was told to come here, she said. —Here to you. At this hour.

—Yes?

—I was told to report to the general after second prayer.

—To the general, he repeated.

—That's right.

—And who gave you these instructions?

She bit her lip a moment. —Ziar Khan.

—Ah! Ziar Khan, said Sattar. —In that case, little brother, pass on.

The bulk of the depot was burned out and roofless, a bomb-shattered ruin, and she followed the only passable corridor to a door inscribed with the names and deeds of long-dead mujahideen. Characters had been scratched into the wood with knives and bayonets and bullet casings, some carefully, some hurriedly, and blacked in with soot from the floor and the walls. She stared at the names, letting her vision go slack and out of focus, watching the letters curl and writhe together. No language on earth was more beautiful to look at, more beautiful to speak. The beauty of austerity. The beauty of no quarter. Tears stood in her eyes when she knocked on the door.

It came open at once and the man she still knew only as the driver beckoned her in without interest, as though she'd long been expected, then shut the door firmly behind her. The room she had entered was stifling and dark. Pipe smoke curled in the half-light. She made out Nazir's slumped silhouette behind a desk in the corner and asked him to pray for her. He made a queer chuckling sound and said nothing.

—They said to come, she managed to mumble in her graceless Pashto. —To come to you and talk.

—Is that so, he answered in Arabic. He hummed to himself. —Were you also told that you might choose the hour?

Someone else was in the room. In an armchair behind her. She fought the urge to turn her head and look.

Nazir leafed deliberately through the papers on his desk. She had never seen him without his crutches and it was apparent now that his entire left side was palsied. His left hand shook badly and as she watched him riffling with excruciating slowness through that loose heap of maps and documents the compulsion to dart forward and snatch them from his hands was all but irresistible. She was being punished, she was sure of it, but for what transgression she could only guess. For being undisciplined, perhaps, or for being insubordinate, or for being American. Perhaps simply for the general's amusement. Perhaps for the amusement of the man she couldn't see.

—I've come about the Helpers, she said finally. —About the new company.

—I see. He pulled a stack of passports toward him. —I thought you came because I wished to see you.

—I want to fight with Pashtuns, she told him in Pashto. —Not with Arabs and Chechens. I want to fight with you.

The smile he gave her then was almost shy. —With me? he said in Arabic. —With me, Suleyman? Not with another?

—Let me stay with my company, General. I may be worthless to you but Brother Khan will have me.

—Will he? Why?

—I don't know. She took a breath. —He seems to think I bring him luck.

—I see. You are a luck-bringer to him. *Taveez*.

—*Taveez?* she said. —I haven't learned that word.

—A fetish, the man behind her said in English.

She would have known him by his cultured voice alone. He sat wrapped in a shawl in the room's dimmest corner and his white beard streaked with henna seemed to draw and trap the light. He looked younger than he had in that echoing white room in Peshawar and he sat with his legs folded beneath him and his amber cat's eyes shining and expectant.

—If you are a luck-bringer to our brother Ziar Khan, said Nazir, —you might be one for us as well. Perhaps I'll take you with me to Kunduz.

She willed herself to turn back to Nazir. —Only God brings victory, General. I know that very well. I'm not sure what Brother Khan sees in me.

—You brought no luck to the man who guided you across the mountains, Suleyman Al-Na'ama. None at all. You brought the opposite.

She bowed her head. —Yes, General.

—Or to the other American. The one in Mansehra. The one who is dead.

She opened her mouth and closed it.

—What was that, Suleyman?

—It's true, General. I've brought no one else luck.

—What is the nature of the luck you bring to Ziar Khan, precisely? said the man in the corner. —You have not yet fought together, I believe.

She shook her head.

—I thought not. What then?

—You would have to ask him, mu'allim.

—The boy calls me *mu'allim*, the man said to Nazir. —I've told him I'm not any mullah. But he persists in his error. A most stubborn boy.

Nazir's drooping eyes seemed to brighten. —No doubt he means it as a gesture of respect.

The henna-bearded man sat forward, resting his delicate hands on the arms of the chair. —Do you remember what I told you, boy, when we last spoke together? About certain men in the city of my birth? In Kandahar?

—I remember.

—This luck that you bring Ziar Khan. He nodded to her. —Is it luck of that kind?

—No, mu'allim.

—Swear it, boy, said Nazir.

—I swear before God and all His angels it is not luck of that kind.

Silence fell. The old man stroked his beard and studied her. She could hear the sound his nails made as he passed them through his hair.

—I still can't put a name to it, he said at last. —This quality you have.

—What quality? Nazir said before she could speak.

The man shook his head and said nothing. He wound the red tip of his beard around his thumb.

—Come forward, Nazir said. —Come here to this desk.

She crossed the floor in three small steps. A wedge of light fell from a soot-coated window and the desk had been turned sideways to receive it. Nazir squinted up at her briefly, as though she had only now come into focus. Then he coughed into his fist and unrolled the largest of the maps and weighted it with a passport at each corner.

—You can read?

She nodded.

—Read in English, he means, said the man in the corner.

—I can, General.

Nazir jerked his chin at the map. —And this?

—How may I serve you, General?

—*This*, he said again, more sharply. —This is English?

She bent carefully over the desk while Nazir moved his palsied hand from point to point, name to name, and waited haughtily for each translation. A map of the city of Kunduz and its environs by the

National Geospatial-Intelligence Agency. They went through it in detail, from the upper left-hand corner to the lower right, and she took great pains to answer him precisely. When they'd finished Nazir pushed away from the desk with a sigh.

—There now, little brother, said the man in the corner. —And to think you told the general you were of no use to him.

She flinched as if he'd slapped her. He'd outplayed her so quickly. In her tent and on her way to the depot she'd run through her argument time and again, rehearsing her tone of voice, even her posture, and none of it had made the slightest difference.

—Perhaps it is well that you interrupted us, Suleyman the Graceful. Perhaps it is auspicious. The old man made a gesture to the driver. —We were about to have our tea. Will you partake?

She hesitated only for an instant. —I'd be grateful.

—Tea if you please, Abu Farq.

The driver stepped out into the hall and returned with a silver tea service balanced on a crimped metal lid labeled R C FIRST AID. Nazir and his guest sat smiling at her blandly. No one will believe this, she found herself thinking. Not even Ziar.

—We were discussing the Helpers division when you knocked, said the man in the corner. —But we were discussing it in the broad sense of the term.

—I'm not sure what you mean, mu'allim.

—Of course not. He blew on his tea. —The new fighting division is to be comprised exclusively of outsiders sympathetic to the cause. You know this much already, I think?

—I wasn't sure how much fighting they'd be doing, she said tentatively. —I thought they might be kept back from the front.

—Oh! There'll be no shortage of fighting, said the man. —The Helper units currently in existence have won great respect in these mountains, by virtue of their preparedness for martyrdom. They are most . . . impatient for it. He turned to Nazir. —Is this not so, my general?

—They fight well, Nazir answered. —Especially among their own kind.

—They certainly do. They fight without inhibition, with righteous abandon, having one foot in the World to Come already. He was quiet a moment. —But the Orchard is not a place of training for the Afghan conflict only. Ours is a jihad on many fronts. Arms and resources flow into this camp from all over the world, Suleyman, and we, in consequence, are beholden to the world. You of all young men must grasp this principle.

—Why?

—Because you are its embodiment.

She gave a slight nod.

—Do you appreciate this principle? This duty?

—I do, mu'allim.

—The boy still doesn't understand, Nazir said cheerfully.

The old man leaned forward. —General Nazir has been requested, by a great benefactor to the Orchard, to ask whether any young mujahid under his command has an interest in pursuing jihad in the shadow countries.

She looked from one of them to the other. —The shadow countries?

Nazir set down his cup. —Countries not illuminated by the teachings of the Prophet. Russia, for example. Or China.

—I'm sorry, General. I've been trained to fight here, in these mountains. For these people. I have no experience of China at all.

The old man pursed his lips. —The boy is right, of course. He has little knowledge even of this country.

—There is only one country the boy has knowledge of, said Nazir.

—Yes, my general. Such would seem to be the case.

Again an airless silence fell. No sound carried in from the hallway or the devastated yard. A question had been asked of her, she was certain, but she hadn't heard a question. She had no idea what the men in that dark room were waiting to hear. Then all at once, without warning or apparent cause, it came to her.

—You want me to go to the States, she said. —You want me to go back to California.

—Not to California, Nazir said, frowning down at his desktop. —I've heard no talk of that.

The old man made a fluttering motion with his fingers, as if urging her to pay no mind to idle chatter. —Is this something you would have an interest in, Suleyman? To seek your martyrdom in the place where you were born?

—You would be of value, Nazir said. —Much more so than here.

The light began to flicker and when she shut her eyes the flickering grew stronger. A vision or a fever dream of herself come home in retribution to the place where she had suffered was projected against her closed eyes like a newsreel in a theater. A faint groan escaped her. She saw herself suspended in the air above those grassy hills and suburbs, supported and exalted by the warm Pacific light. No one in all those tract developments and cakelike Victorians and strip malls and carports could possibly know what was coming. She alone and God could see it. She was arcing toward them like a comet with her clothes and hair on fire.

—Our young mujahid is flushed with desire, said the man. —Do you see it, my general? How the color rushes to his face?

—He has sense after all, Nazir answered. —A sense of proportion.

—No, she said.

Nazir cocked his head. —What does he say now, our Little Executioner?

—My jihad is here, General. I didn't come all this way just to be sent back home. She pressed her hands together. —Please don't ask this of me.

Nazir made a sound in his throat, low and harsh and abrupt, that might almost have been taken for a laugh. The armchair creaked behind her as the bearded man rose.

—You are misunderstanding General Nazir. He is not the person asking this of you.

Helplessly she turned and met his gaze. —Who is it, then? Who is asking?

—The benefactor we have mentioned.

—Is he a Pashtun?

—Saudi, Nazir seemed to mutter.

—He is a Helper, said the man. —A well-wisher from abroad. Like you yourself.

She nodded for a moment. —What's his name?

—You will learn that, little brother, when you meet him.

—Is he here?

—His present location is not your concern. In a month's time, God willing, he will be in Kunduz.

She bit down on her tongue and tried to focus. After what seemed a great while she heard the sound of tea being poured and the clacking of a cup against a saucer. Nazir shifted on his stool. He opened his mouth to speak but she spoke first.

—I'll go, she said. —I'll meet the benefactor.

Suddenly both men were smiling. —That is very well, Suleyman Al-Na'ama. That is excellent. You will find this the most sensible—

—But I want to go to Kunduz with the company I came with. I ask this as a kindness. I want to travel there with Ziar Khan.

Ten days passed before the first ragged constellations of men set out for the northwestern ranges and a dozen more before Ziar came to her tent, ignoring the Yemeni boy sleeping beside her, and whispered that the time had come to go. She rolled her few possessions into her kilim and tied it loosely closed and that was all. She never saw the boy or the Orchard or the Arabs she'd trained with again.

After so many weeks of presenting arms in formation and saluting a makeshift podium and marching in place she'd expected to be sent off with a speech, or at least some perfunctory blessing, but Nazir and his lieutenants seemed already to have left. There were forty men in Ziar's company and they fell in groggily behind him as he threaded his way through the tamarisk grove with the cliffs and hilltops blazing to the west. In time she would come to see the genius in so large a body of men moving in small groups through enemy territory but on that first day it simply seemed undignified. Ziar himself joked that the company looked like a ragpickers' guild, or a stray herd of goats, or a congregation of drunks who'd misplaced their last bottle. But he said it with an air of satisfaction.

For two days they followed the river, fording and refording it times without number, picking their way across it daintily where stones broke the surface, stumbling like mules through the current where circumstance left them no choice. The gorge grew wider and greener as the river descended and she passed the hours looking for songbirds along its banks, stopping and peering into the rushes whenever any movement caught her eye. She counted sixty magpies between the Orchard and the plain of Nangarhar and countless smaller passerines besides. She often found herself wishing for her father's clothbound U.S. field guide, though she knew it would have been no help to her: no creature they encountered on all that long march to the front could have been found within its glossy, dog-eared pages.

The ancient terraced valley through which the Kabul River ran sedately eastward was so verdant and well-tended as to seem a vestige of some lost and temperate age. They kept well clear of Jalalabad but she could make out its walled gardens and the minarets of its mosques and she thought of the old Pashtun merchant she'd met on the flight to Dubai, the dealer in fabrics, and of the pride with which he'd told her of that valley. It shamed her now to think of that kindly pious man sitting across from her in the dimly lit cabin, listening to her self-important talk about the war that still raged in the land of his birth. Nangarhar, she recited as they marched in single file across the floodplain. Cradle of Peace. Forever Spring.

An hour into the foothills they came to a scattering of mud-and-wattle cottages in front of which a crowd stood four men deep around a ring of beaten earth. Thus far in each village heads had appeared in doors and window frames to watch them, emerging smoothly and spectrally out of the dark, but in that place not a single head was turned. Scattered about in the grass were wicker domes half the size of a man, covered in patterned blue cloth, like field tents for a host of tiny soldiers. She could no more imagine what purpose they served than she could guess what the villagers stood watching so intently. Ziar gave them a wide berth and so did the others. It had just struck her that certain of the domes looked like castaway burqas when the cover was lifted from one of the baskets and she caught sight of an oblong silver body and a blood-colored bill.

—Chukar, Ziar said, gesturing toward the basket. —The fighting birds of Laghman Province are well-known.

She bent down for a moment and watched the partridge strut and forage, making gurgling noises, metallic and fluid. —They're beautiful.

—They're expensive, he said without slowing. —And expressly forbidden. In Kandahar these men would be in prison for gambling. Or taken out and beaten in the street.

Above the village the road narrowed to a cattle trail and climbed in grassy switchbacks to a pass. As they reached the first turning a cry went up below them and she looked back to see two villagers poised like dancers with their arms outstretched and baskets at the ready. A brother whose name she hadn't learned stood spellbound a few steps ahead of her, neither moving nor blinking, and Ziar struck him good-naturedly on the nape as he passed and cursed him for a profligate and sinner. She could make out nothing of the fight itself but a cloud of silver feathers and the ring of ruthless faces and she was grateful when the sight passed out of view. There seemed little difference between that circle of men and the one that had drawn itself around her ten weeks earlier, at the cemetery gate, when the guide had been dropped hog-tied at her feet.

For a fortnight they continued northward and westward, eating whatever they could beg or steal or scavenge, sleeping in stables or in ditches and on rare nights in woodstove-heated rooms as honored guests. In each successive valley there were strongmen to be pacified and elders to be attended to and timeworn protocols to be observed. In the third week she was taken by cramps in the stomach, a pain that seemed to sound some vague alarm, but by then many in the company were suffering from malnourishment and her misery drew nobody's attention. The days seemed continuous, little more than hours in some greater, more pitiless day, with intervals of lightlessness between. Ziar kept them moving from dawn until sunset: if not for the five mandated prayers they'd have had no rest to speak of. The men grew more religious by the day.

At the frontier to Panjshir a company of Kabuli Taliban met them by chance, likewise headed north to Kunduz by the Laghman trail. They were a far larger body of soldiers, self-disciplined and silent, their clothes and guns immaculate and black. They seemed warriors in some different cause entirely. Abu Suhail and the other men regarded them with awe.

The Kabuli captain wore a camel-hair greatcoat in spite of the heat and chewed on a blade of grass as he conferred with Ziar. The two were in conference for nigh on an hour and it seemed to her as she watched them that some momentous event must have occurred. Some cataclysm. Ziar was excited in a way she'd never seen before: he was playing the part of the statesman, preoccupied and solemn, for the benefit of the soldiers sprawled around him in the grass. She decided that Kunduz had been lost, or that the northern line had broken, or that the Great Emir in Kandahar was dead.

At last the two men stood and embraced and Ziar gave orders for a meal to be prepared. Someone asked if they should pray first and he roused himself from his reverie and answered that they should. The captain had returned to his men and was directing the assembly of a field radio. The others were unrolling their prayer rugs but she stayed as she was and observed him. With his straggling beard and his preposterous coat he looked less like the bearer of solemn tidings than a beggar costumed in a rich man's clothes. But his men with their jet-colored vestments and their new and gleaming ordnance looked like martyrs on their way to Paradise.

—They aren't praying, someone behind her whispered. —Why aren't they praying?

—They must have prayed before we got here.

—Have you been sleepwalking, brother? We got here at the same time.

—He's a warlord, said another. —They're not Taliban at all.

—Of course they're Taliban. Look at their clothes. Look at their weapons.

—If those are Taliban, then what in hell are we?

Everyone laughed but Ziar. He had yet to say a word. His expression might have been one of exultation or dismay.

—I know what that machine is, Abu Suhail said proudly. —It's a kind of radio.

—A field transmitter, Ziar said. —For talking to Kabul.

—He's using it now, said the second man. —Do you hear?

—I thought music was forbidden, the man who'd made the joke said sullenly.

—It's not that kind of radio, you donkey. It's for talking to one person.

—That's right, Ziar said. —It's for receiving orders, brothers. And for getting news.

Something in his manner hushed them. The wind carried the sound of the radio to them in soft unintelligible rushes. Ziar ate his flatbread and sipped at his tea, nodding to himself as if he were alone. When she couldn't stand it any longer she asked what the captain had told him.

—It's America.

—America?

He looked toward her now. —A strike, he said. —An attack. In the capital and in another city.

She slumped slightly forward. —What kind of a strike?

—A plane, they say. Two planes. He shook his head. —Some sort of conflagration.

No one spoke for a time. She felt them all watching. The radio's chatter paled and brightened in the wind.

—What does this matter to us? came a voice from behind her. She turned and saw the man who'd been enraptured by the cockfight. The confusion in his eyes made her want to embrace him. —It wasn't Pashtuns that did it. I'm sure of that much.

—How can you be sure? she asked.

—Because of this, he answered, holding up his rifle. —This old blunderbuss could never shoot so far.

A few brothers laughed. Ziar gave no reaction.

—Our guns don't shoot so far, he said at last. —But their guns do.

A man with burn marks along his jawline raised his right hand like a student in a classroom. —There was a nation which passed away, he recited. —They have earned their reward, and you have earned yours. You will not be held responsible for what they did.

—Well and truly spoken, said another. —What happens in America is no concern of ours. No nation is exempted from God's judgment, my brothers. And surely that one least of all.

—What do you think, Suleyman? said the man who'd spoken first.

She shook her head stiffly. She was thinking back to Nazir's office and the bargain she had made. Her clothes and hair on fire. She asked Ziar who had carried out the strike.

—I can't say, little brother.

—Not us, said the man who'd made the joke about the rifle. —It was no Pashtun, brothers. No Afghan at all.

—Why can't you say, Brother Ziar? Because you don't know?

—Suleyman—

—Or is there some other reason?

The others turned as one to look at her. She ignored them all and waited for his answer. The radio fell sharply into focus. A young man's voice, speaking Arabic with an unfamiliar accent. When no answer came she stepped out of the circle and walked through the grass to where the captain sat hunched over his crackling apparatus like an alchemist transmuting dung to gold. Two boys sprang up to block her approach, their hands already at the knives in their belts, but the captain waved her forward. He'd taken off his coat and rolled up his sleeves and his fingertips and palms were dark with grease. She waited for him to address her. The young man on the radio was reporting on the weather in Kunduz.

—*Khe chare*, sahib, she said in her impatience. The boys shook their heads at her lack of decorum. The captain set his tools aside.

—The American, he said in English. —The American pays us a visit.

—Yes, sir.

He beckoned her closer, flaring his nostrils as though the smell of her were difficult to bear. —I would ask you the reason, he said. —But on this day I imagine I can guess.

—I'd be thankful for whatever you can tell me.

—The city of Manhattan? You know of this city? The great financial district at its center?

—What happened?

—There is no financial district any longer. There is no trade tower. There is no stock exchange. These things have passed away.

The smallest sigh of disbelief escaped her. The air seemed to thicken. She saw herself in faded video, her image degrading, her outline blurred by violence. In spite of all her subterfuge America had found her. She closed her eyes and saw a grid of streets subsiding into history. No escape was permitted. She was on the ground and she was in the planes. She had gone to the opposite end of the earth, to the void zone on the map, and America had found her. It had found her so quickly. She thought of her small drab life in Santa Rosa, of the mosque in the strip mall, of Decker asleep beside her on her narrow childhood bed. She opened her eyes. These things have passed away.

The captain stood just as before, observing her reaction, making no attempt to camouflage his hatred. She knew what he was looking for and knew also that if he found it she would not have long to live. She remembered what Ziar had said to her the day they crossed the border: You must take pains to be one thing to them only.

She spat ostentatiously into the grass. —Were many sinners killed?

—Oh yes, brother. Everyone was killed.

—That's not possible.

He smiled. —As to the unbelievers, the doubters and the sleepers, they shall have their wage in time.

She pointed back up the slope. —Some of the brothers say America will come here to make war. Up into these mountains. Here to us.

—What do you yourself say, little brother?

She shook her head. —Only if they think that we're to blame.

—And are we to blame? What do you say, as an American?

The urge to shriek gripped her. —Those who suppress what God has revealed of the Book: Those shall eat only fire. God shall not speak to them—

—I did not ask your opinion on theological matters, said the captain. —In any case, your country knows it was no Talib who did this. The entire world knows, or will learn it soon. He held out his hand, keeping his eyes fixed on hers, and one of the boys placed a pair of jeweler's pliers into his palm. —As for you, little brother: the truth will be disclosed to you in time. Go back now to your protectors and petition God for patience.

—I already know who it was, she said. —I didn't come for that. I just wanted you to tell me what he'd done.

He turned back to the radio. —You know nothing. Go back to your company.

—It was a Saudi. A wealthy Helper. Benefactor to the Orchard and the Mountain.

For a moment the captain kept still. Then he gestured with the pliers and his adjutants began to disassemble the radio and pack its components into leather cases lined with pale blue silk. She had spoken impulsively, with no thought of consequences, and it was clear that she had caught him by surprise. The disgust he felt toward her or toward his notion of her was even more explicit than before.

—You think you know a secret, he said. —By now the whole world knows this Saudi's name.

She took a step forward. —What was the reason?

—The reason?

—I'm asking you to tell me, if you know. I'm begging you, sir. So I can understand.

The captain knelt and ran his hands through the grass until he was satisfied his fingertips were clean. —Are you asking me the reason for his actions, little mujahid? Truly? I do not believe that you are. He took up his camel-hair coat and shook the grass from it and draped it regally about his narrow shoulders. —It is impossible that you should be here, in this valley, and not understand the reason. Did you not come here yourself, in good faith, to take up your sworn jihad?

—I've been trained for this fight, she heard herself answer. —Not any other. To protect a Muslim state against its enemies. The warlords of the north.

—And who are you to decide who our enemies are? He brought his face so close to hers that she could see the silver crowns on his back teeth. —Are you the Emir of the Faithful, perhaps? Are you a general?

Are you a prophet? Were you such a fool as to imagine that if you traveled far enough into these mountains, in the company of peasants, the country of your birth need not concern you?

—This war has nothing to do with America, she managed to stammer.

—There is no such war anywhere on earth, Suleyman, the captain said quietly. —America itself has seen to that.

The village they reached the next day at midmorning was the most beautiful she'd seen in all that country. It sat high and exposed on a ridge, like a notch cut in a tree branch, and matched the dun-colored landscape so perfectly that she heard the shouts of children before her eyes could tell the houses from the hillside. Its buildings were made of straw-battened earth, like virtually all those she'd seen, but here the doorframes and rafters and eaves were embellished with carved florets and twisting vines and figures that looked to have been cut before God's word had ever reached those pagan mountains.

The valley had only recently been retaken and the brother with the burn marks, whose name was Sahar Gul, told her that its women had gone about bareheaded a few brief weeks before, without even the pretense of modesty. He cautioned her that the village was a wicked place, depraved and impious, but somehow she couldn't make herself believe him. Of all the settlements they'd seen, this one looked most like the country she'd kept in her mind's eye through the long months of training, the country she'd imagined herself fighting to defend. She prayed that they might stay there for a year.

They pitched camp in a grove of birches just outside the granite columns that marked the southern boundary of the village. The columns were warmed by the early sun and encircled by mulberry bushes, sweet-smelling and heavy with fruit. Sahar Gul and a few others set about gathering the ripe white berries, humming tunelessly to themselves as they worked, their beards and their fingertips glistening with juice. Two men were sent with goatskins to fetch water. Ziar lay down in the sunlight and shaded his eyes.

She sat with her back against the silvery trunk of a sapling, listening to the wind in the crowns of the birches, feeling the light on her skin and the quivering of the wood against her spine. America seemed distant and unlikely. The only image she could call to mind was of her mother in the bedroom, slump-shouldered and sullen, staring out the window with her dogs arrayed around her. She thought about the captain and what little he had told her. *The entire world knows, or will learn it soon.* She wondered whether there had truly been some kind of an attack. It was easy enough to doubt it as the wind drew through the trees.

The men with the goatskins were gone a long time, long enough that Ziar grew impatient, and they returned with two young Talibs dressed entirely in black. She recognized them as soldiers of the Kabuli company and she tried to imagine them picking mulberries, or lying in the sun with the ends of their headscarves draped over their eyes, but she couldn't imagine them doing anything but standing at attention. They stood shoulder to shoulder with their rifles at three-quarters and requested Ziar's presence at a hearing on a matter of law. He asked them who would be presiding and was told that he himself would be, along with the captain and a mullah from the village. The sooner he could come the better, as the hearing was already underway.

Ziar told the soldiers that he would happily discharge his duty to them and to God and yawned and passed a hand across his mouth. Birch leaves clung to his kameez and he brushed them away with no great urgency.

—I believe this grove may be enchanted, he said to the men. —It's a lucky thing you came to fetch me, brothers. Another hour and we might have lost our discipline.

The Talibs exchanged glances and nodded to him gravely and withdrew.

—You still have leaves on your back, she said once they were gone.

—Do I? He yawned again and slipped into his sandals. —Where, little brother?

—Here on your right side. She brushed them away. —The side you were lying on when you were sleeping.

—You know me better than that, Suleyman Al-Na'ama. I never sleep.

He gave her a tired smile. —Will you accompany me on this errand? You understand the Recitation better than all these bumpkins and fanatics put together. Perhaps you'll shine a light into their darkness.

At close quarters the village's squalor was more evident but still it seemed a place uniquely favored. Even the reek of its ditches was less severe, it seemed to her, though perhaps this was due to the cold. Ziar's breath rose thinly as she followed him up those winding alleys and she watched it catch what little light there was. A cat darted ahead of them, keeping always the same token distance, looking back aloofly at each turning. Fair-haired children peered down from porticoes and high unshuttered windows. No one on the street returned her greeting.

At the highest point in the village a cobbled square fronted a small wooden mosque and they arrived to find soldiers from the Kabuli company holding a throng of stone-faced villagers at bay. The men and women in the crowd spoke in thick toneless murmurs and it was impossible to guess their intention. The soldiers kept their rifles raised as high as they could manage, at the tips of outstretched fingers, and this posture made the scene seem somehow pious. The murmurings of the villagers might almost have been prayers.

Ziar stopped short as they drew near the mosque, as though a sudden thought had struck him, and just then the crowd surged forward. Some of the women held their palms upturned like beggars. She told herself that the company had most likely brought medicine from Kabul, or sweets for the children, or tablets to make the water safe to drink. She took a step and Ziar caught her by the arm.

—What is this hearing about?

—Nothing, he said to her. —Not anymore.

—What do you mean?

—It's done, that's what I mean. They have their verdict.

He said this in a careless voice, already turning back, but she slipped free of his grasp and pushed ahead. The women before her stood buzzing together like bees in a hive and she was able to pass them without any trouble. She recognized one of the captain's adjutants among the line of soldiers and he saw her as well and widened his eyes at her and bared his teeth. She was trying to guess what his wild look might mean when he fired his Kalashnikov into the air and the crowd fell back in a series of spasms and the object of its interest lay plain to see before her on the ground. She knelt down beside it. From the rings on its fingers she understood it to be the body of a woman or a girl of marriageable age, crumpled and inanimate and steaming in the cold. The burqa she wore was open at the crown and the linen beneath it was heavy with blood. Scattered around her lay chips of slate and cobblestones and fist-sized chunks of brick. A man's voice was shouting. The crowd pushed forward again to the edge of the blood, indifferent to the Talibs and their rifles. She stared down at the body. So slight and so shapeless. A shroud of black hair hung across what might have been a face.

She was halfway to the birch grove before Ziar spoke her name. The name she was known by, the one she had chosen, not the name her family had given her. For the first time it rang foreign to her ears.

—Remember what I told you, Suleyman. However bestial our comrades-at-arms may seem, our enemy—

—Did you know what was going to happen? Did you know what you were taking me to see?

—You forget yourself. Mind how you speak to me, little brother. Bear in mind that you are under my command.

—Tell me what her offense was.

—It was foolish of me to take you there. He shook his head. —I was a fool to go myself.

—What had she done?

—She was a low woman. A person without faith. A prostitute.

—A prostitute? Here in this village?

—She had relations with soldiers. With the enemy's soldiers. Tajiks. Before this valley was retaken.

For a time they walked in silence. She saw the columns and the birch grove and the flickering of a campfire through the trees.

—Who told you this? Those Talibs from Kabul?

—Those men are our brothers, Suleyman. The ones we'll fight and die beside. Not the people of this godforsaken village. He shook his head. —You've seen how they look at us, how they hiss at us, how they shrink from us when we meet them in the street. The people here are Muslims in nothing but name.

—It's not in the Qur'an, what those soldiers did. It's nowhere in the teachings of the Prophet.

—How young you still are, Suleyman. How innocent. How childish. She continued down the trail.

—It was the villagers who stoned her, not the soldiers from Kabul. Are you listening, Suleyman? It was the villagers themselves.

As if her wish had been heard and mocked in its fulfillment the company spent the next three weeks encamped below the village. Though the peace of the birch grove was linked in her mind now with the stillness of the crowd around the body, with the mute and impassive violence of that place, each day dawned more blue and perfect than the last. Food was plentiful, the men had no duties to speak of, and in spite of the chill at night their strength was soon restored. Soon even those among them most inclined to idleness grew restless and impatient to move on.

Ziar himself was the most restless of all. Each morning after first prayers he walked up the hill to the graceful stone-walled house that the captain had requisitioned for himself and came back preoccupied and ill at ease. Orders by radio from Kabul were to await further orders. Rumors circulated that Kunduz had fallen, or that a cease-fire had been declared, or that the Emir of the Faithful had met with American generals at an undisclosed location in the south. It was said that the president of the United States had declared war, though on whom was unknown. Sahar Gul said Saudi Arabia, Abu Suhail said Palestine, and Ziar kept his own counsel. There were few further signs of unrest in the village but this reassured no one. Some great change was approaching, irresistible and sure as the onset of winter, through the daylight and the quiet and the chill. When she held her breath it seemed that she could hear it. As days and then entire weeks went by she told herself that she was ready for the next trial, the next ordeal, whatever it might prove itself to be. But she couldn't seem to picture what was coming.

On the Day of Assembly they prayed with the captain and his officers in the little wooden mosque. Its interior was warm and nearly lightless and smelled of centuries-old oak and the pine needles that lay strewn across the floor. O believers! Enter the fold of peace, all of you. Do not follow in the footsteps of Satan, for he is to you a manifest enemy. If you slip after clear signs have been revealed to you, be assured that God is Almighty, All-Wise.

Are they truly waiting for God to come to them in the shadowy folds of clouds, with His angels, when judgment is pronounced and all revert to God?

They prayed swiftly and quietly, as if they were trespassing, and in fact when they left the mosque they found a hundred men waiting to enter. Her eyes were attuned now to the menace in the villagers' expressions and she asked herself as she crossed the sun-warmed square how she could ever have felt safe there. Ziar recognized it as well and glanced over his shoulder twice before they'd left the square. The adjutants rolled their eyes at him and laughed at his concern.

The captain's quarters were unheated and spare, as befit a righteous Talib and protector of the faithful, but the kilim he invited them to recline on was the thickest and most intricate she'd ever sat upon. The owner of the house was a dealer in carpets and when he brought in the tea he cast a sorrowful eye on the circle of soldiers resting their unwashed feet on his most prized possession. As his son filled their cups the dealer assured them in Dari and Arabic and Pashto that it was a great and sacred privilege to offer shelter to such highly favored warriors. His son was too young to disguise his resentment but this was not what caught and held her interest. The boy's every movement was carefully rehearsed, painstaking and deliberate, as though he were priming a mine. He put her in mind of someone, some long-lost acquaintance, but he left before she'd thought of who it was. The dealer lingered for a time at the window, looking apprehensively down at the street.

When the talk turned to military strategy he wished them a blessed Juma'a and withdrew.

—I trust that bowlegged Tajik less and less each day, the younger of the adjutants announced.

—A considered view, Brother Zaeef, the captain replied good-naturedly. —But you'll find that our host gets on quite well without your good opinion.

Zaeef stared red-faced at the carpet amid the laughter of the men. Only Aden kept silent. She felt the captain's black eyes on her as she helped herself to tea. Eventually he heaved a sigh and spoke.

—Boys have a keener sense of a man's trustworthiness, in my experience, than a toothless old warhorse like me. They are closer to childhood, when the spirit remains free of worldly blemish. He nodded to himself. —What does your American think, Brother Khan? Are these Tajiks to be trusted?

—I don't have an opinion about it, she said before Ziar could answer.

—Young men always have opinions, said the captain. —I certainly did, little brother, when I was your age. In spite of my pure heart I was stubborn and pigheaded. But perhaps your heart is not so pure as one might first assume.

—Have you had word today from Kunduz? Ziar asked him, sitting forward.

The captain pursed his lips. —My orders have not changed.

—I'd like to use the radio, if you have no objection.

—All in good time, Brother Khan. Kindly curb your impatience. We are drinking our tea.

Silence fell. Zaeef exchanged a look with the other adjutant that made her want to throw the tea tray at his eyes. Ziar bowed and smiled tightly and agreed that there was certainly no hurry. It was the Day of Assembly, after all, and a time of repose. He praised the fineness of the china and the thickness of the carpet.

—We want to know why we're still here, she said to the captain. —It doesn't make sense.

His kohl-rimmed eyes widened. —Who is this 'we' you mention, little brother?

She set down her teacup. There was no disavowing the words she had spoken. Ziar said something under his breath and the captain told him to keep his mouth shut. The walls seemed to tighten. In her mind's eye she saw herself just as she was, as no other living soul saw her, a girl among men, a deceiver, a changeling. She asked herself why this vision should have come to her there, in that moment of all moments, in that place of all places. Then the son returned and caught her eye and suddenly she knew.

—Suleyman, came Ziar's voice. —The captain has asked you a question.

It was all she could do to maintain her composure. —I beg your pardon, sir. It's the men in my company. There are rumors—

—I know of these rumors, said the captain. —They poison morale. The question I have is who is spreading them.

—Perhaps our American is right, said Ziar. —A few words of explanation, to set the brothers' minds at ease—

—I await your answer, Suleyman Al-Na'ama.

—You haven't asked me anything.

—My apologies, brother. I am asking you now. Who is spreading these rumors?

The air seemed to fill with the clacking of china as the merchant's son gathered the cups. She kept her eyes downcast and struggled to focus. She was staring at the floor but she could see them so plainly. A room full of murderers. Just then the son stumbled on a fold in the kilim and the captain's arm shot out and caught him by the wrist. He gave a childish squeal of pain but by some miracle he kept hold of the tray. The captain pulled downward until he was kneeling. The son's face had gone ashen and his girlish lips quivered.

—Yusuf is your name, boy, is it not?

The son gave a moan.

—I wonder, Yusuf, if you'd do us a kindness. I cherish your opinion as an honest boy, a Muslim boy, whose vision of this world is unpolluted. He gestured with his free hand to where she was sitting.

—This other boy here, with the unfriendly look. Is this one to be trusted?

The son's eyes met hers but this time she was ready. She had decided not to let herself believe what she was seeing. If she had believed it then she might have cried out loud.

—He is, said the son.

—What's that, Yusuf? He pulled the son closer. —What's that you say?

—He is, sir. I think so. He is to be trusted.

To her astonishment the captain nodded and relaxed his hold. He seemed almost chastened. Even when the son twisted free and two cups fell to the carpet the captain did nothing. Ziar cleared his throat loudly and engaged him in a discussion of the village's strategic strengths and the particulars of its defense in the event of hostile action from the south. After a brief delay the officers joined in. She was careful to keep herself slumped and small-bodied and still. No one addressed her. She had fallen back into invisibility.

It was agreed that any attack would by necessity come from down-valley, since the steepness of the ridge gave them protection from above. It was observed that the village's antiquity was a direct result of its remoteness and favored position. The talk flowed around her. At some point she realized the merchant's son had disappeared.

—In addition to which, the captain said sedately, —the nearest body of troops is a week's hard march west, on the Badakhshan border. We'll have ample time, in any case, to shore up our positions.

Ziar nodded along with the others. —Will you nevertheless indulge me, brothers, in discussing what our plan might be if, God forbid, we find our first positions overrun?

The officers looked to the captain. The captain smiled at Ziar and said nothing.

—In that event, a man with a reddish beard began,—that is to say, in the worst of all outcomes—

—We'd take to the caves, said another.

—The caves?

—You've never fought here, Brother Ziar, said the captain. —I'd forgotten.

He said this in a soft voice, almost flirtatious, and she knew then that his anger hadn't left him. His anger hadn't left him and it had passed beyond appeasement and every man in that room was subject to its sway. She understood now that he meant to kill her. He would kill her because she was American and because she was an agent of a foreign power. These would be his justifications. The prayer in the mosque and the invitation to tea and even the discussion of the caves above the village comprised a ritual meant to end in execution. She knew this as well as she knew her own name.

—These are famous caves, the redheaded man was saying. —The granite there is pink and hard as iron. The lowest are shallow, no more than folds in the rock, but the ones above are wide and very deep. They are excellent caves. A dozen mortars at their mouths could cover the whole of the valley approach. They are cool and clean and sheltered from the wind. The village mullah tells me that the deepest cave is visited by angels.

Someone just past Ziar gave his opinion of the mullah and the younger men laughed. The son returned and collected the cups that remained, doing his best to draw no one's attention. Again she felt the captain's eyes on her. He waited until the son was out of sight before he spoke.

—I believe in that boy's gift for seeing the truth, Brother Khan. Especially the truth that is hidden. He shook his head fondly. —Perhaps because that boy is not a boy.

Ziar returned his smile uncertainly. —What do you mean by that, brother?

—Exactly what I say. Our host has confided in me that his son is in fact his daughter, raised to be what we call *bacha posh*. You are familiar with this custom? In a household without sons, a girl is dressed in boys' clothes and taught to walk and speak and reason like a man. Have you no such practices across the border?

She was on her feet before the captain had finished. She asked their forgiveness for the interruption and wished them all a blessed Day of Assembly and explained to them that she was feeling ill. She was thick-tongued and unsteady on her feet and it was possible that some of them believed her. The room had fallen silent and their faces seemed to darken and she knew better than to wait for a reply. She was halfway down the stairs when nausea overtook her, as though her lie had willed it into being, and she doubled over in the dark and crouched there heaving as the house revolved around her. She could still hear the men in the room overhead and she prayed to God that she might make no sound. She prayed to Him sincerely though she knew He must despise her. She could feel His disavowal in her chest and in her skull and she could feel it as a droning rising up out of the earth. She bit her tongue to keep herself from heaving. The droning grew deeper and more powerful with each breath she drew until it seemed to shake the mortared vault above her. It was only once she'd managed to stagger out onto the street that she saw that it was coming from the sky.

—Suleyman! came Ziar's voice. —What in God's name are you doing? Can't you see the planes?

—He wants to kill me, she said.

—I can't hear you, Suleyman. If you'll just—

His voice was sucked up into the droning and she shook her head and kept walking, staring down at the cobbles, her right arm extended in case she should fall. She heard shouting behind her and quickened her step. However dangerous the sky had become the merchant's house was more dangerous by far. She walked down the sunless slant-walled alley to the mosque without meeting a soul. Two streets ran downhill from the square's southeast corner and when she reached it she turned left again into the old bazaar. Down a covered passageway she glimpsed a group of children darting from one stall to another and she seemed to see the merchant's son among them. The noise from the sky was shrill enough now to break glass but there was no glass anywhere for it to break. She passed stalls with images crudely painted on their shutters of the wares for sale within, sandals and tinware and handmade plastic roses tied in Pakistan or China, and felt a childish urge to force their locks and hide there from the droning. Now that the truth had been revealed she felt no fear, not even sadness, but only a hopeless clearheaded exhaustion. She was walking like a girl again, like an eighteen-year-old girl and an American. She hadn't forgotten. She undid her headcloth as she walked and let it hang down from her shoulders. Perhaps some buried part of her exulted. A Tajik in a sequined cap came running up the street and knocked her over, excusing himself elaborately as he stumbled on.

She was almost to the first of the terraced barley fields above the village when she heard Ziar behind her. The droning had dimmed and she could hear the wind in the holly oaks bordering the path and his footfalls on the gravel and his hard insistent breathing. Though his eyes were wild he kept his distance from her. He carried a Kalashnikov slung from his shoulder and clutched his cap in his hands so that he stood before her as bareheaded as she was herself. She'd seen fervor in his eyes before, even some unnamed species of desire, but never the helplessness she found there now. His desperation was plain in his faltering walk and in the pleading voice with which he spoke her name. Suleyman? he murmured, climbing circumspectly toward her. On his lips her name became a question and the question seemed addressed to all the world.

—Can you see them? she said.

—I can't hear you.

—Can you see the planes?

—They aren't planes. He seemed relieved to be asked a question he could answer. —Not the one I saw. Too small. No pilot inside.

—Missiles, then.

—Not missiles either. There's been no explosion.

—Why? she said. He was within arm's reach now. —Why hasn't there been an explosion?

—I can't tell you why. God help us, Suleyman. I have no idea.

She leaned toward him then and took his hand in hers. It felt as smooth and unresponsive as a piece of polished wood. She was opening her mouth to ask his forgiveness when the house behind him disappeared and a wall of stunned air knocked them flat and strafed them with debris. Ziar cried out but his cry was oddly muted. Life returned to her limbs as a spasm of fear and she lurched onto her feet just as the second shock wave hit. The mosque was gone and its courtyard was gone and so was the schoolhouse behind it. It seemed to her not that missiles were colliding with houses but that houses were rising up into the clouds. It seemed more a weather pattern than a technological event. She was aware of shrieks in the intervals between the explosions and of the hail of falling matter and of men firing frantically into the clouds but none of this detracted from the stillness. There was only stillness now though she could see smoke raveling upward behind streaks of yellow tracer fire and two women running naked through a brightly burning field. She hadn't seen a woman's legs or arms since California and the women were very beautiful and in all that landscape they alone seemed understandable and real. The first was running barefoot with a kameez pressed to her bosom and the second wore nothing at all. Then the edge of the field was lifted like the corner of a carpet and the women were gone and Ziar was running toward her through the stillness and the smoke.

—Are you hit?

She gave no answer as he steered her by the shoulder up the path. She could walk without much trouble but she couldn't feel her feet. She could feel her feet but not the ground beneath her. The collar of her shirt was damp and this troubled her vaguely and when she turned her head she saw that the flesh across his knuckles had been sheared down to the bone. She told him he was bleeding and he shook his head and pushed her forward. She felt bloodless and white but if anything Ziar's weathered skin was darker than before. His beautiful skin. Every last thing was darker and she felt her legs buckle beneath her.

—Suleyman, he said. —Look here to me now. Are you injured?

She told him she wasn't and he took her by the hair with his unhurt hand and pulled her to her feet. Her eyes were streaming from the pain but she could feel the ground again and hear Ziar ahead of her, wheezing and stumbling, cursing her and the missiles and the village and himself. The hideous stillness had passed and they were high above the rooftops now and she tried to find the planes but couldn't find them. The planes were behind the clouds, behind the mountains, perhaps already in another country. Ziar forced her onward. She remembered enough of her training to ask him why they hadn't taken shelter.

—This is shelter.

—What is?

He pointed past her to the lowest of the caves. Even in that cata-clysmic twilight she could see the deep rose color of the granite. He told her to hurry but already she was climbing faster than he could manage and she reached its arched mouth well ahead of him. She'd expected to find provisions inside, sacks of grain or munitions or a cache of arms, but she found nothing but droppings and empty soda cans and the ashes of a long-extinguished fire. Above it was a second cave and above that yet another. Ziar said to keep climbing, his face gone white at last from loss of blood, and she found herself deferring to his weak-ness as she'd once done to his strength.

At the seventh or eighth mouth Ziar could go no farther and she passed her arm around his waist and helped him to lie down. She pulled the loose folds of her headcloth from her neck and made a cushion for his head, surprised at the softness of his matted graying hair. He apolo-gized to her without saying what for and she pressed a palm to his fore-head and told him to hush. A flap of skin hung wetly down across his fingers and the exposed ligaments spasmed in a way that made her stom-ach turn. Water was trickling from a furrow in the granite and she tasted it and found it clean and bitter. She caught some in her hands and brought it to Ziar where he lay with his head propped against a milky outcropping of crystal, the cushion she'd made him already discarded, and he lapped it from her cupped palm like a cat. Then he asked her to bring him ashes from the firepit she'd seen in the first cave.

On her way down she kept her eyes on the footpath before her, steep and glittering with quartz, but returning with her fists full of ashes she forced herself to look back at the village. What few buildings remained stuck out at incongruous angles like scorched and shattered teeth. She tried not to think of the beauty of those ancient pagan houses or the cen-turies of shelter they had given. She tried not to think of the people inside. She tried to view the wreckage as an elegant abstraction, a study in ballistics, an object lesson in the vagaries of war.

She found Ziar huddled at the cave-mouth, stooped and impassive, squinting down into the hanging smoke.

—I see the carpet seller's house, he told her. —Can you see it?

She looked out past the ruins of the mosque and the bazaar and answered that she could.

—The stone walls are what saved it. A rich man suffers less, even in war. That's one of the sayings of our Prophet. He managed to smile. —Or it ought to have been.

—Even its roof looks all right, she said, shading her eyes.

—The roof is in perfect condition. The roof is untouched. Your friend the captain is an excellent judge of houses.

She said nothing for a moment. —The bombing's done. I guess we should go back.

—We can't go back.

—Why not?

—You know why not, he said.

He'd washed his hand while she was gone and replaced the flap of flayed skin and affixed it in some way she couldn't grasp. He instructed her to wet the ashes and pack them in a poultice against the wound. She tore a strip of cloth as wide as her palm and wound it carefully around his hand and tied it at the wrist. Then they sat together arm-in-arm and watched the village burn.

—How do I call you? he asked her that evening.

Most of the fires had been put out, though a scattering of cinder heaps still smoldered. The setting sun shone straight into the cave and she saw that it was deeper than she'd thought. She felt caught in the sun's glare, exposed and at risk, set on a sacrificial stage for all to see.

—Let's go back in, she said.

—I could call you Suleyman Al-Na'ama, I suppose. I find it still suits you.

—I don't think it does, she said. —Not anymore.

—What name, then?

—I don't know. You could call me Sawyer.

—Sawyer only?

—My given name was Aden. Aden Grace.

He turned the syllables over on his tongue for a time, acquainting himself with their contours and weight, and she corrected him shyly. The color had come back into his cheeks now and his eyes were hard and clear.

—Aden Grace Sawyer. So be it.

She watched him. —Tell me something.

—Yes.

—How long have you known?

—Since you left the carpet seller's. Longer than that, possibly. He looked down at his bandaged hand. —Possibly since the beginning.

—There's a precedent for this, you know. A precedent in scripture.

—A precedent for what, Aden Grace? He laughed. —For the two of us together in this cave?

She sat up straight. —Umm Sulaim took up a dagger on the Day of Hunain. She took it up in battle at the Prophet's side and promised to protect him. This is written in the Hadith.

—Yes?

—It's written that the Prophet even turned to her and smiled.

—I see. He coughed into his fist. —And is it written what God's Messenger did next?

She hesitated. —He smiled. That's all I remember.

—I'm no mullah, God knows, but I do recollect this passage. The Messenger, may peace be upon him, said to Umm Sulaim: God is sufficient, and He will be kind to us. You do not need to carry this dagger.

—But He didn't forbid her from carrying it. And He smiled at her.

—What is your fear, Aden Grace Sawyer? That I'll cast stones at you? He grinned. —I don't blame you. There are plenty to choose from in this place.

—No, she said slowly. —That isn't my fear.

For a moment all was quiet. His eyes were hard and clear and the color had returned to his skin and he reached for her with arms like polished wood and pulled her to him. He gripped her roughly but she offered no resistance. Her own arms were useless and she fell heavily against him and lay with her face in the folds of his shirt, stubborn and gasping, like a fighter taking shelter from a blow. He took her by her useless arms and pushed her to the ground. She asked herself what his experience of women might have been and what the appropriate conduct was for a Muslim in her situation and laughed at the grotesqueness of the thought. Ziar mistook her laughter for a cry of pain and told her that he hadn't meant to hurt her. He breathed into her ear that what was happening was glorious and a reverence to God and all His seraphim and that she herself must be an angel come to earth to ease his grief. Come to him even in his waywardness, even in his pride. He told her that there might be a small pain at first, but only for an instant, and she laughed again at all he didn't know.

—Now, she whispered. —Let it happen now.

She took hold of him surely and guided him forward. Now it was Ziar who put up no resistance. He was above her and the daylight caught the vault of quartz behind him and he was moving as she wanted him to move. She was shaking with cold but not with the cold of that place. She had brought the cold with her. She had felt it since their crossing, since the Mountain, since Karachi, since the farthest point her memory could reach. He was moving above her and the light was behind him and she clenched her jaw to keep her teeth from chattering. She was shivering as a child will shiver coming into a warm and well-lit room out of the snow.

They spent a full night and day between waking and sleeping, looking down at the village as if from a cloud bank, taking care not to be caught out in the light. She slept so much that it astonished her. Each time she awoke she felt lightheaded with hunger and each time as Ziar spoke to her the feeling passed away. Never had she felt so confident of Paradise or so sure of damnation. She wondered if it could be true that God loved sinners best, as her mother often claimed, and though she knew the thought was heresy she was helpless to refute it. It was the only explanation she could think of.

Ziar assured her they were presumed dead and therefore free, as free as ghosts or djinn or creatures of the air, and she kissed him and agreed it must be so. At times he would leer at her when he made such pronouncements, as mischievous as a schoolboy, and at other times his eyes would lose their focus. He looked through her then, as if she truly were a phantom, and she could sit back and observe him at her leisure. His wind-chapped hands, his hooded eyes, the delicacy of his close-set teeth.

That evening when the line of dusk was just shy of the cave-mouth she opened her eyes to find him looking down at her, already fully clothed. She sat up at once and wrapped her shirt around her.

—We're going, she said.

He smiled at her. —We must.

—Why are you smiling?

—To think that you made me ask myself whether I had a fondness for dancing boys, like some Kandahar degenerate. That was not very charitable of you, Aden Grace.

—What would you have done?

—What do you mean?

—If I had been a boy. Here with you in this cave.

He answered without hesitation. —I'd have done as I did. To do otherwise would have been beyond my power.

—That makes me happy.

—Yes. He nodded. —You may take heart in that. You have not been to blame.

She watched him as he adjusted the dressing on his hand and refastened his belt and ejected the clip from his rifle and slid his thumb into the firing chamber to check that it was clean. The cave was drowned in sunlight, rose-colored and shadowless, exactly as it had been two days before.

—To blame? she said at last.

—The sun will be down presently. We'll leave when it has set.

She waited for him to look at her.

—I'd like to keep clear of the village altogether, to be sure we don't encounter our friends from Kabul. It's best if we hold to the slope.

—Where are we going, Ziar?

—To the birch grove, of course. To our company.

—What about me?

He cocked his head slyly. —Whatever can you mean, Brother Suleyman?

—No, Ziar. I can't do that. They'll know.

—And how will they know? Were any of them at the carpet seller's house? Were any of them with us in this cave?

She stood and braced an arm against the wall. —They'll know as soon as they see us. They'll know right away.

—They've had weeks to see us. They've had months. No one guessed.

—But we didn't know yet, either. We didn't even—

—Of course we did, Aden. We knew very well.

She said nothing to that. It was obvious when he spoke again that he'd chosen his words with great care.

—What we've done is between us and the sky and God's angels. No one else can condemn us. We can leave it in this cave if we desire.

She took a step toward him. —Don't make me do that.

—Get dressed now. We'll have need of this light.

—What about the captain? What about his officers?

He shortened the strap of his Kalashnikov and stepped into his sandals. —We leave for Nangarhar after first prayers tomorrow. There's no sense now in holding this position, let alone in marching for Kunduz. I don't need the captain's radio to tell me that.

—Don't go yet. Don't go out there.

—Nonsense. It's time.

—Ziar, listen to me. I can't— She felt her head shaking. —I can't go back to how things were before.

It seemed to her that she could see the sky darkening instant by instant as he stood motionless as a statue with her shalwar in his hands. His face was hidden by the light and she was grateful not to see it.

—You'll come now, he said. —Or you won't come at all.

Night had fallen by the time they reached the birch grove and they took their brothers wholly by surprise. They had posted no sentries and started no fire. Of the forty who'd set out with Ziar from the Orchard fourteen were unaccounted for, six were known to be dead, and seven had left for Nangarhar already. The remainder sat huddled together around a propane lamp, talking in whispers. Sahar Gul sprang to his feet when he heard them and discharged his rifle but the firing pin jammed and no damage was done. When he saw who it was he broke into tears and embraced them both fiercely and brought them into the circle and begged their forgiveness. No one asked where they'd been. It struck her that their manner toward her had changed in some elusive way but perhaps this was due to the bombing. None among that company had ever witnessed such a massive strike, Ziar included. What awed them most was that the planes had been so small.

They left before light of day, stumbling and furtive and sadly diminished, muttering verses to themselves and glancing skyward at the slightest noise. She learned from Sahar Gul that six of the company had been in the bazaar when the first strike had hit and three more had burned to death fighting a fire. Abu Suhail and two others had been crushed under a wall. She asked Sahar Gul where they'd been buried and he pretended not to hear.

At noon they overtook the first deserters. The youngest of them sat in the middle of the trail with his knees drawn in to his chest, answering the questions of his companions with diffident shakes of the head. She'd expected Ziar to show anger, to mete out some kind of punishment, but he greeted them straightforwardly and asked what ailed the boy.

—Nothing ails him, Captain. He'll be up and walking soon.

—He was in the mosque, said another.

—Not in the mosque, the first man said. —But near it.

—Was he hit? Ziar asked in the same forthright voice. —Can he walk? Is there a problem with his legs?

—Nothing ails him, Captain. He's just being mulish.

—If that's the case, then get him walking.

The men exchanged looks. The boy paid no attention. He sat hugging his knees in the dirt, humming quietly. Ziar signaled a halt and knelt beside him.

—Your friends say nothing ails you, Brother Hamza. Is this so?

The boy gave no answer. It hurt her to see him. Ziar bent lower and said something else, too quietly for her to understand. Then to her astonishment he turned and beckoned to her.

—Brother Suleyman is with us, Brother Hamza. You remember Brother Suleyman, I think?

The boy's eyes darted toward her, or past her, perhaps, to where his companions were standing. He let out a groan and clutched himself more tightly. Ziar took her by the arm and pulled her closer.

—Of course you know Brother Suleyman. He was with us when we crossed the border. Through the snow with that old guide. That old hypocrite. Ziar shot her a glance. —We need you to keep walking, Brother Hamza. To rejoin your comrades. You can't keep sitting here. It isn't safe.

The boy hummed more loudly and lowered his head.

—You remember that old guide who wouldn't stop preaching? You remember when General Nazir found us, don't you, and lined us up against the cemetery wall? Look here at me, Brother Hamza. Do you remember when Brother Suleyman put that old man to death?

—Captain Ziar, she heard herself stammer.

—Not a martyr's death, brother. A far cry from that. Eight rounds in the chest and an unhallowed grave. You remember. You saw for yourself.

The boy's head rested on his knees now and Ziar put a hand on the back of his neck. As she watched them the ground moved under her as it had during the strike. She backed away and closed her eyes to keep from being sick. She opened them to find Ziar before her. His lips were pale and he seemed to be fighting for air.

—I can't do this, Ziar. Don't ask me to do this.

—What have I asked of you? I've asked nothing of you. Only that you stand beside me. And even this small token you refuse.

—That boy is hurt. Anyone could see it.

He watched her for a moment, panting softly. —It would seem you've forgotten your training.

—The hell with my training.

—Be careful, Suleyman. You may find—

—Don't call me that now. Call me by my real name.

—And which name is that? Aden Grace Sawyer? You told me that name in a hole in the ground. Out here I am your captain and I call you Suleyman.

She nodded very slowly. —I won't do it.

—I've asked nothing of you. Nothing. Only to stand at my side. He smiled at her strangely. —But if I said that you will shoot this boy, that you will take the rifle from my hands and shoot him through the neck, then you would do exactly as I say.

—I've heard you say all sorts of things, she told him in English. —You said I was an angel.

—Suleyman—

—You said that in the cave when you were taking off my clothes.

—Look around you, Suleyman. All our brothers are watching. You are fortunate that these men have no English.

—It doesn't matter what you say to me. Not if all those other things were lies.

He drew back from her as if she'd been screaming. Perhaps she had been. He grinned a moment longer, an involuntary tic without significance, then took the boy by the collar and pulled him up onto his feet. The boy's companions mumbled their servile thanks and led him off. The column began to move again and she stood in the parched brown grass below the trail and watched it go. Ziar himself was the last of them to pass.

—You asked me once what he had done, he said.

—Who?

—Your friend. The childish one. The one who died.

He watched her, gauging the effect of his words, and she returned his stare blankly. To deny him that pleasure. But she seemed to be falling back into herself.

—Ali, she said at last. —You mean Ali.

He nodded. —Now you have your answer.

She reached for him then but he was already gone, shouting orders down the line, so no one was there to catch her as she sank into the grass. She sank into the grass and stood unmoving in the dust. She stood motionless and gasping as the column passed away. She was following her brothers and she was falling smoothly backward. She followed them as the dead grass caught her and she closed her eyes in sleep.

—Listen to me, she said to him that same night. They were camped above the village where the fighting birds had been. —Listen to me, Ziar. I have an idea.

It was a cold night and windless and the lights of Jalalabad discolored the sky to the south. He'd been sleeping with his shearling coat draped over him at a distance from the others. When she spoke to him his breathing changed and he raised his head and asked her what she wanted.

—We'll be in Jalalabad tomorrow. Is that right?

—By God's will, he said, passing a hand over his face.

—What will happen to us then? To the company, I mean.

—There is no company anymore. Not enough men. Either more men will be found or we'll be added to some other.

—They would do that?

He sighed. —He has influence, that Kabuli captain. It's possible that I'll lose my command.

—Because of me?

—For any number of reasons. He hesitated. —But you may have been right, Suleyman. It may have been better to have stayed among the dead.

—Run away with me, she said quickly. —As soon as we get to the city. I'll go anywhere you want.

—Ah! Suleyman Al-Na'ama. You're a child still. I'd almost forgotten.

—You wanted me to kill someone today. Would you have asked that of a child?

—Don't mistake me for Nazir, Suleyman, or for the company he keeps. I would never ask that of you. He sat up heavily. —And you, for your part, must not ask this of me.

—Don't talk to me that way, Ziar. I can't stand it.

—What way?

—Like some wise old uncle. Like my father. It makes me want to die.

He sat mutely then for a very long time. He was looking past her, looking through her, exactly as he'd done back in the cave. She dug her nails into her calf to check her panic. She stared into his eyes and found no recognition there.

—I'll tell them, she whispered. —If you don't come with me I'll tell them.

—Have you lost all reason, Suleyman? You have no—

—I'll tell them as soon as we get to the city.

—Consider what you're saying, idiot. Bear in mind the punishment you witnessed in the square. That woman was guilty of half what you've done.

—Not what I've done, Ziar. What we've done. The two of us together.

—Shut your mouth, he hissed. —Shut your mouth now, Suleyman. And move away from me.

—I told you once already. I won't answer to that name.

She was woken the next morning by a calloused palm passed lightly down her cheek. She murmured to Ziar that she was sorry but the voice that answered was another's and she sat up with a start. Sahar Gul sat crouched above her with a finger at his lips.

—Brother Sahar, she muttered. —Did I miss the morning prayer?

—God knows full well who the wicked are, he said.

Fear took hold of her then and she struggled to stand. He held her by the arms and fixed his eyes on something just beyond her line of sight. In a stand of poplars twenty paces distant Ziar stood conferring with three men in whispers. The men wore black robes and headscarves and daggers with silver pommels tucked through their belts. Sahar Gul clucked and shook his head and held her down until the men had gone. Then he stood and walked away without a word.

They marched all that day, halting only for prayers, through the last low foothills leading down to the valley. The country ahead was as green as it had been when they'd crossed it heading north the month before.

Cradle of Peace, she said under her breath. Forever Spring. The words no longer heartened her. The men could barely keep upright. It seemed to her that she could make out impact craters to the east, in the direction of the border, but her sight was oddly clouded. She asked Ziar but he seemed not to hear. He stayed with the column now, haranguing the men with ritual abuses, driving them forward through their hunger and exhaustion. He kept his distance and refused to meet her eye.

After fourth prayers the men were slower than ever to take up their packs. Ziar took his place at the end of the line, shifting from foot to foot in his impatience. When she spoke he had no option but to answer.

—Those men this morning, she said.

He narrowed his eyes, as though the question itself were a betrayal of his trust. —Which men?

—The men from the Kabuli company. I saw them, Ziar. I was awake.

—Of course you were awake. I sent Brother Gul to rouse you.

—What did they want?

—They were coming from Jalalabad with intelligence for their captain. They asked how large the strike had been and how many men were lost. He smiled crookedly. —How many of their own men, of course. No one else's. They were quite surprised to hear I couldn't say.

She watched him. —What I saw looked more like an argument.

—An argument? Not at all. A disagreement perhaps.

She waited for him to go on. He was shading his eyes and looking back over his shoulder.

—What was the disagreement about?

—The information they were taking. I wanted them to share it. He cleared his throat. —It appears that I have fallen out of grace.

She moved nearer to him. She could smell his sweat and the oil from his freshly cleaned rifle and the sourness of his tattered unwashed clothes. The back of his neck was as wrinkled and age-spotted as the neck of an old man. How strange not to have noticed that before.

—I apologize, she said.

—What for?

—For what I said last night. For making threats.

He made a gesture of annoyance, still looking back the way they'd come.

—I won't tell, she said, her voice plaintive and weak. —Have you seen me today? I know that you have. I've been quiet. I've been good.

—Step away from me, he said. —The men will see.

She felt herself flinch. —What do you care, Ziar? Are you afraid of your men?

He turned and touched two fingers to the hollow of her chest. —I am afraid, he said. —I counsel you to be afraid as well.

The tips of his fingers seemed to pierce her as she closed a hand around them. She spoke his name again, disgusted at the quaver in her voice. The capitulation it expressed. The cowardice. God knows full well who the wicked are. You will find them, out of all mankind, those most attached to life.

—Sahar Gul quoted from the Recitation, she said. —When he woke me this morning.

—Is that so?

—Did you tell him what to say?

He shook his head and pulled his hand away. —You've left the binding from your breasts, he said, stepping past her. —Don't become careless.

—I'm sorry, she murmured. —I didn't—

—Mind yourself, Suleyman. Attend well to your conduct. I say this to you now for the last time.

They pitched camp that night in a field within sight of the river. The city was perhaps an hour distant and a rumbling reached them faintly from the Kabul-Torkham road. She lay on her back in the rushes at the edge of the field and stared into the vacant sky and cringed and wept and cursed herself for weeping. She'd been prepared for any suffering but loneliness. She was a foreigner in a remote and hostile nation. She was a sinner and an apostate. She was neither Suleyman nor Aden Grace.

Sometime long after midnight she gave up on sleep and set out in her bare feet across the field. She passed within arm's reach of where Ziar lay sleeping and felt sick with desire to lie down beside him. To feel the warmth of his gaunt body and the cadence of his breathing. To abase herself and beg for clemency. She gave thanks then for the closeness and the power of the river, for the murmuring that drew her onward, for the cool wet air that roused her and the mud that felt so good against the soles of her sore feet. Her arms and back were spasming strangely, as though electric wires ran through them, but there wasn't any pain. She began to make out the headlights of trucks bound for the Khyber Pass and Peshawar. She imagined her past life waiting on the far side of the border, the camp and the madrasa and the town where she'd been born, her school friends and her family, the girl she'd been and long since put to death. Abu Imam and Hayat Khan and Ibrahim Shah and her mother and her father. She pictured Decker waiting for her, impatient as always, his shattered body whole again and lovely. She raised her arms and stepped into the current.

The river was stronger by far than she'd imagined. She sank to her knees in the soft mealy bottom and would have been carried off but for the heavy silt that closed around her calves. She lurched forward, somehow keeping upright, until she reached a ledge of sunken granite. The water was up to her waist and the shock of it thundered through her bones like a command. Like the trucks with their headlights the river was bound for the border with all possible speed and she needed only to surrender to be carried there as well. Already the current was numbing her body. She stood on the ledge with her legs braced apart, wheezing and shuddering, and watched with cool detachment as her last misgivings left her. She could do Ziar no greater good than to pass out of his protection. He'd told her time and time again to reduce herself to one desire only. She would do as he asked now. The river would take her. She took a small step and stumbled and sank to her ribs, still sheltered from the main arm of the current. She was nothing now but numbness and the urge to disappear.

Had We wished We could have created you as angels, to take your place on earth.

A flickering sprang up at the limit of her vision. She looked back and saw the brake lights of a line of covered trucks. They stopped at the encampment and in the pale uncertain darkness she seemed to see her brothers swiftly rise and take up arms. Through the booming of the current she heard a muffled *pop pop pop* as she fought her way frantically back to the bank. She caught hold of a willow branch and hauled her body upward. The cold in her legs made them leaden and stiff, as though she were balanced on stilts, and by the time she reached the company her calves were black with mud. She saw now that the trucks were transports with canvas-covered flatbeds and that the men were being loaded on in pairs. She laughed with relief to recognize one driver as a man she'd drilled alongside at the Orchard. She waved to him and he nodded in return. The shots she'd heard might well have been the backfiring of engines. They would drive to the Orchard now, or to Jalalabad, or perhaps across the border to the Mountain. Reconvene and start over. Petition Heaven for patience.

Merciful to all, she told herself. Compassionate to each.

She made out Ehsannullah Sattar's huge and unmistakable silhouette in the gap between the first and second trucks and she went to him with as much grace as she could muster, salaaming with her mud-encrusted hands. He smiled and returned her salaam.

—God's greetings, Ehsannullah Sattar. May you never tire.

—God's greetings, Little Executioner. I would wish the same for you, but my wishes would appear to come too late.

—You're right, Brother Sattar. I'm more tired than I've been in my whole life.

—Time to climb in, little brother. Time to go. He gestured upward with his rifle. —Planes will come.

—Of course, she said. She hesitated. —In which truck is Brother Ziar?

He smiled again behind his dense black beard, as though they shared some private joke between them. —A place has been saved for you in the last.

The foremost of the trucks was beginning to roll as she scrambled back along the ditch. Sahar Gul called something to her from the second truck as it pitched forward but before he could repeat it someone pulled him down amid a peal of laughter. She could hardly believe that the long march was over. She ran the last few steps and hailed the fifth truck and its driver flashed his lights. A fair-skinned man she didn't recognize hopped down from the cab and took her by the hand. She asked after Ziar and he smiled and touched a finger to his lips. She felt the blood rush to her face. —Ziar, she repeated. He jerked the gate open. The flatbed held nothing but a kilim and a length of copper pipe. She said there had been a mistake and he said very likely. She was shouting Ziar's name as his hand closed over her mouth.

I was dreaming yesterday with my eyes open but asleep. After everything that's happened I don't sleep anymore Teacher. I don't know what to call it. I dream right through all the marching and the stopping and the waiting. All of us do. Someone said it's like praying but I don't believe it. It feels better than praying to me.

Last night a dog or a jackal was sitting next to me staring down into a pool. This was happening in the desert or in the hills above our house. Those dirty hills past Hidden Valley Drive where people dump their trash. Do you remember?

The sand was wet and I was thirsty and the sun was going down. I could feel the heat off the jackal's body so I slid a little closer. It was like one of Mom's old ridgebacks that you hated but its eyes were blue and tired. It just stared into the pool. There was something down there Teacher. A giant dark something. When it moved I could see it. The sunlight cut into the water and I thought if I waited long enough I'd know what that thing was.

The jackal turned and looked at me and then it started talking. I tried to answer but I couldn't speak its language. It needed help Teacher. It was something important. Tears were running down its long sad yellow face into the water. I said I had a father who could help but he was busy. He was a professor with a big desk on the far side of the world.

I said your name a hundred times and hoped to God you'd answer. It got colder and colder. I was frightened and everything was strange and I was maybe five years old. It was getting dark Teacher. I wanted you with me. You were far away and busy but you might have understood.

4

Her eyes came open on a white room bare of any decoration. Light fell coldly from vents in the high vaulted ceiling and a woman in a brown hijab lay huddled on the floor. For a moment in her nausea and bewilderment she imagined that the woman was her own self reflected but when she raised her head the woman did not stir. She tried to speak and her mouth refused to open. Her tongue was somehow fastened to the back side of her teeth.

The woman lay with her face to the wall and her right arm folded winglike underneath her. Half-smoked cigarettes and empty cans of Coca-Cola and foam rubber cushions surrounded her, haphazard and filthy, as though she'd overstayed her welcome at a party. Behind her sat a galvanized tin bucket and a broom.

In time Aden was able to force her jaws open. She freed her tongue and licked her lips and took in breath to speak. Her sight fell on a wrought-iron door a few feet past the bucket. She saw no knob or handle. The top half of the doorframe had been mortared shut with crushed brick and cement.

—Hello, she said.

The sound had no more substance than a voice heard through a wall. She repeated the greeting in Arabic, then in Pashto. At her third attempt the woman's body stirred.

—Please, little mother, she whimpered. She tried to rise and a bolt of pain shot upward from her wristbones to her skull. Her arms were trussed behind her back with insulated wire. Her headcloth was gone and her ankles were bound and her kameez had been cut open at the neck. She felt the prickling of sweat along her hairline. The air smelled of stale smoke and mildew.

—Please, little mother. Little mother, I'm thirsty.

Haltingly the woman shifted. The rustling of her clothing seemed to thunder like a river. Aden closed her eyes and clenched her jaw and felt the building shaking. When she looked again the woman lay exactly as before.

When next she lifted her head the room was the same but the ceiling seemed higher and the woman in the brown hijab was gone without a trace. Sweat ran into her eyes and a cushion lay beneath her where no cushion had been and her clenched teeth were buzzing at a frequency too high for her to hear. The bucket lay overturned where the woman had been. Had there ever been a woman. Again her mouth refused to open and she understood now that her lips had been sewn shut. Her lips had been sewn shut and silver wires had been threaded through her body. She could feel the wires humming. The little door stood open and beyond it she saw flower beds and scintillating fountains. It pained her to see them. Her body was too vast ever to pass into that garden. Too vast and too polluted. There was someone behind her. A rustling sounded in the distance and a manicured hand came down over her forehead and her eyes. She gave a helpless sigh of pleasure. She asked for water and received it. The hand was slowly lifted and that endless room went dark.

Fingers gripped her sometime later and pulled her stiffened legs straight and pushed her gently down onto her back. Her bindings were unfastened and her wrists were wrapped in medicated gauze. She heard a slurring low-pitched voice and saw the woman high above her. The woman might have been speaking Pashto or Arabic or Urdu or some language of her own invention. She repeated what she'd said and still the words were drained of meaning. Her jaw was swollen so severely that her lips seemed not to open when she spoke. She lisped the words again and bobbed her head and filled a chipped green glass with barley tea.

The tea had been sweetened with both cream and honey and Aden realized as she sipped it that she must have had a fever. Days had been lost, perhaps weeks. She drained the glass and set it on the floor and the woman grunted softly and refilled it. It was warm and indescribably delicious. She thanked the woman in Pashto and in Arabic to no effect at all.

When the second glass was empty she rolled back the gauze on her wrists and saw that the cuts from the wire were scabbed over. The cloth she was wrapped in was clean and smelled of bleach and of cedar. It was precisely the smell that her father's shirts had had when she'd been small and she knew this was impossible and as she had this thought she started sobbing. The woman said something urgently in her hideous slack-tongued voice and as Aden tried to answer her the room began to turn. There was no need to guess what the woman was saying. Her bony hands were trembling as she pulled Aden upright and gave her more tea.

—Ziar, she heard herself saying. —Ziar Khan. Do you know him?

The woman's eyes seemed to widen.

—You know him, little mother. I can see that you know him. I need you to give him a message. To tell him I'm here.

The woman gave a warbling moan and stared down at the floor. Aden took her wrist and gripped it. She jerked her arm away and rocked in place and spoke in gibberish. Aden covered her ears with her hands and lay back down and pictured Ziar coming. She closed her eyes and saw him. He was coming in his pickup with a gun across his knees.

A day and night passed and the door did not open. She drank what she was given and slept in brief snatches and let the woman lead her to the bucket. The high white walls began to seem familiar, to kindle some dim memory, but the boundary between her past and what she'd dreamed had been erased. Her last reliable memory was of standing in her bare feet in the freezing Kabul River. Nothing since made sense to her at all.

———

By the time they came for her she'd recovered enough to know why the room seemed familiar. Two men in skullcaps and cream-colored jackets unbolted the door and entered like courtiers or handmaidens bearing gold-embroidered silks for her to wear. She knew by then whose house it was and whose elegant hands had touched her in her delirium and what the lisping woman lived in fear of. The men displayed the clothes without fanfare and laid them in two neat piles on the cleanest of the cushions and left the room again without a word. The woman kept still until the door was shut, then rose and gestured mutely to the squares of folded cloth. The smile she gave was terrible to see.

The men returned for her within the hour. Whereas before they had stared at her unabashedly they now averted their eyes and spoke only in whispers, as though she were a priceless relic in some temple. They requested in careful English that she accompany them and waited humbly for her answer before leading her outside. They guided her by gesture only, never by touch. She followed them through the low iron doorframe, catching her headscarf momentarily, and panic seized them that her hair might be exposed. They begged her to pay more attention.

She stepped dazedly into the full light of day, holding the scarf in place with her right hand, still hoping to find the garden she'd envisioned. She saw a cinder-block enclosure, a gravel-lined courtyard, a reticulated gate of painted steel. She saw the tile-roofed outbuilding where she'd waited with the Arab jihadis in their T-shirts and sneakers a lifetime before. The pebbles she walked on were pale green and speckled, like magpie's eggs, and the gate was a sun-beaten blue. She'd missed such details on her first visit because of the darkness and because she'd been a child then and a fool. But there was no residue of that child left within her, not anymore, and neither was she frightened or confused. She was a woman and the opposite of frightened. She was eager. She walked ahead of her retainers and they fell in line behind.

She found him as he'd been that first night, alone in his chamber with his legs crossed beneath him, his henna-tipped beard all but brushing the floor. His eyes were half shut and his thin lips moved subtly, as though he were in conference with angels. His yellow eyes came open as the door behind her closed.

—Now I know, he said. —And I am satisfied.

—You don't know anything.

—I said you had some quality. A quality that set you apart. He smiled. —You'll not dispute the point, I hope. It would not be ladylike.

—Go to hell.

—I'm acquainted with this practice, of course. This girl-as-boy practice. We too have this tradition. But I had no knowledge of it from your country. He nodded to himself. —I took you simply for a boy, one of rare faith and surpassing beauty. You were a wonder to us all, Aden Sawyer Grace. A sign of God's forbearance and His favor. To some of us you are a wonder still.

—I don't care what I am to you.

—You've never worn hijab before, that much is evident. He ran his tongue along his teeth. —How do you find your clothes?

—I want to see Ziar.

He nodded and appraised her for a time.

—Naghma did a fine job with you, I must admit. But even she cannot work miracles.

—Naghma?

He raised his eyebrows. —By now I would have thought you'd be first friends. Pardon my English. *Fast* friends. Is this the expression?

—Who is she?

—Naghma Benafsha Gul is the most senior of my wives.

—How many do you have?

—A worthy question, Aden Grace. Worthy and apposite. He wound the red tip of his beard around the knuckles of his thumb. —I now have two.

In the silence that fell she could hear children shouting to each other and the hum of the air-conditioning unit and the nearby keening of a muezzin. These sounds came so abruptly that they seemed conjured out of nothing by his answer. But she knew that the sounds had preceded her there and that they would continue after she had passed away. The sounds had always been there and the room had always been there. The platform he sat on was higher than before, the kilim more luxurious and intricately figured. She saw fountains and lilies like those in her dream. A silver antenna taken from a car or from a radio lay at his feet. Its presence confused her.

—You've been ill, said the man. —You must still be quite weak. I give you my permission to be seated.

—I can stand.

—We'll be in this room a long time, child. Days on end possibly. You'd be well-advised to save what strength you have.

She blinked at him, trying to follow, then turned and looked behind her. Her escorts were gone. There was only the platform and the brick walls and the cold fluorescent light.

—You think I'm a liar, she said. —You think that's all I am.

—I think you're a deceiver, Aden Grace, and a consummate one. He pointed at her with a liver-spotted finger. —Look at you now. Dressed as a new bride should be, perfumed and wrapped in silk from head to foot. You are beautiful, my dear. Your boyishness is stripped away completely. And yet it was so wonderfully convincing.

—I'm a whore, she said. —I've been with men already.

—I assumed as much, the man said comfortably. —And so did Ziar Khan.

She wavered for an instant. —But Ziar didn't take me.

—What's that, my dear?

—Ziar didn't take me as his wife.

—Ziar was a proud man, Aden Grace. A man in his prime. I, on the other hand— He pursed his lips. —Old age has its compensations, as you may yet discover. One may profit, for example, from the scruples of the young.

—I'd rather die, she said.

—Beg pardon? said the man, holding a cupped hand to his ear.

—I'd rather die.

—Nonsense. God charges not any soul except with what it can bear. To its credit belongs what it has earned: upon it falls the burden of what it has deserved. He brought his fingertips together. —You won't refuse what you deserve, I trust?

She felt her legs lock under her. —He loves me.

—Who does? The All-Merciful? The man sighed. —Perhaps so. Yet here you stand, forsaken, in this room.

—Ziar, she said.

—What's that, my dear?

—Ziar won't let you do this.

—My precious child! the man said, shaking his head. —Who do you think it was that brought you to me?

She stood for what seemed a great while with her legs locked beneath her and her blurring vision focused on the kilim. He watched her in silence, holding the tip of his tongue between his teeth. It was possible that this was all he wanted. She imagined herself growing old in his house, in his room, in his elegant presence, forgetting her transgressions and her English and her childhood and her name.

—Raise your eyes to mine, Aden Grace. You have my permission.

She did as she was told. She found what she'd expected to find in his face but still it appalled her. He was making no effort to hide what he wanted. She tried and failed to turn her head away.

—Do you remember the last time we sat here together, when you were calling yourself Suleyman Al-Na'ama? Do you remember what it was that we discussed?

She shook her head slowly.

—I asked you what had brought you to the Faith. You gave quite a long answer. You said some things were beautiful in this world our God created. He cleared his throat primly. —You said other things were depraved.

—I never said—

—I have a fine memory, you see, though my hair has gone white. He made a wide and sweeping gesture, taking in all the room. —Tell me, Aden Grace Sawyer, before we proceed. Might not some of His creations be both?

She gave no answer but he bobbed his head regardless. Her expression and her silence seemed to satisfy him fully. He sat back on his heels and ran his palm over the lilies and the fountains and the stars and the rosettes.

—You yourself are both, he said at last. —Come here.

She opened her mouth to speak and heard no sound at all. She shook her head and found herself obeying. Obeying this man who was all that now remained. There was nothing outside, nothing left, of that much she was certain. There was only this chamber with its freshly tiled floor and the hum of the ventilator and the old man on the platform and her body and her clothes. The weakness had passed and her brocaded slippers slid forward and her body seemed to have no form or weight. She came to him shyly. The silk gasped and whispered. She heard the rustling of the costly cloth and knew it was exquisite, a voluptuousness surpassing even her most self-indulgent dreams. The man on the platform knew it also and gathered the raw blue silk into his fist and pulled her closer. Her slippers knocked against the platform's wooden baseboard. He was no longer smiling. His breath smelled of tobacco and turned milk and cloves.

—Show me.

He made a gesture and she bowed her head and felt herself bend forward. Her last fear had left her. He relaxed his hold and she reached down and gathered the silk of her gown at its hem and raised it to her chin. She heard the air catch in his throat. The noise of it resounded off the high white walls like music. He gestured again and she lifted her underdress and now his breath came hissing through his teeth. He let her loose and hooked his thumbs into the stockings she wore and rolled them down to just above her knees. The hand that had passed so tenderly across her forehead in her delirium now took hold of her so fiercely that she cried out from the pain. He ordered her to lower her eyes and when she refused he snatched up the antenna and brought it down across her forehead like a switch. The pain was severe but not unwelcome and when she brought a hand to her cheek the switch came down again across her fingers and her chin.

—Look at me, no one's daughter. Look at me, little blessing. Little godsend. Little wife.

Tears were standing in her eyes as she obeyed him. The pain was such that there was room for nothing else. All thought reduced to a line. She knew only that she was bleeding and there wasn't any blood.

—Little wife, said the man. —Say to me: Yes, my husband.

—Yes, my husband.

—Repeat it, my wife. And do not look away.

—Yes, my husband.

He nodded. —Now ask my forgiveness.

—Forgive me, my husband.

—For what?

—I don't know.

—For what?

—I don't know. I don't know anything.

—That is so, said the man. —You have much yet to learn, Aden Grace. He took her hand and ran the switch across her upturned palm. —But you needn't worry. I have much to teach.

—Yes, my husband.

—Take this off, he said, lowering the switch to her hips.

She thanked him and pushed down her stockings. The light started pulsing. She stepped out of the stockings and kicked them away. The antenna twitched like a cat's tail in his fingers as he watched her. She asked herself what the difference might be between the man who now observed her and the man in that sunlit cave so long ago and she told herself there wasn't any difference. Not from this moment forward. She imagined that vaulted white room as a cave of some kind and herself as a martyr for a cause she had yet to discover. She prayed that she might learn the cause before she ceased to be.

—Raise your garment again. Quickly now. Lift it higher.

She did as she was told. He set the switch aside.

—I ask to see your body before seeing your bare head. You may think this strange.

—No, my husband.

—Of course you do, child. You have no understanding.

She watched him bring his fingers languorously to his lips. His eyes grew distant.

—The hair of the girl is the most private part. It is for this that you

223

wear the hijab. It is the most precious part. The most secret. His eyes found hers again. —This is my personal belief. Others may disagree.

She looked at him and said nothing.

—Remove it, he told her. —Uncover your head.

She undid the silk. She was eager to do it. It was diaphanous and lovely and it crackled in her fingers. She held it out for his appraisal, gathered neatly in her palms. Her hair was parted like a schoolboy's and it stood up in the back. He reached out to touch it. His eyes were hooded and his small creased mouth hung open. She parted her hands until the silk was taut between them. His eyes rolled upward like a mystic's and he said something too breathlessly to hear. She leaned close to him and asked him to repeat it.

—I'm asking His forbearance, he said in a voice leached of feeling. —I'm asking His forgiveness for what I intend to do.

—You're forgiven, she said, and passed the fabric twice around his neck.

Such was his ecstasy that she was behind him before he understood her purpose and by then her foot was braced against his back. He thrashed with more power than she'd have thought possible and it took all her strength and skill to keep behind him. She feared the silk might tear but it was excellently made. She imagined his eyes wide and bulging in surprise and spittle gathering on his lips but she saw nothing but the reddening of flesh along his nape. She wished that she could see his eyes and begged God's pardon for the thought. She brought her full weight to bear on the trench of his spine and arched her back as she'd been taught by her instructors at the Mountain and felt his body give a sudden kick.

—All right, Aden, she said softly. —All right, Aden. It's all right.

She heard the spirit leave his body clearly. A small bright fluid note as from a bell. His left hand closed around her wrist and dug its nails into her skin and that was all. She counted slowly down from ten, as she'd been taught, before letting go of the silk. His forehead met the platform with no sound that she could hear.

A span of minutes or of seconds passed in which colored bands of light obscured her vision and it took all of her resolve to keep from falling. She thought of Decker but Decker was a memory now and nothing more. She thought of Ziar and felt certain he'd been killed. Anything else was unthinkable. She repeated his name as the room turned around her. Her blood seemed to thicken. She hadn't considered what would happen once the cat-eyed man was dead.

She was still standing naked over the body with her arms held out to either side when she became aware of footfalls on the gravel. She crossed the room in her bare feet and listened at the door. A man said something and laughed and another man hissed at him in Pashto to keep quiet. They slipped out of their sandals and came closer and knelt on the doorstep. She could feel them on the far side of the boards. A flickering shroud of blue and silver draped itself across her sight and she rested her fingers on a crossbeam of the door to keep her balance. By the time the shroud had lifted the two men seemed to have gone.

She lost no time now in stripping the body and dressing herself in its clothes. Her legs were too long but she tied the shalwar as low as she could and hid the bareness of her hips beneath the tails of the kameez. She found a bowl of tepid water and drank her fill and used the dregs to clean the powder from her face. She put on the old man's headscarf and arranged it with painstaking care. The smell of him was strong enough that she began to retch and she closed her eyes and let the retch run through her. The men were listening at the doorstep or the men had gone away. The future is the province not of man but the Unseen.

A call to prayer was sounding as she stepped into the light. The whitewashed wall, the gravel yard, the freshly painted gate. The call was coming from a modest tin-roofed mosque outside the compound. The yard was deserted. She crossed it without hesitation and entered the nearest outbuilding and left its door open behind her.

The young men inside had just risen for prayer. They greeted her shyly, still unsure of protocol. There was some confusion as to whether they should pray in the courtyard or in the mosque outside whose muezzin was calling and one of them asked her opinion. She took a prayer mat from a heap in the corner and looked down disdainfully at those few still reclining on cushions and announced that she was going to the mosque. Again the call sounded. Four men in shalwar kameez who were standing at the door with mats already in their hands nodded to her as she led the way out. By this time the others were crowding behind. They passed her in their eagerness and pounded on the gate. Most of them had at least the beginnings of beards and were embarrassed to be guided by a barefaced foreign boy.

A hatch of sorts was set into the gate and they opened it and went out in single file. The third call sounded. She kept to the back of the group but she could see the rutted yellow road and a row of parked trucks and the stucco mosque behind them like a dusty piece of cake. She stumbled over someone's foot and in that same instant saw the men who had brought her wedding clothes standing squarely in the road. They were gesturing to the mujahideen to go back inside and the mujahideen were holding their mats raised like swords or like torches and pushing slowly forward to the entrance of the mosque. One of the two men met her eye for a long, vacant moment, then raised an arm and shouted to someone behind her. She was easing her feet out of her slippers and bracing to run when the man turned away with a look of disgust and shuffled slowly and flat-footedly back to the gate.

She let the group carry her now past the last of the trucks and when they came to the mosque she excused herself from her companions and asked God to bless them and continued very slowly down the middle of the road. A man's voice called her name or seemed to but she didn't turn her head. There was no living soul in all that country who knew by what name she was rightfully called. And as she made her way east and away from the mosque and the compound, from the resettlement camps and the blue border ranges, it occurred to her that she knew least of all.

She passed that night in a ditch by the Peshawar road, clutching her knees to her chest and staring wide-eyed and bewildered at the stars. The moon was a crescent, the moon of banners and of headstones, and

she seemed to see it shiver as it rolled across the sky. The growling of her stomach was the only sound there was. The ditch was steep-banked and narrow, dry as the country it cut through, and she lay behind a screen of brush in case a car should pass. It was cold with no wind and the stars hung so low that she found herself reaching up to them for warmth. All her life lay behind her, every day, every hour, bright and irrevocable and fixed. She saw it so clearly. Ahead was starlit blackness. There was nothing there for her to know or see.

You were right about this place, she seemed to hear a voice repeating. You were right about this place but you were wrong about one thing.

In spite of her precautions someone found her in the night. An hour before daylight a girl half her age came walking up the ditch and sat down on its edge without the slightest sign of fear. Her dark hair fell past her shoulders and her pale face shone bluely and her running shoes knocked playfully against the crumbling bank. She frowned down at Aden. The sky turned behind her. There was a question on her lips and in her gray determined eyes but she said nothing. Perhaps she was afraid after all. Perhaps she was injured. Perhaps she was lost. She spoke not a word, made no gesture of greeting, and it took the last of Aden's strength of mind to understand her question.

She took a breath and told the girl that she was still alive. She told her that she hadn't died, not yet, and that she meant to keep on walking east as soon as it was light. Her life had been spared for reasons unknown to her, reasons hidden from her sight behind a great and shapeless veil, and she had no choice but to take this as a mercy. By no virtue of her own she had been guided to the straight path, the path of those upon whom grace abounds. Although she was a sinner and a murderer the love she harbored for the world was free of sin.

She wept for a time, rocking stiffly in place, and the girl sat on the ditch's edge and watched her. The sky to the east gave off just enough light to disclose the girl's frail body in its loose T-shirt and jeans. She knocked her heels against the clay and hummed a melody. The lettering on her shirt read SANTA ROSA ROUND-UP. Her humming brightened as the stars went dim.

Aden knelt and touched her forehead to the ground and felt herself summon the world into being. She kept her eyes closed and took in the noises around her. The wind off the foothills. The trucks on the roadway. The call of a magpie. The rustling of her garments and the creaking of her bones. She took them in and praised each one and asked the girl's forgiveness. She asked her for patience. She asked her for courage. When at last her eyes came open it was well into the day.

ACKNOWLEDGMENTS

Jin Auh, Nooruddin Bakhshi, Francis Bickmore, Charles Buchan, Jamie Byng, Tyler Cabot, Andrew Chaikivsky, Rajiv Chandrasekaran, Eric Chinski, Brooke Costello, Elizabeth Costello, Kathy Daneman, Kiran Desai, Matt Dojny, Nathan Englander, Isaac Fitzgerald, Jessica Friedman, Sheila Glaser, Bill Hall, Barbara Wuenschmann Henderson, Edward Henderson, Corin Hewitt, Kirk Wallace Johnson, Kirsten Kearse, Alice Sola Kim, Kathleen Alcott, Shamila Kohestani, Suketu Mehta, Tim Nelson, Sangar Rahimi, Jamal A. Rayyis, Sarah Rehmann, Julia Ringo, Bernhard Robben, Akhil Sharma, Adrian Tomine, Thomas Überhoff, Max D. Weiss, Brian Williams, Anni Wuenschmann, Peter Wuenschmann, Andrew Wylie, Sybil Young.